DOGGONE DEAD

A sense of dread settled over me. "Did something else happen?"

"You might say that." Emily paused as if she needed to find enough energy just to say the words. "Early yesterday morning, the police found a body in the woods." Her fingers flicked a wave toward the rear of her property.

"A body?" I gasped.

Emily nodded. "He'd been shot."

"Do they know who it was?"

"His name was Will Grace," she told me in a small voice. "He was my ex-husband . . ."

Books by Laurien Berenson

Melanie Travis Mysteries

A PEDIGREE TO DIE FOR
UNDERDOG
DOG EAT DOG
HAIR OF THE DOG
WATCHDOG
HUSH PUPPY
UNLEASHED
ONCE BITTEN
HOT DOG
BEST IN SHOW
JINGLE BELL BARK
RAINING CATS AND DOGS
CHOW DOWN
HOUNDED TO DEATH
DOGGIE DAY CARE MURDER
GONE WITH THE WOOF
DEATH OF A DOG WHISPERER
THE BARK BEFORE CHRISTMAS
LIVE AND LET GROWL
MURDER AT THE PUPPY FEST
WAGGING THROUGH THE SNOW
RUFF JUSTICE
BITE CLUB
HERE COMES SANTA PAWS
BITE CLUB
GAME OF DOG BONES
HOWLOWEEN MURDER
PUP FICTION
SHOW ME THE BUNNY

Peg and Rose Mysteries

PEG AND ROSE SOLVE A MURDER

Published by Kensington Publishing Corp.

Pup
Fiction

LAURIEN
BERENSON

Kensington Publishing Corp.
www.kensingtonbooks.com

For Glenda Stanley, Phyllis Stanley, and
Charla Allyn Hughes
Three wonderful women whom I am honored to
call family

Chapter 1

On a list of things that bring joy to a mother's heart, the first day of school must surely rank near the top. And the first day of summer camp cannot be far behind. Just the thought of all those melted popsicles, wet bathing suits, skinned knees, and sticky fingers occurring somewhere other than my house was enough to bring a smile to my face.

My two sons, riding in the car with me, weren't similarly amused.

"What?" Davey glanced my way. He was sitting beside me on the front seat.

Soon to turn fifteen, Davey had just finished his freshman year of high school. By his estimation, that meant he was the smartest person in the car. He'd grown two inches over the winter and had recently buzz-cut his hair in preparation for starting his first real job. For the next four weeks, he would be a junior counselor at Graceland Nursery School summer camp.

"It's nothing," I said quickly.

"No, it's not." He looked suspicious. "You're smiling."

"Is that a bad thing?"

"I'm smiling too!" Kevin crowed from the back seat.

My younger son was five, and an optimist by nature. A blond-haired, blue-eyed bundle of energy, he was looking forward to spending the next month swimming, hiking, and making new friends. Kev had been to preschool—indeed, he'd graduated from Graceland in the spring. But camp would be a new adventure. Now he had one arm looped around the neck of the big black Standard Poodle sitting next to him.

The Poodle was Faith, my constant companion for the previous nine years. A glance in the rear-view mirror confirmed that she had drawn close to Kevin on purpose. Poodles are an empathetic breed. She'd sensed that, for all my son's bravado, he was a bit nervous about his first day.

"I'm smiling because I'm happy," I said to Davey. "You should be too. Having a job is something to be excited about."

"I'm excited about the prospect of a paycheck," he said with a grin.

I slanted him a look. That wasn't what I'd meant, and he knew it.

"Okay, yeah. Maybe I'm looking forward to trying out my cat-herding skills."

"Cats?" Kev piped up, surprised. "There are going to be cats?"

"Not real cats," I told him. "Davey means you, and all the other campers in the younger groups. He's saying it's hard to keep an eye on a dozen five-year-olds at once."

"We're not cats," Kevin grumbled.

Davey twisted around in his seat. "It's just an expression, munchkin. You're not supposed to take it literally."

"And I'm not a munchkin." Kev crossed his arms over his chest. "Nicknames are for babies."

"No, they're not," I said. "Nicknames are for people you love."

"Eww," said Davey.

Kev laughed and joined in. "Ewww . . ."

Faith wagged her tail happily. I could hear it thumping up and down against the seat. She didn't know what the boys were complaining about, but she liked the sound of their protest.

Graceland Nursery School was situated on five acres of rolling land in the northeast corner of Stamford, Connecticut. Founded eighteen years earlier by teacher Emily Grace, the small preschool was noted for its friendly atmosphere and its adherence to the principle that early learning should be fun. Kevin and Davey had both attended the school, and Davey had also been a camper when he was young.

I pulled through the gate, and we followed the driveway until we came to two weathered, clapboard buildings. They were angled apart from each other and connected by a low covered walkway. The main building in front of us housed the classrooms, plus a gym and a locker room. The smaller building off to our left held several administrative offices, a storeroom, and the school cafeteria. Emily lived in an apartment upstairs.

Behind those structures was a spacious lawn with a

playground and a soccer field. An enclosed swimming pool sat off to one side. On the other side, an incline sloped downward toward a picturesque pond where campers sailed toy boats and attempted—usually unsuccessfully—to catch frogs. The school property ended in a thick belt of woods that merged its rear boundary with that of its neighbors.

The compact parking lot near the admin building was flanked by a row of leafy maple trees. I bypassed the drop-off area in front of the main structure and pulled the Volvo into a shaded parking space. As the boys got out of the car, I opened all the windows. Faith would have to wait here for a few minutes while I got Davey and Kevin situated.

Since it was opening day, new counselors had been told to check in thirty minutes before campers were due to arrive. For now, the yard in front of the school was still mostly empty. I knew from past experience, however, that it would soon look like bedlam, with hordes of children trying to figure out where they were supposed to go.

At the moment, there were only a few people in sight. A group of teenagers, all neatly dressed in khaki shorts and white polo shirts, was gathered near the entrance to the other building. Davey's fellow counselors, I presumed.

A young woman with a rounded figure and an eager smile stood ready to assist us at the end of the sidewalk that connected the driveway to the school. I immediately recognized Emily's cheerful assistant, Mia.

She had a clipboard in her hands and a pen tucked behind one ear. The bun on top of her head was starting to come loose, tendrils frizzing into curls in the summer heat. Mia had a name tag affixed to the front of her shirt, with her name written in large red letters. She'd used a purple marker to add a smiley face next to it.

"Hello, Ms. Travis. Hi, Kevin!" she called in a bubbly voice as we approached. "Welcome to the July session of Graceland summer camp."

"Thanks," I said. "We're delighted to be here."

Mia turned to my older son. "You must be Davey. We're happy to have you as a new addition to the staff. And it's nice to finally meet you. Kevin talks about you all the time."

"He does?" Davey sounded surprised. And maybe a little pleased.

Mia nodded.

"I do," Kevin confirmed, sounding quite pleased with himself.

Mia looked down at her clipboard. "Davey, you'll be working with Courtney. The two of you will be in charge of our Jellyfish group." She pointed toward the group of teens. "Go introduce yourself to your fellow counselors. See the guy with the red hair? That's Brian, and he's in charge. He'll tell you everything you need to know."

"Terrific." Davey turned and strode away, leaving us without even saying goodbye.

I stared after him. I probably had a disgruntled look on my face because Mia giggled.

"Teenagers," she said with a shrug. "What can you do?"

Mia was less than a decade beyond her teenage years herself. But she had a point. If Davey'd had his way, I'd have dropped him and Kev off at the end of the driveway so he wouldn't have to be seen arriving at camp with his mother.

"I'm going to be a Sunfish," Kevin announced.

"Yes, you are," Mia agreed. "Your counselors are

Kayla and Luke, and several of your former classmates will be in the group with you."

She looked up at me. "Why don't you take Kevin inside and get his things stashed in his locker? A few other kids have already arrived. They're hanging out in the music room with one of the older counselors. You can leave Kevin there."

"Thanks, I'll do that," I said. "Is Emily here this morning? If she is, I'd like to say hello."

Actually, I'd been surprised not to find Emily out here ready to greet the new arrivals. After all, Graceland was her school.

"Of course." Mia's head bobbed a quick nod. "She's in her office now, but I expect her out here shortly. I'm sure she'll be happy to see you."

Kevin and I entered the main building. We found his locker and placed his backpack and lunch inside. Then I walked him to the music room, where a teenage girl was leading half a dozen campers in a sing-along. Without missing a beat, she beckoned Kevin into the room and dismissed me with a cheery wave.

Now that he was on familiar ground, Kevin's earlier trepidation had vanished. He went skipping in happily to join the others.

In less than ten minutes, I'd gotten both boys to their assigned places. That had to be some kind of record. I hurried back outside to retrieve Faith from the car.

The big Poodle was waiting for me with her head poked out the open window. When I opened the door, she hopped out of the Volvo with her tail wagging. Faith had no idea what we'd be doing next, but it didn't matter. She was just happy to be part of the plan.

All dogs are wonderful, but Poodles are particularly

perfect. I live with five of them, however, so I may be somewhat biased about that. Faith had entered my life when she was a young puppy, arriving as a gift from her breeder, my Aunt Peg.

I'd quickly discovered that Poodles are smart, easy to live with, and always entertaining. They're companion dogs who will gladly adapt to just about any lifestyle as long as they can be with their people. Poodles also love a good joke, especially one at their owners' expense.

Faith is a Standard, the tallest of the three Poodle varieties. Her head comes to just above my waist, so she's within easy reach for either a pat or a conversation, both of which happen often. She has dark, intelligent eyes and a short blanket of dense black curls covering her body. Faith is both a clown and a sage. She's also my best friend. I hope she lives forever because I can't bear to think about the alternative.

My ankle twinged as Faith and I strode across the parking lot to the smaller building. I'd broken my fibula in February. Although the break had healed well, it still ached sometimes when I walked on hard ground. The accident that had caused the break had been my own fault, so I tried to think of the pain as a useful reminder to watch my step.

When I slowed down, Faith ran on ahead. Nose to the ground, she checked out all the unfamiliar scents while also keeping an eye out for errant squirrels. She circled back as I reached the building, and we entered it together.

Emily's office was halfway down the hall. She must have heard us coming because before we reached the doorway, she was already stepping out of the room to meet us.

I'd known Emily Grace for more than a decade. In all that time, she hadn't changed much. Now in her mid-forties, she had a slender, well-toned frame and long blond hair that swung loose around her shoulders. The crow's feet etched at the corners of her eyes were new, but she remained as lovely as ever.

Emily loved her job, and she was very good at it. Maybe that was why she almost always seemed to be smiling. She wasn't doing so now, however. Even as we exchanged a quick hug, she still looked preoccupied.

"What's the matter?" I asked, when we'd drawn apart.

"Nothing," Emily replied quickly. Perhaps too quickly. Then she shrugged. "Oh, you know, just first-day jitters." She reached down and scratched beneath Faith's chin. "Hello, pretty girl. It's nice to see you again."

"Don't think you can change the subject by talking to my dog," I said.

"You're kidding, right?" Emily almost laughed. "You talk to that Poodle more than most people talk to their spouses."

There was that.

"Come on in and sit down." She waved me to a comfy seat, then pulled out the chair behind her desk. "I have a few minutes before I need to be out front. Let's catch up."

"You probably don't have to hurry," I told her. "Mia seems to have everything under control."

"I'm sure she does. Mia is a whiz at getting things done." Emily frowned slightly. "That girl loves to make herself useful. She solves problems before I'm even aware that they exist. In the six months she's been here, she's managed to make herself all but indispensable."

"That's a good thing," I said. "Right?"

"Yes . . . of course. I guess. Although, to tell the truth, sometimes her constant activity drives me a little batty." There was a threadbare rug on the office floor. Emily paused to watch Faith turn two full circles before lying down. "Or maybe it's just that Mia makes me feel old. I remember when *I* had that much energy . . . and it seems like a long time ago."

"I don't believe that for a minute," I said. "Any more than I think you have first-day jitters. You're an old hand at this. It's what, your fifteenth year of running the camp?"

"Something like that. But it feels like every year is a new challenge. Or maybe just a new chance for something to go wrong."

I stared at her across the room. That wasn't at all what I'd expected to hear. "Is there something in particular that you're concerned about?"

Emily finally managed a small smile. "Because being entrusted with the care and custody of nearly fifty four- to seven-year-olds isn't enough of a worry?"

"Okay, I get that." I smiled with her. "In your place, I'd probably be a basket case. But you're terrific at what you do."

"So are you. Don't think I've forgotten that summer all those years ago when you got roped into filling in when I needed a substitute counselor. You did a great job; the kids all loved you."

I couldn't help but notice that Emily had deftly changed the subject. Perhaps my probing had touched a nerve.

"Now Kevin's a camper," she continued. "And Davey— who was a Sunfish back then—is a counselor himself. That must feel like déjà vu to you."

"More like things have come full circle, I think." Looking back, it seemed as though the previous ten years had gone by in a flash.

I was about to mention that when there was a tremendous crash in the room above us. I winced and ducked to one side. It sounded as though the ceiling had cracked.

Faith was just as startled as I was. She leapt to her feet and began to bark. I went to grab her. I wanted to calm her down—but the Poodle eluded my grasp. She'd never done that before.

When Faith became upset, I paid attention. Now that made two of us wondering what the heck was going on.

Chapter 2

Faith wasn't the only one on her feet. Emily had jumped up too.

"Those damn dogs," she said.

Dogs? What dogs?

Then, abruptly, I remembered. In the spring, Graceland School had become home to three rambunctious Dalmatian puppies. Occasionally, I'd catch a glimpse of them when I was dropping Kev off or picking him up. The spotted trio had been roly-poly youngsters when they'd appeared in April. Now they must be around six months old.

Not a good age to have been left alone without supervision. That thought brought me to my feet as well.

"Where are your puppies?" I asked.

Emily pointed toward the ceiling—which, remarkably, was not in tatters on the floor around us. "Guess."

"That's your apartment, right?" I'd never seen it, but I knew it was there. "You live upstairs?"

"I do if the place is still in one piece. Right now, I'm thinking the chances of that are about fifty-fifty."

I wouldn't have taken those odds myself. Apparently, the puppies were loose up there by themselves. And it sounded as though they were having a great time.

"You didn't want to crate them?" I asked.

She shrugged. "I might have, if I owned crates."

Yes, that definitely would have been helpful.

I started to say something else, then stopped. My relationship with Emily had always been cordial, but she and I only really knew each other in a professional capacity— either as teacher and parent, or briefly as employer and employee. I hoped my curiosity about the Dalmatians wasn't causing me to overstep some unspoken boundary.

"I usually try to keep the puppies with me," Emily said. She sounded apologetic. "Or at least somewhere nearby. But this is the first day of camp, and you know what that's like. Today, I just wanted them out of the way, in a place where they couldn't cause any trouble."

If that had been her goal, it appeared she'd failed miserably.

Another thump—this one not nearly as large as the first, came from above us. Emily and I both gazed upward with trepidation. Yup, there was definitely a crack in the ceiling.

At least Faith was no longer barking. Now she'd returned to stand with her body pressed against my leg. Clearly, she was feeling apologetic too.

I reached down and gave the big Poodle a pat. Her ear-lier transgression was forgotten. She and I were good.

Emily sighed. She briefly closed her eyes. She was probably imagining the damage being done upstairs. I figured I probably shouldn't mention that; when my fam-ily's male dogs were in the mood to make some serious mischief, they'd been known to attack our couch cush-ions.

"Don't you have a pen for the puppies out back?" I asked. I was pretty sure I'd once seen the Dalmatians confined behind the school.

"Yes."

"Why didn't you put them in there?"

"That's just it. I did."

I frowned. "You did what?"

"I got up this morning and took them for a long run to wear them out. Then I put them in their pen. Early. It was before seven o'clock. I knew today was going to be hec-tic. I figured it was the safest place for them to be."

"But they're not there now," I pointed out.

"I know that," Emily snapped. "Something went wrong, I have no idea what. Next thing I knew, Mia was calling to tell me that the puppies were loose and playing in traffic out on the road. She'd seen them when she was driving in. She said they nearly caused an accident."

"Yikes." No wonder Emily was upset. That was every dog owner's worst nightmare.

"I ran right out to get them. But then they wouldn't lis-ten to me. Those little stinkers thought we were playing a game. It took me twenty minutes to round them up. By that time, I was covered in dirt and sweating like a pig. In the end, I had to bribe them with hot dogs."

Entertaining as that visual was, I didn't dare laugh. Apparently, Emily had yet to train her puppies to pay attention to her. If only she'd required the same respect from them that she did from her students, that whole misadventure would have played out differently.

"At that point, I didn't dare put them back in the pen," Emily continued. "Because I didn't know how they got out the first time. So I was afraid they'd just escape again."

"Good thinking," I agreed.

"I was running out of time, so I brought them up to the apartment with me. The puppies were worn out by then. They fell asleep while I was making myself presentable again." Emily's expression turned glum. "Now it sounds as though they've gotten their second wind."

You think?

"But I can't do anything about that now, because they need to stay locked up until after morning drop-off. So remember earlier, when you asked me what was the matter?"

"Yes," I said. "And now I get it."

Emily sagged back against the edge of her desk. Suspicious noises were still coming from the room above us. "Why don't these things ever happen on a quiet weekend morning?"

"Because that would make life entirely too easy," I replied. "Tell me what I can do to help."

Unexpectedly, Emily grinned. "Last time you asked me that question, you ended up working here for the summer."

Good point.

"Not this time," I said, but I was smiling too. "Why don't we go and have a look at your pen? Maybe the puppies dug their way out. Or maybe there's something wrong with the latch."

Emily walked over to the window. It overlooked the parking lot and the school entrance. Cars were beginning to form a line down the driveway, but drop-off was proceeding in an orderly fashion. Mia and the head counselor, Brian, appeared to have everything under control.

"I guess I can spare ten minutes," she decided. "I still feel frazzled from all that running around. This'll give me a chance to catch my breath. Me standing out front and looking like a crazy lady is not the first thing parents should see when they arrive to entrust their kids to our care."

Emily and I headed for the door. Faith fell in beside us.

"That jittery feeling is adrenalin," I told her. "It should fade soon. Those puppies must have given you quite a scare."

She nodded. "All I could think was, what if one of them got hit by a car? Or, even worse, caused someone to crash? It could have been a disaster."

A door at the far end of the hallway took us out the back of the building. We walked past the playground, with its swing sets, slides, and elaborate climbing equipment. Beyond it was the puppies' pen.

Six feet wide and ten feet long, the enclosure was constructed of tall, chain-link fencing. It looked solid and well-built. There were no gaps between the fence and the ground. Nor had the puppies dug any holes that I could see. But the door to the pen was standing half-open.

Emily frowned as we approached. "I'm sure I closed that gate this morning."

Faith trotted on ahead of us and began to sniff along the outer edge of the pen's wire fence. She'd never met

Emily's Dalmatians, but she was already forming an opinion about them.

"Today you were probably more distracted than usual," I pointed out. "And maybe you were in a hurry?"

"I suppose it's possible that I wasn't careful enough." She sounded annoyed with herself. "It's opening day, and I had a million little details to think about. But could I really be such a scatterbrain that I didn't remember to latch the gate?"

"Let's find out."

I examined the metal locking mechanism. It was simple enough. Just a horseshoe-shaped bar that slipped up so the gate could be opened, and then down again to hold it closed. I locked the gate and rattled it hard. It made some noise but held firm.

"It's pretty sturdy," I told her. "I can't imagine that the puppies were able to open it themselves. That's the good news."

Emily shot me a sideways look. "And the bad news is that I'm an idiot. Right?"

"I wasn't going to put it exactly that way."

"I'm always telling the kids that honesty is the best policy." She sighed. "I guess I should practice what I preach."

I rattled the gate again. "More good news. Now that you know the pen is secure, you can bring the puppies back out here, rather than letting them continue to tear up your apartment."

"That's the best idea I've heard all day," she said.

We turned to head back to the school buildings. Her inspection of the pen complete, Faith came skipping along behind us.

"I know the puppies have been here since spring," I said. "But where did they come from?"

"It's a long story." Emily didn't sound happy about that. "Short version, they were a gift."

"Three at once?" I looked at her in surprise. "I'm not sure if that's a gift or a burden."

"Believe me, that was my first thought too. But they've turned out to be a big hit with the children. You know, because of the movie? Everybody's seen it. So the kids are excited to get to meet three live Dalmatians. And the puppies have been wonderful with them. Posey likes to lick noses."

"Cute name."

"Thanks. The other two are Poppy and Pansy. The nursery school was in session when they arrived, so I let the kids name them."

"It sounds as though they're all bitches?"

"Bitches?" Emily repeated. She looked shocked.

"No insult intended," I told her. "That's the correct term for a female dog."

"It is? *Really?* Now I am insulted. Who do you suppose came up with that?"

"I have no idea." Actually, I'd never wondered about it before.

"What's the term for a male dog?"

"Dog." I grinned.

"Seriously?"

"I kid you not."

Emily shook her head. "There's something wrong with that system."

I couldn't argue with that.

* * *

My family lived in North Stamford too, so when Faith and I left Graceland camp, we were home in just ten minutes. Home was a colonial house in a quiet residential neighborhood. Two-acre zoning meant that none of our neighbors were close enough to be bothered by the fact that we had six dogs who often ran around outside in our enclosed yard.

Six dogs hadn't been the plan in the beginning. But somehow they just kept accumulating. Five members of our canine crew were black Standard Poodles, all retired show dogs. Eve was Faith's daughter. My second husband, Sam, had brought two Poodles of his own to the marriage: an older bitch named Raven; and Tar, a gorgeous young male. Augie came along when Davey was old enough to have a dog of his own.

Then there was Bud. He was a small, spotted dog of indeterminate lineage, whom Davey and I had found one day by the side of the road. Initially, we'd intended to get him healthy and find him a home. But Bud had other ideas. He'd immediately attached himself to Kevin, and that was that.

Before I even turned in the driveway, I saw the maroon minivan parked beside the garage. Faith knew what that meant. She stood up on the seat and pressed her nose against the window. Her tail began to whip back and forth.

Aunt Peg is here!

"Yes, I know," I said with a sigh.

This will be fun!

Of course Faith would think so. Aunt Peg loved all

dogs without reservation. People were another matter. She and I had a complicated relationship, made all the more difficult by the fact that she refused to acknowledge any of the many ways she continued to drive me crazy.

When Aunt Peg showed up unexpectedly, it usually meant she wanted something. And her requests seldom turned out to be simple. Or easy. Which was probably why she brought them to me—because I'd never success-fully figured out how to say no to her.

Aunt Peg was in her seventies, but the passage of time hadn't affected either her energy level or her mental acu-ity. She was six feet tall and built like a brick wall. Her store of knowledge was vast, and she was insatiably curi-ous about the things she didn't know. Aunt Peg asked too many questions, believed strongly in her own opinions, and couldn't abide foolish people.

Some days it was a challenge just holding a conversa-tion with her.

A longtime breeder of superb Standard Poodles, Aunt Peg was now a respected dog show judge. She was ap-proved for the Toy and Non-Sporting Groups, and lately she'd been eyeing several of the Herding breeds to add to her roster.

I pulled the Volvo up beside Aunt Peg's van. Faith quickly jumped out and ran to the gate that led to the backyard. Sam and Aunt Peg must have been outside on the deck. I briefly contemplated sneaking into the house through the garage. It was only wishful thinking, but I took a moment to enjoy the idea anyway.

Having heard our arrival, the other Poodles began to gather near the fence. Then Bud came running over. He and Faith touched noses through the gate. The spotted dog began to pop up and down like a jack-in-the-box. He punctuated each leap with a shrill yip.

Bud might have been a small dog, but he had a big bark.

Sure, I thought. Tell the whole neighborhood I'm home.

Now I had no choice but to go find out what Aunt Peg wanted this time.

Chapter 3

When I reached the gate, Sam was already standing on the other side. He shooed the dogs away so he could open it long enough for me to slip through.

Big black Poodles eddied around both our legs as I looked up to thank him with a quick smile. Sam was six inches taller than me, and he filled out a T-shirt and shorts handsomely. His shaggy blond hair was swept back off his forehead. Blue eyes, much like Kevin's, gazed down at me.

"Did everything go okay at camp?" he asked. "I thought you'd be back half an hour ago."

"It was fine," I said as I reached down to greet each dog individually. Tar pushed his way to the front of the group and nearly knocked me over. Eve hung back and waited for me to come to her. "There was just one minor complication."

"Oh?" Aunt Peg was on the deck, reclining on a lounge chair with a cup of Earl Grey tea within easy reach. She loved complications. I'd known that would pique her interest. "What happened?"

"Here's a better question," I replied. "What are you doing here?"

Aunt Peg straightened in her seat. "Is that any way to greet your favorite relative?"

Favorite? Aunt Peg was giving herself entirely too much credit. I was pretty sure she wasn't even in the top five. And that was before I started adding the Poodles to the list.

"I think I'll go inside and refill my coffee," Sam said to no one in particular.

"Please bring me a cup too?" I asked. Whatever Aunt Peg was up to now, it was sure to go down better accompanied by a strong jolt of caffeine.

"Of course." Sam disappeared with alacrity.

Bud followed him inside. The little dog had been skinny when we brought him home. His weight was fine now, but Bud still never missed a chance to visit the kitchen. He seemed to believe food would magically fall into his mouth when he was there. And sometimes—especially when Kevin was around—it did.

"So?" Aunt Peg prompted. "You were in the middle of a story."

"I was?"

"Indeed. It was about complications."

"Oh." I grinned. "I only said that to get your attention."

"Well, it worked. I'm all ears. Tell me the rest."

"It was about Dalmatian puppies."

"I see." Now she looked skeptical. "Were there more than a hundred of them? And a woman with a white streak in her hair?"

"No, just three." I sat down in a rattan chair with a thick cushion on its seat. "And the woman is a blonde."

"That sounds like Emily Grace." Sam reappeared with a mug of coffee in each hand. He'd added a splash of milk to mine, just the way I liked it. He settled into a matching chair beside me.

I noted that Bud had remained behind in the kitchen. He was probably busy nosing around the pantry. The Poodles, meanwhile, had run off to play a game of tag around the trees in the yard.

"Who's Emily Grace?" Aunt Peg wanted to know. "And why does she have two first names?"

"She's the proprietor of Graceland Nursery School." I took a welcome sip of coffee. "And Grace is her last name."

"And she has three Dalmatian puppies?" Aunt Peg asked. "All at once? Is she a breeder?"

Of course that was the conclusion she would leap to. Most of Aunt Peg's best friends bred purebred dogs.

"No, nothing like that," I said. "The puppies were a gift."

"From whom?"

"She didn't say."

"Aha." Aunt Peg smiled. "A woman of mystery. Despite her name, I like her already."

"You would like Emily. She's smart and capable. She runs her own business and mostly makes it look easy. You would call her a useful person."

Aunt Peg should have been pleased by that. Useful

people were her favorite sort. Instead she snorted under her breath. She was probably reserving judgment until she could meet Emily and decide for herself.

"The puppies' names are Poppy, Posey, and Pansy," I said. "The children named them."

"We can tell." Sam grinned.

"Three bitches then," Aunt Peg said. "How old are they?"

"They were youngsters back in April," I told her. It was just after the Fourth of July now. "So around six months, I would guess."

"Has Emily made plans to get them spayed?"

"I don't know. I didn't ask."

"Well, you should. Reproductive responsibility is important. Especially when dealing with puppies that apparently showed up out of nowhere."

"The puppies didn't come from nowhere," I told her. "They were a gift."

"So you said. But I'm not sure I believe it. Who would give someone three Dalmatian puppies at once? All the same age, so probably from the same litter. It seems much more likely that they escaped from somebody's backyard and your Emily Grace took them in."

"As it happens," I admitted, "they do seem to be accomplished escape artists. They got out of their pen this morning and ran out to the road in front of the school."

"The plot thickens," Aunt Peg muttered.

"Actually, that's pretty much where the plot ends."

"I hope no one was hurt," said Sam.

"Thankfully, no. By the time we arrived, Emily had recaptured the puppies and locked them away."

Aunt Peg was not appeased. Judging by the frown on

her face, she was thinking about the lecture she wanted to deliver to Emily.

I took another sip of coffee and repeated my earlier question, "Aunt Peg, why are you here?"

"Apparently, I came to listen to a story about Dalmatian puppies," she retorted. "And not a very good one at that."

As if I would believe that. Aunt Peg had never even heard of the puppies until five minutes ago. The woman was the queen of ulterior motives. I knew she had to be up to something.

The Poodle pack came circling back to us. Tar and Augie were exhilarated by their run. The two males looked ready to take another lap around the big yard. Faith, Eve, and Raven joined us on the deck to lie down in the shade.

I put my mug down on a side table and went inside to fill a bowl with cold water for the dogs. I expected to find Bud in the pantry. Instead he was in the kitchen, sitting in front of the refrigerator and staring at the closed door hopefully. Faith knew how to open the appliance, but thankfully she hadn't taught that trick to Bud.

"There's nothing in there for you," I said as I picked up the water bowl from the floor and rinsed it out.

Bud hopped to his feet. His stubby tail wagged so energetically that his hindquarters were wiggling from side to side. That little dog was cute, and he knew it.

"I can't feed you," I told him when I'd turned off the tap. "Otherwise, I'd have to give the Poodles something too."

They're outside! Bud shimmied some more. A black-spotted ear flopped up and down over one eye. *I won't tell!*

Oh, for Pete's sake. I set the full bowl of water down on the counter, then crossed the kitchen in three quick steps. There was an open bag of kibble in the pantry—now stored high enough that Bud couldn't reach it. I put my hand inside and pulled out two small pieces.

Bud was right behind me. His mouth was open and ready. His pink tongue slipped out and flicked the kibble out of my fingers. Bud didn't even bother to chew before swallowing.

"Happy now?" I asked.

He jumped up to dance on his hind legs. *Again! Again!*

I didn't even dignify that with a reply. Instead I went to get the water dish, then made sure that Bud came too when I went back outside. I set the big bowl down on the deck, and Raven and Eve drank noisily. Tar and Augie had run off again. Faith was lying underneath my chair.

"What did I miss?" I asked Sam.

"We were talking about the dog show on Saturday," he said. "Peg thinks Coral will have a good shot at taking the major in Standard bitches."

Of course she thought that. The woman never lacked for confidence. Plus, she was Coral's breeder. So, in the way of good dog breeders everywhere, she was predisposed to admire her own bitch.

Which was not to say that Coral didn't have many admirable qualities. She was a lovely Standard Poodle, the product of numerous generations of Aunt Peg's superior breeding. Had Aunt Peg been planning to show Coral herself, the win probably would have been a lock. Instead, fourteen-year-old Davey would be in the show ring at the end of Coral's leash.

That partnership had been formed the previous summer when the Poodle was just beginning her show career. Aunt Peg, Coral's owner, was busy with her own judging duties. Also, she was loath to appear in other judges' rings and perhaps incite talk of impropriety.

After Davey had shown Augie to his championship, he'd been eager to continue honing his handling skills. When Aunt Peg asked for his help, he'd quickly agreed. In theory, the alliance should have benefited both of them. In reality, the pair often found themselves arguing over who was in charge.

Coral had won five of the fifteen points needed to become a champion by the time she turned a year old. At that point, she'd taken time off from the show ring to grow into her new adult trim.

The young bitch now looked very elegant in her continental clip, with a large coat of mane hair covering the front half of her body, rounded bracelets and rosettes on her lower legs and hips, and a glorious pompon on the end of her tail. Since February, she and Davey had amassed an additional five points. That meant Coral was now in need of two major wins to finish her championship.

In dog show competition, points are awarded to the Winners Dog and Winners Bitch based on the number of same-sex dogs beaten on the day. The number can be as low as a single point or as high as five. Included in the total of fifteen, a dog must also win two "majors," meaning he must defeat enough competition for the win to be worth three or more points.

Major wins are hard to come by and highly prized. At times, that level of competition can also be difficult to find. Coral was now in the unenviable position known in the dog show world as "stuck for majors."

So this upcoming dog show, with its healthy entry in Standard Poodle bitches, mattered a lot. To all of us.

I narrowed my eyes and stared at Aunt Peg. She'd brought Eve up onto the lounge chair beside her, and her fingers were tangling idly through the Poodle's topknot.

"Davey's looking forward to the show," I said. "He's ready."

"I'm sure he thinks he is," she replied. "But one can never be too prepared."

"What does that mean exactly?" Sam asked. In the past, we'd both been frustrated by Aunt Peg's attempts to micromanage everything about Davey's performance.

"I was just thinking that a little tune-up of his skills wouldn't be a bad thing." She smiled complacently. "I'd be happy to step in and give him a handling lesson."

No way, I thought. Aunt Peg's constructive criticism had about as much finesse as King Kong had used to swat down pesky airplanes.

"I'm sure that won't be necessary," I said.

"Let's not forget, there's a major on the line."

There seemed to be very little chance that any of us would forget *that*. Which was why ratcheting up the pressure on Davey to put in a stellar performance was precisely the wrong way to go about things.

"If it will make you feel better, I can work with him this week," said Sam.

Aunt Peg frowned, then nodded. "I suppose that will have to do." She nudged Eve gently to one side and stood up. "I'll be going then. Thank you for the tea and the lovely company."

It was unlike Aunt Peg to give in so easily, I thought. Could that truly be all she'd wanted?

I glanced over at Sam. He just shrugged. He was baffled too.

"We could have had this conversation over the phone," I pointed out.

"What would be the fun in that?" Aunt Peg asked. "Besides, I thought you two might be lonely, with both boys out of the house now. There's a name for that, isn't there? Empty nest syndrome?"

She had to know that referred to teenagers leaving for college. And adulthood. Not nursery school summer camp. But whatever.

Sam and I followed Aunt Peg to the gate. Hand resting on the latch, she paused as if something had just occurred to her. "Oh. There was one other thing I wanted to mention."

And here it came. Finally.

"What will you be doing a month from now, say around the second week of August?"

Sam and I shared a look. It was summer vacation. Who bothered to plan that far ahead? Certainly not us.

"Umm . . ." I said.

"Good answer," Aunt Peg replied. "I was hoping I could count on you to do me a small favor."

"Sure," Sam replied.

I kicked him in the ankle. Hadn't his long association with my family—and particularly with Aunt Peg—taught him anything? Never make a promise until you find out what you're getting into.

"You know Willow," Aunt Peg said.

Sam and I both nodded. Willow was one of Aunt Peg's Standard Poodles. A beautiful bitch, she was also Coral's dam.

"She's pregnant."

"What?" I yelped. That was a surprise. "Since when?"

Sam didn't need to ask. He was already counting backward.

"Early June," Aunt Peg informed us blithely. "I wasn't sure the breeding would take, but it did. Since there's nothing on your schedule, I was thinking you two might like to whelp a litter of puppies for me."

Chapter 4

"Holy moly," I said. "How did that happen?"

"Quite on purpose, I assure you," Aunt Peg replied. "A great deal of planning and forethought went into this mating."

"But why didn't you tell us?"

"I'm telling you now. I didn't mention it to anyone beforehand. It's madness for someone with my schedule to even consider having a litter of puppies. But what choice did I have? Willow isn't getting any younger. This will be her last litter."

"Puppies," said Sam. He had a goofy grin on his face.

I probably did too. Who didn't love a litter of puppies?

"There was just one thing I couldn't control," Aunt Peg said.

We all knew what that was.

"Of course, Willow came in season at an inconvenient time," she continued. "But I didn't dare let her go by again. So I went ahead and did the breeding, even though I'd already committed to an out-of-state judging assignment the week the litter will be due."

"Who did you breed her to?" Sam asked. He and Aunt Peg could spend hours discussing Standard Poodle families and pedigrees and all the possible ways to combine them.

Aunt Peg named a West Coast dog whose progeny she had judged and admired. The dog's owner was an old friend of hers, and their bloodlines had mingled throughout the years with excellent results.

"Good choice," I said.

Aunt Peg nodded. If the mating hadn't been a good choice—or, more accurately, an excellent choice—she wouldn't have done it.

Somehow, I couldn't stop smiling. I'd known Aunt Peg was up to something, but I'd never expected this.

Caring for a litter of puppies was a big commitment. Even when they weren't your own. Maybe especially then. Puppies needed plenty of quality care and attention. They took over your house. And your lives. Maybe Sam and I should discuss this before agreeing . . .

Oh, who was I kidding? I thought. Puppies were more fun than anything else in the world.

"We'll do it," I said.

Aunt Peg unlatched the gate and let herself out. "Of course you will. I never doubted it for a minute."

"She takes us for granted," I said to Sam as we watched Aunt Peg drive away.

"Yes, but this time I don't mind." Sam's smile was back. "We're going to have a litter of puppies."

"No, Aunt Peg is going to have puppies," I corrected him. "We're just the surrogate parents."

"Close enough. Wait until the boys find out."

Yikes. I hadn't even thought about that.

We turned back toward the house. "And here I'd thought we were going to have a nice quiet summer," I said.

Sam looked skeptical. "Did you ever actually believe that?"

"I was trying to."

"Good luck with that," he said.

Predictably, when they heard the news, Davey and Kevin were even more excited about it than Sam and I were.

Kevin and Bud danced around the living room together. Kev's sneakers squeaked on the hardwood floor. His T-shirt, rumpled and stained from camp, twisted around his narrow waist as he and Bud spun circles around each other.

"A new puppy for me!" he cried. "I'm going to name him Fluffy."

"Not so fast," I said.

Kev stopped dancing. So did Bud. The two of them stared at me with wide eyes. I hated always having to be the bad guy.

"You were the one with the goofy grin," I said to Sam. "You explain it to him."

Sam nodded. Then instead, he changed the subject. He hunkered down to Kev's level. "How was your first day of camp?"

Kev's face lit up. Suddenly, he was happy again. "It was grrreat!"

"Did you make lots of new friends?"

"Yup."

"Swim in the pool?"

"Yup."

Davey started laughing. A teenager, he was usually the one with the one-word answers.

"How about you?" I asked him.

"What?" As if he didn't know.

"How was your first day of being a counselor?"

Davey considered the question. He was munching on an apple he'd nabbed in the kitchen. "Not bad," he decided after a minute.

"Care to elaborate?" asked Sam.

"Not really."

Ookay.

"Aunt Peg came by this morning," I told him. "She wanted to talk about Saturday's dog show."

"I know it's a major," Davey said. "And that it's a big deal. I'm good to go. She doesn't need to check up on me."

"That's what we told her."

"For real?"

"For real," Sam replied. "You and I can practice with Tar this week if you want. But it's up to you."

"Nope." Davey shook his head. "I'm good."

"He's good," Kevin echoed solemnly. "I'm good too."

"Well, that's a pleasant state of affairs," I said. "Let's hope it lasts."

* * *

We made it all the way until Thursday before something went wrong. Three days without a major problem turning up? In my house, that means we're doing great.

Davey looked upset when I picked the boys up at camp that afternoon. "What's the matter?" I asked.

He glanced at Kevin and shook his head. I understood that shorthand. I'd often used it myself. Davey and I would talk when we got home.

Sam was working in his home office, so I got Kev settled in the living room with a video game and a juice box. Yes, I know. But sometimes when you're a mother, expediency wins out. Besides, Kevin had just enjoyed an active day at camp. So I was pretty sure that one hour of lazy parenting wouldn't ruin his life.

Davey and I sat down in the kitchen. The Poodles fanned out on the floor around us. Bud was on the couch with Kev. At least I hoped he was.

There were three peaches in a bowl in the middle of the table. I offered one to Davey, then took one for myself. He stared at the piece of fruit in his hand as if he wasn't sure what to do with it.

I hadn't yet heard a thing, and already I didn't like the way this conversation was shaping up.

"Something happened today at camp," Davey said. His expression was grave.

"To Kevin?" I asked quickly. I started to rise.

A slight shake of Davey's head made me sit back down.

"To you?"

"Kind of. But not really."

"You're going to have to explain things better than that."

"It was weird."

Weird, I knew. Weird was my stock in trade. But it wasn't Davey's.

I gave him a few seconds to gather his thoughts. I waited while he ate two bites of his peach. Juice dribbled down his chin. I got up to get him a napkin, then sat back down. Still waiting. I made myself take a deep breath and slowly let it out.

"No pressure," I said. "Start at the beginning. Or anywhere else that makes sense."

"Ms. Grace keeps an old pickup truck at the school," he began. "It's, like, ancient. Probably a classic. Maybe you've seen it?"

I nodded. That truck had been around for as long as I'd been going to Graceland. It was a Chevy of some kind, painted a ridiculously shiny shade of red. Usually, it sat parked inside a carport behind the main building. I'd never seen anyone drive it. When Emily needed to go somewhere, she zipped around in a Toyota.

"What about it?" I asked.

"Actually, it's kind of a cool truck." Davey had always been fascinated by anything with an engine. "Way back when I was a camper, I asked Ms. Grace about it. She told me it was from the 1960s."

"No wonder no one ever drives it," I said. "I wonder if it even runs."

"It did today," Davey told me. "That was the problem."

"What problem?" I asked. Belatedly, it occurred to me that I probably shouldn't have told him to start at the beginning.

"It ended up in the pond."

"Emily's truck?"

Davey nodded. Now that things were finally getting interesting, he paused to take another bite of his peach.

"How?" I asked. "When?"

"Right before lunch. Courtney and I were at the playground with the Jellyfish kids. Suddenly, we heard someone screaming behind the other building. Courtney said she had our kids under control, so I went to see what was wrong. When I ran around the corner, I couldn't believe it. The red truck was rolling down the hill toward the pond."

"Who was driving it?" I asked.

"That's just it. There wasn't anyone inside. The truck must have been in gear with its brake off. It went flying down the incline, bumping up and down over the lawn."

"That's bizarre," I said with a frown. "Who was screaming?"

"It was Sarah. She and Tom are the Goldfish counselors. It looked like they'd just had their kids down at the pond, and now they were coming back up the hill for lunch."

I sucked in a breath. "Was the truck heading their way?"

"Not exactly. But it was heading for where they'd been a few minutes earlier. Sarah and Tom were quick to pull all the kids off to the side. The truck missed them by at least twenty feet. It rolled past and kept going until it landed in the pond with a big splash."

"And everyone was all right?" I asked quickly.

"Yeah, they were fine." Davey didn't look nearly as upset as I felt. "I went over to see if Sarah and Tom needed any help. Their kids thought it was a big adventure. They were all pointing and laughing, like the whole thing was really funny."

It didn't sound funny at all to me. "Then what happened? Did the truck sink?"

"Not all the way. It must have gotten caught up in the mud because it stopped before it was fully submerged. The cabin was mostly underwater, though. The door wasn't shut, so you could see inside. The water came all the way up to the seats. Ms. Grace isn't going to be happy about that."

"I'm sure she's even less happy that some of her campers were put at risk," I told him. "How did it happen?"

"Dunno." Davey shrugged. "When I got there, the truck was already on its way."

"What did Tom and Sarah have to say?"

"Pretty much the same thing. Because they were down near the water, they'd both been keeping a close eye on the kids. Neither one of them was paying any attention to what was happening at the top of the hill."

"Do you think someone had gotten the truck out to use it?" I asked.

Davey shrugged again.

"There's a man who does maintenance around the school," I remembered. "What's his name?"

"Mr. Bobbit. But I don't think he was there today."

"What about Ms. Grace?" I asked.

"I know she didn't get it out, because she was as shocked as the rest of us. Ms. Grace came running outside just before the truck hit the water. When that happened, she shrieked and covered her mouth with her hands. By that time, Sarah, Tom, and I had all the Goldfish campers in a group behind the building. And Courtney was bringing the Jellyfish kids around to join us. The rest of the campers were already inside the cafeteria."

"What did Ms. Grace do then?"

"She looked like she was going to faint right on the spot." Davey looked like he was biting back a smile.

"But she didn't," I said firmly. Emily was made of sterner stuff than that.

"Nope. Instead, she made us line up all the campers who were outside, and then she took attendance like six times. After that, she checked out each of the kids individually to make sure everyone was all right. Then she told the counselors to take everyone inside for lunch, and not to worry about the truck because she'd take care of it."

"That's all she said?"

"Yup."

"She didn't offer any explanation of how something like that could have happened?"

Davey gazed at me across the table. Suddenly, he looked older than his almost fifteen years. "I don't think Ms. Grace had an explanation. If she did, she didn't want to share it with us."

The next morning, when I drove the boys to camp, I left Faith at home. Now that we were nearly a week into the session, morning drop-off proceeded like clockwork. Mia greeted the arrivals and turned them over to their respective counselors. Each group waited until all its campers were present, then everyone moved on to their first activity.

Today, however, after the boys got out of the car, I didn't head back down the driveway. Instead, I pulled out of line and parked the Volvo in front of the smaller building.

Mia glanced in my direction as I walked toward the

entrance. She hailed me before I could open the weathered wooden door.

"Are you looking for Emily?"

I nodded. "Is she here?"

"Yes, but not in her office. Last I saw her, she was in the gym, unpacking the decorations."

Another car pulled up in front of Mia. I was quickly forgotten as she leaned down to open the door and help two small siblings disembark.

I crossed the walkway to the main building. The gym was on the other side of the school. It was mostly put to use on stormy days or in the middle of winter. I wondered what kind of decorations Emily was putting up.

I was almost to the gym when I heard yelling coming from inside the room. "Hey, cut that out! Right now! Do you hear me?"

Quickly I strode to the door and shoved it open. I started to enter, then jumped back. Two black-spotted Dalmatian puppies went flying by. Each was holding one end of a red, white, and blue banner in her mouth. The bunting dragged on the floor between the pair as they raced around the corner. A third puppy was just behind them in hot pursuit.

Emily was up on a ladder that she'd propped against a side wall. She gave me a small wave before climbing down and coming over. "They're not supposed to have that," she said unnecessarily.

I laughed. "I could have guessed."

"Sorry about that. Sometimes those three act like little hoodlums. They're not great at doing what they're told."

"It's hard to train three at once," I said. "They'll learn much better if each one gets some exclusive time with you."

Emily looked surprised. "You mean they're like kids."

"Precisely." I hunkered down close to the floor and clapped my hands. "Hey, puppies, over here! Come and say hello."

I'd never met a puppy that didn't love a friendly stranger, and this trio was no exception. In seconds, the Dalmatians had abandoned their prize to come racing toward me. I opened my arms wide and braced myself for the onslaught.

Aunt Peg would have immediately begun to catalog the Dals' virtues and faults. All I knew was that the three puppies were adorable. All had pretty faces, muscular bodies, and long tails that were wagging an enthusiastic greeting. One puppy began to sniff my legs. Another jumped up to lick my nose.

"That's Posey who's giving you kisses," Emily said. "She loves to be the center of attention."

"They all look alike to me," I said with a laugh.

"Right," she replied. "Because black Standard Poodles are easy to tell apart."

Oh. She had a point.

I gazed around the gym. Aside from the banners, Emily had unpacked tri-color pompoms and pinwheels, along with several flags and wreaths. "Fourth of July was last week," I mentioned. "Aren't you supposed to be taking that stuff down rather than putting it up?"

"Normally, yes. But you know how kids love holidays. And since this year Fourth of July fell on the Friday before camp started, we missed the whole thing. So we're celebrating Bastille Day instead. The colors are all the same. Nobody will notice the difference, right?"

I wouldn't be too sure about that. But right now, it

seemed to me that Emily had bigger things to worry about than a missed holiday.

One of the puppies grabbed the edge of a red-and-white-striped tablecloth that was hanging out of a nearby box. She tugged on it until it reached the floor. Then the puppy lay down and began to chew.

Emily looked over and frowned. "I probably should have put these guys away before I started decorating. I guess I'm a little scattered this morning."

"I don't blame you," I said.

Her gaze lifted. "So you heard about what happened."

I nodded. Emily didn't look happy.

"I'm taking a break," she said abruptly. "Let's take the puppies outside for a walk."

Chapter 5

"I asked the counselors not to say anything about that," Emily said unhappily as we left the building. "I guess they didn't listen."

Campers were arriving in front of the school, but the area behind it was still mostly deserted. The three Dalmatians followed us outside; then they took off in three different directions. Emily didn't appear to be paying any attention to them. I hoped the puppies wouldn't go too far afield.

"By 'they' you mean Davey," I clarified.

She nodded shortly. "Although I'd imagine he wasn't the only one who blabbed about it."

"It wasn't fair of you to make them complicit in your silence," I said. "And by asking the teenagers to keep quiet, you made them think the accident was a bigger deal than they'd thought."

"Actually, it was a pretty big deal," she admitted.

"So I heard. Where's the truck now?"

"One of my neighbors has a tractor. He came and pulled it out of the pond for me. Then AAA took the truck down to the repair shop. It's sitting there until it dries out. After that, the mechanics will be able to assess the damage."

"Will you get it fixed?"

Emily shrugged. "I guess we'll have to see."

"It's an old truck," I said. "It might not be worth the cost of the repair."

She turned to look at me. "I actually have no idea what it's worth. Though I doubt it's much. The truck belongs to my ex-husband. He found it in a junkyard and restored it. The project was more a labor of love than something he planned to profit from."

"Ex-husband?" I had no idea Emily had been married.

"Very ex-husband," she said. "You're not the only one who didn't get it right the first time. Although in my case, I knew better than to try again."

I might have argued with her about that. All things considered, my second marriage was working out to be pretty damn great. But I didn't want the conversation to get sidetracked. I had more important things to discuss.

"How did the truck end up in the pond?" I asked.

"Good question. I wish I knew."

I wasn't as complacent about that lack of knowledge as Emily appeared to be. "Apparently, it narrowly missed hitting a group of campers."

Emily stiffened. "I hope you're not accusing me of negligence."

"No," I replied carefully. "But I am trying to figure out what went wrong."

"So am I," she retorted. "The truck's been sitting in that carport for years. Occasionally I get it out when I need to haul something, but other than that, it never moves. It's certainly never decided to take itself for a joyride before."

"I'm guessing that wasn't the truck's idea."

She frowned. "You know what I mean."

I gazed around the open field behind the school. It was beautiful land. Once, all the properties in the area had been as large as this one. Now, with development encroaching on all sides, they'd become a rarity.

"Have you ever had a problem with neighborhood kids playing pranks?" I asked.

Emily paused to think about that. While she did that, I checked on the puppies. Thankfully, all three of them were still visible. Now they were busy chasing a squirrel. They followed it to the base of a tree, then jumped frantically against the trunk, daring the squirrel to come back down.

"No, never," Emily replied after a minute. "Graceland School is a kid-friendly place, and everyone around here knows it. Lots of the local kids started their educations here—so I know most of them by name. If someone started acting up, I'd probably nab them by the collar and put them to work."

I could imagine her doing exactly that. "So what's your theory then?"

Emily didn't reply.

That was okay. I had time. I waited her out.

When she spoke again, however, Emily changed the

subject. "I opened Graceland Nursery School here, on this property, nearly twenty years ago."

I nodded. I knew that.

"It's funny to think how young I was back then. And how sure of myself. To believe that I could open my own nursery school and actually make it work. Practically, logistically, and financially, I was like a babe in the woods."

"But one with a vision," I pointed out. "And you did make it work."

"I did," she agreed. "But I couldn't have done it without help. Do you know who Malcolm Hancock was?"

The name sounded familiar, but I couldn't quite place it. I shook my head.

"At one time, he was a major property owner in North Stamford. This land we're on is his. Malcolm believed that the arts, music, and education are the pillars of civilization—and that it was important to make them available to as many people as possible. When he and I met, this property had been used as an artists' retreat for a number of years. But applications had been dwindling, and Malcolm was looking for a new way to put it to good use."

"And you showed up with a plan for a nursery school that would offer good teachers, affordable fees, and strong art and music programs."

Emily smiled at the memory. "Malcolm liked my idea. Even better, he believed in it. He believed in *me*. You have no idea what a thrill that was for a girl in her mid-twenties with a degree in education who was barely scraping by in an entry-level job. When Malcolm offered me use of this property and told me to see what I could make of it, I felt as though he had handed me the keys to the world."

Two Dalmatian puppies came circling back toward us. Poppy and Pansy? Posey and Poppy? I had no idea.

Luckily, Emily did. "Oh, you guys," she moaned. "What have you gotten into now? Where's Posey?"

"Over there." I pointed.

The third puppy was digging a hole at the base of a nearby bush. Dirt flew backward between her front legs as she tunneled energetically. Posey was going to be filthy by the time she finished. Plus, there'd be a big hole in the yard.

"Stop that right now!" Emily called. She and I strode that way.

The puppy lifted her head, glanced at us briefly, then resumed digging. These three could definitely use some obedience training.

Emily grabbed Posey's collar. I got Poppy and Pansy turned around, and we all headed back toward the school buildings. The three puppies were panting. I'd have to be sure to check their water supply when we got back.

"Finish your story," I said to Emily.

"Oh, right. So Malcolm offered me a lease on the property at very affordable terms. Nowhere near what it would have cost on the open market. And I worked day and night to fulfill my dream. I created Graceland School and turned it into"—she waved her hand through the air—"all this."

"It's an amazing place," I said.

Emily sighed. "It's an amazing place that will probably have to shut down next year."

"Wait . . . *what*?" I turned and stared at her. "Why?"

"Malcolm died last year. His grown children inherited this property along with everything else. Originally, Malcolm and I had signed a ten-year lease. When it ended, we renewed it. But it's up for renewal again in about eighteen months."

"And the rate you've been offered this time isn't nearly as affordable?" I guessed.

"Not even close. It's not like I can blame Malcolm's heirs. This land was worth a lot more than I was paying when I opened the school—I was well aware that I was getting a great deal. And you know what property values are like in Fairfield County. Everything has only continued to appreciate. I know the heirs have had offers to sell the land as soon as they can get me off of it. Thankfully, they've resisted so far."

"That's gracious of them," I muttered.

"Actually, it is," she said. "They could have grabbed the money and run. At least they've offered me a chance to stay in business. Only it's not much of a chance if I can't afford the new rent they're planning on charging."

"What about raising the school fees?" I asked. "Would that help?"

"About as much as sticking my finger in a dike. Plus, it would go against everything Malcolm believed in. The whole point—one that he and I both agreed on—was that this nursery school should be accessible to kids who might not get the same kind of opportunities in other aspects of their lives."

"I'm really sorry to hear that," I said. "This is a wonderful school. It would be a huge shame if it wasn't able to continue operating."

"I agree. I've been trying to think of any way I can make some extra money. I'm applying for grants, looking for tax breaks, and wondering how much I can cut the staff and still maintain the quality of education. The whole thing has been keeping me up at night." Emily sighed again. "So, believe me, I know I'm not at my best right now."

My thoughts immediately went back to the runaway truck. "You know that's how accidents happen," I said gently.

"I'm well aware of that. But yesterday's incident wasn't an accident."

"What makes you think that?"

"The truck has been stored here forever. Nobody ever goes near it but me, and it almost never leaves the carport. I checked yesterday after it ended up in the water. The only set of keys was still in my office."

One of the puppies nudged her nose into my hand. I reached down and scratched behind her velvety ears. "So you're saying that someone must have deliberately pushed the truck to the top of the incline?"

"That's the only thing I can think," Emily replied grimly.

"To what end? Why would someone want to terrorize the campers?"

"I don't know. I don't understand any of this." Emily's expression was bleak. "Maybe it's someone who wants to harm me."

That put an interesting spin on things.

"It could be that Malcolm Hancock's heirs aren't as gracious as you think," I said.

Saturday morning started early.

Our whole family enjoyed going to dog shows, so it

wasn't surprising that Davey and Kevin were both up and dressed before I was even out of the shower. What was surprising was that the two boys had also let the dogs outside, fed them breakfast, and then set out breakfast for the human members of the family too.

Okay, it was just juice, cereal, and bananas. But still.

"Did you do that?" I asked Sam. He was already seated at the kitchen table when I got downstairs.

"Not me." He looked up from the newspaper that was sitting beside his plate. "Davey's in charge this morning."

"I'm in charge too." Kevin banged his fist on the table. A dribble of milk sloshed over the side of his bowl.

"Of course you are." I kissed the top of his head. Not only did Kevin's shorts and T-shirt match, his sneakers were already on and tied. Davey had been busy.

I shifted my gaze my older son's way. "Well done."

Davey nodded. "Today's going to be a good day."

"You know it," Sam agreed.

I liked their confidence. And I really hoped they were right.

Aunt Peg had spent the previous several days meticulously clipping, bathing, and blow-drying Coral's coat. We did our part by schlepping to the dog show all the supplies necessary for preparing Coral for the ring. Those included a wooden crate and a rubber-matted folding table, plus an assortment of combs, brushes, wraps, bands, hair spray, and a misting bottle, all neatly stowed inside a multi-level tack box.

A state park in Dutchess County, New York, provided an idyllic outdoor setting for the dog show. As always, my heart lifted when we arrived and I saw the level, grassy field with its familiar configuration of rings—two parallel rows of eight, with a center aisle between them covered by a green-and-white-striped tent.

A second, smaller tent provided a shaded grooming space where exhibitors congregated to prepare their dogs to be shown. Beautiful dogs of all colors, shapes, and sizes were relaxing or being groomed on their tabletops. Numerous exercise pens ringed the outside of the handlers' tent. The whine of a dozen generators buzzed in the air.

Sam pulled his SUV up beside the tent to unload. We each had a job to do. Sam put the big wooden crate on a dolly. I rested the grooming table on top of it. Davey grabbed the tack box and the hanging bag that held his sports coat. Kevin was drafted to carry his bag of toys. That left me with the cooler that held snacks for us, as well as a baggie of dried liver that Davey would use in the show ring to focus Coral's attention.

"I see Aunt Peg," Kevin announced gleefully.

Actually, she was hard to miss. Standing taller than anyone in the vicinity and waving her arms above her head, Aunt Peg now had half the people and dogs under the tent staring in her direction.

"Good." Sam began to maneuver the dolly between the tightly packed setups. "That must mean she saved us a spot."

Drawing near, I saw that Aunt Peg had Coral sitting on a table borrowed from the neighboring setup. It belonged to professional handler Crawford Langley and his assistant, Terry Denunzio. The two men had been a couple for years and had celebrated their wedding on Valentine's Day.

"It's about time you got here," Terry said under his

breath as I approached. He was line-brushing a black Mini Poodle, who was lying on his side on another table.

I grinned at him. Terry and I were best buddies. He was cocky, outrageous, and always entertaining. At any event, Terry could be counted on to have the best gossip and the best hair. Today's coiffure was black and spikey. On him, it looked almost normal.

"Is Aunt Peg driving you crazy?" I asked in the same low tone. Heaven forbid she should overhear us.

He rolled his eyes, as if the answer was a given. "Did you know there's a major today in Standard bitches?"

"Of course. That's why we're here."

"Peg has reminded us three times since she arrived. Worse, she's been pacing back and forth across our setup waiting for you to arrive."

"I bet Crawford loves that."

I must have spoken louder than I'd intended because the handler, who was busy at the other end of the big, multi-table setup, turned around to face us. Crawford was in his late sixties, a time when many men would have been contemplating retirement. But after decades spent handling glorious dogs to notable wins, Crawford was still at the top of his game. It was a position he had no intention of relinquishing anytime soon.

"Good morning, Melanie," he said. "Are you two talking about me behind my back?"

"We're trying to." I gave him a cheeky smile. Crawford and I had worked through issues in the past. I was happy our relationship was now back on solid ground. "But since you're onto us, I guess we'll have to stop."

"I've been telling Terry for years that you're a bad influence. But he never listens."

"Au contraire, O Mighty One," Terry shot back. "I value every pearl of wisdom that passes your lips."

Crawford stared for a moment, then turned his back to us again. "Sheesh," he muttered. I nearly laughed out loud.

"You there." Aunt Peg waved imperiously in my direction. "Quit goofing around. Come over here and make yourself useful."

While I'd been talking to Terry, Sam and Davey had set up the grooming table and wedged the heavy crate between two others of similar size. The cooler was now stashed under the table, and the tack box was open on top of the crate.

It looked like we were open for business.

All we needed now was a Standard Poodle. Striding past Coral, I paused and patted my chest. The big black bitch hopped into my arms. Two steps later, I deposited her on top of our grooming table.

Coral nudged Davey with her nose and woofed happily. "I know," he whispered into her ear. "Me too."

Aunt Peg observed their interaction with an arched brow. "You too, what?" she inquired.

"I think Coral told him she was looking forward to having a great time in the ring today," I said. "And Davey agreed."

"Oh?" Aunt Peg was not amused. "Today is serious business. We didn't come to have fun."

"Speak for yourself." Sam was as eager to deflect Aunt Peg's high-pressure tactics as I was. He flapped a hand at her. "Now shoo."

"Shoo?" She folded her arms over her chest. "I don't think so."

I expected Davey to protest. In similar circumstances, he and Aunt Peg had clashed before. And none of the previous shows had been as important as this one.

"Fine," Davey said. "If you don't believe that Sam and I have everything under control, you can stay. On one condition. You can't say a single word."

"But—"

"Not one," he warned. "I mean it."

Aunt Peg glared at me. Davey was my son, after all.

Inwardly, I cheered. On the outside, I just shrugged.

Aunt Peg's fingers grasped the top of my arm. She spun around and left the setup. I had no choice but to follow.

"Kevin's with you," I told Sam as she yanked me away.

My husband merely nodded, but I was pretty sure he was trying not to laugh. Terry didn't even make the attempt. The sound of his snickering followed us out of the tent.

Chapter 6

"That was rude," Aunt Peg said as she and I headed toward the rings.

"I agree," I replied. Thank goodness, she'd released my arm. Any minute now, the circulation should start returning to it.

She shot me a suspicious look—as if she didn't trust that we were talking about the same thing. Which we most definitely were not.

"It's going to be a long day if you keep trying to make trouble," I told her.

"And an even longer one if Coral doesn't win," she muttered.

"Jumping down Davey's throat isn't going to make that happen."

"I was merely offering to help."

"And he was merely refusing," I replied. "Get over it."

Aunt Peg swung around to face me. I expected her to snap out a pithy retort. I really hoped that she didn't threaten to take Coral away from Davey. Because that would really make me mad.

Not for the first time, however, Aunt Peg surprised me. She stared down at me. The expression on her face almost looked like respect. "All right, then," she announced. "I'm over it. Let's talk about something else."

Great idea. I said the first thing that popped into my head. "Emily Grace's school is in trouble."

"Emily Grace. You mentioned her the other day. The lady with complications. Is this another puppy problem? Don't tell me they got away again."

Of course she would ask about the dogs first.

"No, the puppies are fine—"

"That's good. Though I assume that means that something else isn't. Is it something we should care about?"

"Money," I told her.

"Oh." Aunt Peg frowned. "Everyone cares about that. Dogs, however, would have been more interesting. How do you feel about Collies?"

Collies? "I don't have an opinion about them one way or another," I said.

"That's not good." Aunt Peg sidled up to the first ring we'd come to. Three smooth Collies were gaiting around its perimeter. "They're lovely dogs. We'll stop here and watch for a bit. While you tell me about Emily Grace's money problems, I will endeavor to educate myself about another Herding breed."

It only took a few minutes for me to outline everything Emily had told me the day before. Aunt Peg listened to me with both eyes trained on the Collie ring. I figured that meant she was devoting about half her attention to what I was saying. I was tempted to give her a quiz at the end to see how much information she'd retained, but I was pretty sure that wouldn't go over well.

The smooth Collie Best of Variety class entered the ring. Aunt Peg and I both paused as the judge evaluated his four entries: two champions, plus the Winners Dog and Winners Bitch. It was easy for me to tell which dog Aunt Peg found the most deserving. Luckily, the judge agreed with her. Otherwise we would have had to have a discussion about that too. Instead we were able to return to our conversation.

"Malcolm Hancock," she said thoughtfully. "I've heard that name."

I explained briefly who he was. "I'm surprised you didn't know him."

Some days it seemed as though Aunt Peg knew everybody.

"No, unfortunately, he and I never crossed paths. But Graceland School sounds like a fine institution. It's a shame it might be forced to close. Did Emily say how much of a financial shortfall she's looking at?"

"We didn't go into specifics. But I'd love to be able to help her in some way."

The smooth Collies had filed out of the ring. Now the rough coated Collies were being judged.

"Those look more difficult," I said.

Aunt Peg cast me a glance. "Hmm?"

"You know, to judge. With the smooth variety we could see the dogs' bodies and movement quite easily. With these Collies, almost everything is hidden by the hair."

"Most people would say the same thing about Poodles."

I hadn't thought about that.

"With smooth coated dogs, a judge can perform most of her evaluation by sight alone. But in a long haired breed, good grooming can cover a multitude of sins. You really need to get your hands down into the coat to feel for yourself what's there." Aunt Peg watched with approval as the judge in the ring did exactly that.

The rough Collies only took ten minutes to judge. When they were finished, two medium-sized, reddish-tan dogs with foxy faces and bushy tails entered the ring. They gaited around together.

"Icelandic Sheepdogs," Aunt Peg said before I had a chance to ask. "Quite an appealing breed."

Frankly, her endorsement didn't mean much. Aunt Peg thought all dogs were appealing.

She waited until the judge had awarded the ribbons, then turned to me. "Have we wasted enough time yet?"

"Excuse me?"

"You know perfectly well what I mean. Have we been away from the setup long enough that we can go back to see how things are progressing?"

"Not even close," I told her.

She harrumphed under her breath. "We've been waiting nearly six weeks for a major entry."

"I know."

"And Davey's only fourteen. At his age, he can benefit from proper guidance."

"You trusted him to handle Coral because you thought he had potential," I pointed out. "And he's improved steadily since the two of them became a team. Now you have to sit back and let Davey show you what he's capable of doing."

"I hate sitting back and doing nothing," she huffed. "It makes me feel useless."

"Fine," I said. "Then help me come up with an idea that will save Graceland School."

"Funny you should ask," said Aunt Peg. "I've been thinking."

When? I wondered. Barely fifteen minutes had passed since we'd finished discussing it.

"Dog people love to pull together for a good cause," she said. "Look at all the good Take the Lead has done. Not to mention the Poodle Club of America Foundation."

"Sure," I agreed. "But those are dog people helping other dog people. Or working for the betterment of their breed. Emily isn't a member of the dog community."

"You're right, she isn't," Aunt Peg said. "And right now, that might be just what we need."

"What do you mean?"

"Look around," Aunt Peg told me. "What do you see?"

I knew I would see the same thing I'd seen at virtually every dog show I'd ever attended. Nevertheless, I obliged her. I let my gaze roam slowly down the row of rings in front of us, where half a dozen different breeds were strutting their stuff. Then I turned around and looked back toward the handler's tent. By the time I'd finished, I was smiling.

"I see many wonderful dogs," I said. "All of them meticulously groomed to look their best, all having a great time interacting with their owners or handlers. You know perfectly well that a dog show is a dog lover's paradise."

"It is indeed," she agreed. "But if that's all you saw, you were only looking at the surface."

That punctured my happy mood. It sounded as though I was in for a lecture. Better me than Davey, however.

"Let me tell you what *I* see," Aunt Peg continued. "When I look around, I think about the fact that every dog here today is the product of many generations of focused, intentional breeding. Each different breed was carefully developed with a specific purpose in mind. Each was bred to have those traits that would enable them to do their jobs and do them well—whether that job might be herding cattle, locating lost hikers, or flushing game."

I nodded and remained silent. I already knew that. But when Aunt Peg was on a roll, it was safest just to stay out of her way.

"Conscientious breeders have worked hard to preserve those attributes that define their breeds. It's not mere chance that Bloodhounds have big noses and long, floppy ears. Or that Salukis can run like the wind."

"Or that Poodles love to dance on their hind feet."

Aunt Peg glared at me.

"Sorry." I bit my lip. "I couldn't help myself."

She was not amused.

"I feel like you're making a point with this lesson," I said. "I also feel like I have no idea what it is."

"That's because you haven't been paying attention."

I could have sworn that wasn't true.

"Since you still don't get it, I shall continue," she informed me.

This looked like it could take a while. There were two empty chairs beside the ring, where Beaucerons were now being judged. I walked over and sat down. Aunt Peg watched the judging for a minute before coming over to join me.

"The bitch at the end of the line is quite lovely. She'll be Winners Bitch," she murmured, just loud enough that only I could hear.

I knew she'd be right. If Aunt Peg had been born three hundred years earlier, she'd probably have been branded a witch.

She turned her attention back to me. "As I was saying, not only has the dog world developed and nurtured a multitude of breeds that remain remarkably consistent in their looks, their temperaments, and their abilities, we've also made huge strides in the areas of canine disease control and genetic testing."

I nodded again. Really, at this point what else was there for me to do?

"In practical terms, what that means is that if someone wants to add, say, a Labrador Retriever, to their family—and they seek out a reputable breeder—they may be assured that the puppy they bring home will be a good-sized, solid, fun-loving dog who is wonderful with children and remarkably fond of tennis balls."

Time was passing. The Beaucerons had left the ring. Now the judge had his hands on a Pumi. If I didn't stop her now, Aunt Peg and I might be here all day.

"What does that have to do with Emily and Graceland School?" I asked.

"If only you would be patient, I was getting to that."

Said the Queen of Patience herself. I sighed and waited for her to go on.

"It's no secret that the world of purebred dogs now finds itself in a precarious position. The animal rights groups are controlling the narrative, and 'Adopt, don't

shop' has become the mantra of the day. Responsible
breeders find themselves being lumped in the same category as puppy mills, when nothing could be farther from
the truth."

I totally agreed with her. But again . . . Emily Grace?

"So I had a thought about your friend and her school,"
Aunt Peg said. *Finally.* "What if we got a group of breeders together and held a benefit for her?"

That came as a surprise. I paused and considered the
idea. "What kind of benefit?"

"I'm thinking of something like a purebred dog showcase. We could call it Meet the Breeds, or maybe Meet
the Breeders. We would introduce our lovely dogs and
our friendly selves, plus add in other kinds of entertainment. I bet people would be willing to pay a reasonable
admission fee for that. Think of the educational opportunities."

I was. And Aunt Peg was right. The idea had merit.

"I know plenty of dog show people who would be
willing, even eager, to take part in an event like that," she
said. "We might be able to attract as many as fifty or sixty
different breeds. It could be a win-win for both Graceland
School and dog lovers."

Suddenly I was really liking the sound of this. "I bet
we could hold it right at Graceland," I said. "There's
plenty of room. And that would give people a chance to
see all the good Emily is doing there. Then they could
make a direct donation to the school too."

"What if we held some silly competitions?" Aunt Peg
proposed. "Longest tail, biggest nose, most spots, that
type of thing. We could let the children who were there
do the judging and hand out the prizes."

I could picture the whole thing happening. And it looked wonderful.

"Aunt Peg, you're a genius," I said.

She nodded, accepting her due. "We wouldn't make enough to pay off the whole lease, but our proceeds might be able to carry Graceland School for an additional year or two. And if the event is a success, we could think about making it an annual occurrence."

"You're sure you'll be able to get enough breeders to take part?"

"That will be the least of our worries," Aunt Peg said with confidence. "You leave that to me. Once I put the word out and we start taking names, I predict we'll have an overflow of entries."

"Don't start yet. I need to get Emily's approval first. She may not like the idea."

"Nonsense." She snorted. "What's not to like? Emily's in need of a fundraiser, and dog breeders could use some good PR for a change. Everybody benefits. I don't know why I didn't think of something like this sooner."

Probably because she'd been too busy worrying un-necessarily about Coral and Davey. Abruptly I glanced down at my watch.

"We need to get moving," I said. "Standards start in twenty minutes. Let's stop by the ring and pick up Davey's armband, then head back to the grooming tent."

"I thought you'd never ask," said Aunt Peg.

Chapter 7

Coral was nearly ring-ready when Aunt Peg and I got back to the setup. The big Poodle was standing on her table while Davey layered a liberal amount of hair spray into her copious topknot and neck hair. Meanwhile, Sam was using a pair of curved shears to snick tiny bits of hair off of her rounded front puffs.

"Momeee!" Kevin was sitting in the grass nearby, looking at a picture book. He jumped up as we approached. "Did you bring me a hot dog?"

"No." I thought back. "Did you ask me for a hot dog?"

He stuck out his lower lip. "I thought you would just know."

Is there a mother anywhere who doesn't feel guilty about something most of the time? If so, I hadn't met her.

I walked over and opened the cooler. "How about a peanut butter and jelly sandwich?"

"What kind of jelly?" Terry asked from next door. "Don't say grape."

Crawford was already up at the ring, where Minis were currently being judged. Terry had their white Mini special standing beside him on a tabletop. One hand was beneath the dog's chin, the other was rubbing the base of its tail. The Mini entry wasn't large, which meant that Terry would need to leave soon.

"You're in luck. It's raspberry." I held up a baggie with the sandwich inside. "Want one? Maybe you can hold it in your third hand."

"Shush. Play nice." Terry leaned over and lowered his voice. "Crawford's going to win nearly everything today in Toys and Minis, which will clear the way for you"—he nodded in Coral's direction—"in Standards. We'll all come back here afterward and celebrate with peanut butter and jelly."

"It's a deal," I told him. "Except for one thing. You guys aren't the only ones we have to beat. There are twelve Standard bitches entered."

"Yes, but ours is the one you have to worry about because other than Coral, she's the best." Terry swept the white Mini off the table and hurried away.

Aunt Peg stared at me from the other side of the setup. "What were you two talking about over there?"

"Nothing important," I said breezily. Aunt Peg was superstitious when it came to dog shows. She didn't need to know that we'd been discussing potential results.

"I hope you weren't trying to bribe Terry to throw the win with peanut butter and jelly," Sam said with a grin.

"Coral won't need any underhanded assistance to do well today," I said. "She looks great."

Davey stepped away from the table and took a look too. "She does, doesn't she?"

For a minute, we all stood and admired the beautiful Standard Poodle in front of us. Now twenty months old, Coral had grown into her adult trim. Her topknot and ears were glorious, and her neck hair and mane coat had filled in. Her topline was level, the swoop of her beautifully angulated hindquarter was just right. Her tail stood straight up in the air. Coral's pretty face stared right back at us. She knew today was her day.

"Hey," said Kevin. He was clearly not as impressed as the rest of us were. "Where's my sandwich?"

I gave Kev half a sandwich and told him to bring it to the ring with us. It was almost time to go. Sam helped Davey into his sports coat, then banded Coral's number to the top of his arm. Aunt Peg checked to make sure Davey had bait in his pocket. I unwrapped Coral's ears and combed the long hair into place. Then Sam carefully lifted the bitch off the table and set her on the ground.

As soon as Coral found her footing, she gave her body a long, luxurious shake. When she was finished, I grabbed the comb and fixed her ears again. Sam unspooled her narrow leash and handed the end to Davey.

As we were heading out, Crawford and Terry came hurrying back to the setup with their Miniature Poodles. Both men were carrying ribbons. Purple and gold meant Best of Variety. Red and white was Best of Opposite Sex. Blue and white was for Best of Winners.

Terry's prediction had been correct: Crawford had won everything in Minis. That helped.

The two men stashed the Minis on tabletops and grabbed their Standards. Crawford was showing an Open bitch. He also had a champion dog for Best of Variety. I looked at his class bitch critically. She looked great. That wasn't unexpected—every dog Crawford showed looked great. But she wasn't as nice as Coral. I hoped today's judge would agree.

We arrived at ringside when the Open Dog class was being judged. Sam and Davey took Coral off to one side, protecting her from being jostled by the crowd of people and dogs beneath the center tent. I was holding Kevin's hand. We went with Aunt Peg to find a good spot from which to watch the action.

Kev was finishing his sandwich. There was a smear of jelly across the front of his T-shirt. It figured.

"When's Davey's class?" he asked.

"Not for a few minutes. There's a major in dogs too. See?"

I gestured toward the ring, but Kevin lost interest when he heard it wasn't Davey's turn yet. He reached for my catalog instead. He opened it and began to look at pictures.

As always, I was fascinated by the scene in front of us. We'd missed two earlier dog classes. Six Open dogs were now in the ring. The judge, an older woman, appeared to be making short work of her entry.

"Who's going to win?" I asked Aunt Peg.

She reared back and stared at me in outrage. "How would I know that?"

Seriously? She always knew that. Witness our earlier

exchange at the Beauceron ring. Now, apparently, she'd decided to be circumspect.

I tried again. "What kind of dog does Alida Rudolph like?"

I'd never shown under the woman nor seen her judge, but I knew Aunt Peg would be well aware of Mrs. Rudolph's preferences. After all, she'd made the entry for Coral. So if this judge favored white Poodles or was known to reward dogs who didn't move well, we wouldn't be here.

"Pretty," Aunt Peg said out of the side of her mouth. In keeping with ringside etiquette, she kept her voice low.

Check. We had that covered. "What else?"

"She'll give Coral's front a thorough inspection, and she cares about good feet."

I added a few more checks to the list. So far, so good.

"I assume she doesn't mind owner handlers?" Politics could be a problem for amateur exhibitors. Some judges cared only about the connections of the handlers in their rings.

"No, but . . ." Aunt Peg paused as Mrs. Rudolph rearranged the order of her Open dogs. She was about to send them around the ring one last time.

"Go on," I prompted. A "but" was never a good thing.

Aunt Peg exhaled as Mrs. Rudolph motioned a handsome silver dog over to the first-place marker. I assumed he was the Poodle she'd secretly been rooting for.

Two handlers waiting outside the gate hustled the winners of the earlier Puppy and Bred-by-Exhibitor classes back into the ring. The three dogs lined up in class order to compete for Winners Dog—and the all-important points that came with the award.

Mrs. Rudolph stared at the trio from across the ring.

Aunt Peg stared at Alida Rudolph, as if she was trying to pick the judge's brain.

"But?" I said. Davey would be entering the ring shortly. If this was something he needed to know, I wanted to hear about it now.

Aunt Peg spared me a glance. Apparently I wasn't nearly as interesting to her as what was happening in front of her. "Alida demands a good performance. She wants her exhibitors to be on their toes and paying attention. She won't tolerate any sloppiness or fooling around. The handler doesn't have to be a pro, but she wants to see a professional level handling job."

Oh. That explained why Aunt Peg had been on Davey's case this week.

"You might have mentioned that earlier," I said.

"And you might have trusted me to know what I was doing. Apparently we both failed to do our jobs."

I tried to look on the bright side. Surely, there had to be one somewhere. Preferably, one that didn't involve Aunt Peg's hopes and dreams resting on the slender shoulders of my fourteen-year-old son.

"Davey's ready for this," I said, with more confidence than I felt.

Aunt Peg frowned. "He'd better be. Because ready or not, he's about to join the big leagues."

Winners Dog went to the silver Standard. After that, the Puppy Bitch class with its three entries seemed to go by in a flash. There were nine bitches in Davey and Coral's Open class. When the handlers entered the ring and set their Poodles up in a long line, they took up one entire side of the enclosure.

The steward had asked for catalog order, which put Davey and Coral in the middle of the line. That was too bad. It was much easier to stand out when a dog was positioned at one of the two ends.

Once Davey was in the ring, Sam came over and joined us at the rail. Terry was close behind. There wouldn't be time to go back to the handlers' tent between now and Best of Variety, so Terry had Crawford's Standard special with him. He held the big white Poodle with his fingers cupped gently around the dog's muzzle. We all moved over to make room for him in our group.

I leaned down to Kevin's level. My son was eyeing the massive coat on Terry's Poodle. "Don't touch."

"I know." Kev smirked. He'd only been told a thousand times. "Besides"—he extended his hand over the low railing to point into the ring—"there's Davey. It's almost time for him to run around."

I quickly pulled his hand back, then held onto it. Heaven forbid he come in contact with anyone's Standard Poodle, even accidentally.

Mrs. Rudolph was making her first pass down the long line. She appeared to favor Coral with a few extra seconds of scrutiny, but that could have just been hopeful optimism on my part.

Crawford was at the head of the class. The judge told him to take the Poodles around the ring, and he glanced back to make sure everyone was ready. As the line began to move, Davey paused for a moment, giving the Standard bitch in front of Coral a head start. With a little extra room, Coral wouldn't have to hold back her longer stride to make it fit.

"Good job," I heard Aunt Peg mutter under her breath as Coral flew around the ring, showing off her lovely outline and extension.

Sam and I shared a pleased look. Terry grabbed my

hand and squeezed it hard. Much as he loved Crawford, I was pretty sure that today he was rooting for us.

Each of the first four bitches was individually examined and sent to the back of the line. Coral's turn was next. As the Poodle before him was finishing her performance, Davey walked Coral forward into a perfect stack. Then he moved around to stand in front of her.

One of his hands had her leash. The other held a fuzzy toy mouse he'd pulled out of his pocket. Coral eyed the toy. She arched her feet and went up on her toes. Her tail wagged back and forth.

Whether it was luck or perfect timing, Mrs. Rudolph chose that exact moment to turn around. When she saw Coral posed in front of her, looking like the living embodiment of the Poodle breed standard, a smile lit up her face. Then she quickly shuttered her expression and got down to business.

"Did you see that?" Terry whispered gleefully. He pounded on my shoulder with his fist.

"I did," I told him. By the time this day ended, I was going to be black and blue. Hopefully, it would be worth it.

"Be quiet, you two," Aunt Peg commanded. "I'm trying to concentrate."

Coral gaited down and back across the diagonal of the ring. Then Davey trotted her around the perimeter to the end of the line. Mrs. Rudolph's gaze followed her the entire way. The ringside did too. Coral possessed that kind of charisma.

The judge finished her individual examinations, then gazed once more down the line. She beckoned Crawford out to the center of the ring with his pretty bitch. Then she indicated that Davey and Coral should join them. Next, she pulled out a mature brown bitch presented by another pro. The remaining six bitches moved back against the outer rail as Mrs. Rudolph asked the three handlers in the middle to show off their Standard Poodles.

The head-to-head battle would be the acid test of Davey's skills and Coral's quality. Did my son have what it took to hold his own against the pros? We'd soon find out.

In Davey's place, I'd have been intimidated. My son, however, seemed oblivious to the pressure. He ignored Crawford and the other handler. He didn't care what they were doing. His attention never left Coral for a moment.

The black bitch responded in kind. What a wonderful team they made. Coral was having the time of her life. When Davey swung her out to the end of the lead to reposition her, the Poodle turned her head and gave Mrs. Rudolph an adoring look.

The judge melted. I saw it happen. Everyone else must have too—because Terry started pounding on me again.

Mrs. Rudolph lifted her hand and motioned Coral to the head of a new line. Crawford's bitch was placed behind her. The brown bitch was third. The judge plucked a bitch from the other six to put fourth. As soon as the line was reset, she pointed to each of the Standard Poodles in turn to pin her class.

Kevin jumped up and down. He pumped his small fist in the air.

"Wait," I told him. "It's not over."

I didn't realize it yet, but I was wrong. The decision had already been made. Because when the Puppy class winner returned to the ring, Mrs. Rudolph only waited long enough for the handler to move his bitch into position before she pointed to Coral a second time.

"You're my Winners Bitch," she said to Davey.

And just like that, Coral had won her first major.

Chapter 8

The judging wasn't finished yet, but we didn't care. Davey and Coral had already accomplished what we came for.

Crawford's bitch was Reserve Winners. The handler stopped on the way out of the ring and shook Davey's hand, congratulating him on a job well done. Coming from Crawford, that was high praise. I knew Davey would be almost as pleased about that as he was about the win.

The Best of Variety judging was next. Crawford switched Poodles with Terry, then re-entered the ring with his specials dog. Two other champions took their places behind him. The Winners Dog was after that, followed by Coral.

Now that the pressure was off, Davey showed Coral with a huge grin on his face. When Coral was awarded

Best of Winners over the dog, it was just the icing on the cake.

Davey collected his third ribbon of the day, then exited the ring and walked over to where we were standing. He dumped his loot in Kevin's waiting hands. Then he turned to Aunt Peg. "Am I allowed to say I told you so?"

"No," I answered quickly.

"Yes," Aunt Peg said at the same time. "You may." Suddenly she was smiling too. "That was quite a performance the two of you put on."

Davey's cheeks grew pink. "This is quite a nice bitch you bred. Thank you for allowing me to handle her."

"Thank *you*," Aunt Peg replied.

Our mutual admiration society looked quite pleased with themselves. Meanwhile, Coral was bouncing up and down on her hind legs. She wanted some of the credit too. Aunt Peg wrapped an arm around the Poodle's neck and gave her a hug.

Terry cleared his throat loudly. "Before you mess up her hair too much, you ought to think about having a picture taken."

"Oh!" Aunt Peg gasped. "Of course."

She immediately nudged the Standard Poodle down to the ground. Sam produced a comb from his pocket. Davey grabbed a can of spray from Terry. Quickly, they made repairs to Coral's coat.

Kevin had tucked the three ribbons into the waistband of his shorts. Now he watched the flurry of activity surrounding the Poodle with a frown on his face.

"Aunt Peg touched," he announced. "That's not allowed."

"You're right," I said. "But Coral belongs to Aunt Peg.

So if she wants to do something wrong, we can't stop her."

Out of the corner of my eye, I saw Aunt Peg's head swivel my way. I refused to meet her gaze. This was too good a day for arguments.

"Come on, Kev," Davey said happily as he reclaimed Coral's leash. "We're going back in the ring to have a picture taken. Will you come with us and bring all the ribbons so the judge can hold them?"

"Okay." Kevin checked out his collection. "But only if I can be in the picture and hold a ribbon too."

Davey paused. He wasn't sure if that was allowed.

"Alida Rudolph is a grandmother." Aunt Peg smiled. "I'm sure she won't mind a bit."

We floated home on a pleasant cloud of euphoria. Coral was now just one major away from finishing her championship. Although Sam and Davey had done most of the work, we all felt a sense of accomplishment. Even Kevin.

"I helped," he said happily.

"Of course you did," I told him.

"What did he do?" Davey wanted to know from the back seat.

"Kevin is your biggest fan," I said. "He always roots for you to win."

Davey thought about that for a few seconds. Apparently, that hadn't occurred to him before. He looked over at his little brother. "Thanks, munchkin."

Kev grinned. He didn't even object to the nickname.

All in all, it was a good day.

* * *

The new week had started uneventfully, but unfortunately that didn't last. On Tuesday, I was emptying the dishwasher when my phone rang. Faith was lying in the corner bed, supervising. Bud was hiding under the table, ready to react if something edible dropped on the floor.

I glanced at the screen before answering. It was Davey. He shouldn't have been using his phone in the middle of a camp day. I quickly lifted the device to my ear.

"What's up?"

"I need to talk to you," he said.

"Okay." That didn't sound too bad. "Why are you whispering?"

"Because I'm not allowed to have my phone out of my locker."

"I know that," I said. "Where are you? It's lunchtime. Don't you eat lunch with the campers?"

"Usually yes. But today everything's crazy."

The dishes could wait. I pulled over a chair and sat down. "Crazy how? What's going on?"

"There was a fire—"

I shot back up to my feet. Faith startled and did the same. That made Bud jump up too. The small dog began to bark.

I quickly shushed him and said, "When? Where? Is everyone all right?"

"Yeah, everyone's okay. It was in the kitchen. A stove caught fire or something. Pretty much everyone was outside or in the other building when it happened. But Brian—he's the head counselor—saw smoke and went to investigate."

"Did he call nine-one-one?"

"Right away," Davey told me. "By the time the fire

trucks got here, Ms. Grace and Mia had already put the blaze out with fire extinguishers. I guess it wasn't real big."

"Okay." Suddenly my legs felt weak. I sat back down. "That doesn't sound too bad. Could the firemen tell how it got started?"

"Maybe. I don't know. Nobody's telling us anything." I could tell Davey was frowning about that. "Ms. Grace just gathered everybody up and told us we were going to have a picnic outside under the trees. If we hadn't seen the fire trucks come roaring up the driveway, we wouldn't even have realized anything was wrong."

"What about the campers? Were they upset?"

"Not that I could tell. They're just little kids, you know? They all thought it was exciting."

Kevin would, I thought. He loved fire trucks.

"Something's wrong," said Davey. "Things are happening here that don't make sense. I got Courtney to cover for me so I could go talk to Ms. Grace. She said everything's fine, and that I was overreacting. But I'm not."

I didn't think so, either. Davey was usually pretty level-headed. If he was disturbed, there was a reason.

"Is there anything else I should know about?" I asked him.

"First thing yesterday morning, I went into the locker room to stash my gear. When I walked in, every single locker was wide open."

"So?"

"The last thing the counselors are supposed to do before we leave is make sure all the benches and the shelves are clear, and that the doors are closed up tight. And I know we did."

"Yesterday was Monday," I said. "Maybe a cleaning crew came in over the weekend?"

"Maybe." Davey didn't sound convinced. "But that's not all. Something else happened."

Faith came over and laid her head across my lap. I buried my fingers in her thick coat. Her warm presence always made me feel better.

"Tara showed it to me," he continued. "She's one of the counselors with the Angel Fish group. Someone had written on a blackboard in one of the classrooms. It said, 'Watch out. You're next.'"

Holy crap. Abruptly, I straightened in my seat. Faith lifted her head and gave me a reproachful look. I deserved that.

"Did Tara know who wrote it?" I asked Davey.

"No. Neither one of us had any idea. She showed it to Ms. Grace too."

"What did Emily say?"

"Nothing much." Davey sounded frustrated. "She just erased the blackboard right away and told us to go on with our day."

I didn't like the sound of any of this.

"How come I'm just hearing about this stuff now?" I asked. "Why didn't you say something yesterday when you got home?"

"Because Ms. Grace said it wasn't a big deal and I wanted to believe her. And she's my boss, so I'm supposed to do what she tells me. Plus . . ."

I waited a beat for him to continue. He didn't.

"Plus, what?" I asked.

"No offense, but I didn't want you to overreact either."

Okay, maybe I would have done that. But now there'd been a fire. Which meant it was definitely time for someone to react. Davey must have felt the same way or he wouldn't have snuck away to call me.

"Where's Ms. Grace now?" I asked.

"I don't know. Maybe in her office? She's always around somewhere when camp's in session. Do you want me to find her for you?"

"No, I don't want you involved. Go back to wherever you're supposed to be. I'll drop by this afternoon and have a chat with her."

"You're not going to make her mad, are you?"

"Of course not." I crossed my fingers beneath Faith's chin.

"Because this is my first real job, and I don't want you to get me fired."

"I don't want that either," I said firmly.

Let's hope it didn't come to that.

I put down the phone, then stuck my head in Sam's office. The dishes could wait. Finding out what was going on at Graceland camp couldn't.

"I'm going out," I told him.

"Fine." Sam barely looked up. He was engrossed in something on his computer screen.

"The dogs are here with you."

"Fine," he said again.

"I'm going to buy exploding fireworks for the boys," I said, just to see what would happen.

"Whatever you think is best," Sam replied.

Apparently I didn't have to worry about being missed.

Faith watched me pick up my purse and car keys. She followed me to the door that led to the garage.

I crouched down to rub the sides of her muzzle with

my thumbs. "Sorry, but you can't come with me this time."

I'll be good!

"I know you will," I agreed. "You're always good. But you'll be better off here. Keep an eye on Bud for me."

Faith sighed with resignation. Nobody enjoyed that assignment.

When I arrived at Graceland camp, all the doors to the smaller building—where the lunchroom and kitchen were located—were standing open. I could hear the sound of kids playing out back in the pool and on the playground. A faint smell of smoke hung in the air.

The small building also held Emily's office, so I headed that way. I was pretty sure I'd find her somewhere inside. I was almost there when one of the Dalmatian puppies came flying out through the open doorway. My ankle twisted as I jumped quickly to one side, narrowly avoiding a collision. I hopped for a step or two, then put my foot down gently. Thankfully, it held.

"Hey, sorry about that!" A teenage boy burst through the doorway behind the puppy.

He was tall, and skinny, with gangly limbs and ears that were too big for his head. His red hair was matched by a shading of peach fuzz on his upper lip. I was betting he hoped that made him look older. It didn't.

The boy looked familiar, and after a moment, I realized why. He was Brian, the counselor to whom Mia had directed Davey on opening day.

"No problem," I said. The Dalmatian had gone running past me. Now she was headed toward the covered walkway. I hoped she'd cross it to get to the back of the buildings. "I thought those puppies always traveled in threes."

"Usually, they do." Brian smiled. "But that's Poppy, the renegade. Sometimes she likes to go off and do her own thing."

I gave him extra credit for being able to tell the members of the spotted trio apart. "You're Brian, right?"

"That's right." He sounded surprised that I knew his name. "Can I help you with something?"

"I'm Melanie Travis, Davey and Kevin's mother. I'm looking for Ms. Grace."

"She's inside. But this isn't really a good time. Ms. Grace is a little . . . umm . . . busy right now."

"I can imagine. I heard you had some excitement here earlier."

"It was nothing," Brian said quickly. "Just a little accident. But everything's fine now."

I sincerely doubted that. A fire, even a small one, could do plenty of damage in no time.

"You were the first one to see the smoke," I said. Better to leave Davey's name out of it. "Do you know how the fire got started?"

"No idea." Brian shook his head. "Once I realized there was a problem, I immediately went back outside and called for help. There was no time to waste. These buildings are really old, and they're made of wood. Luckily, Ms. Grace keeps a fire extinguisher in every room."

"She and Mia must have gotten the fire under control pretty quickly."

"They did. By the time the firemen got here, it was already out. Mia told me it was mostly contained in one spot. There's an old cast-iron stove in the kitchen that nobody ever uses. She thinks the fire started in the oven."

"Of a stove that nobody uses?" I said. "That seems odd."

"I agree. But I'm just glad that nobody got hurt." Brian moved past me. "If you don't mind . . ."

"No, go ahead." I waved him by. "Sorry to hold you up."

I waited until Brian had followed the same route the Dalmatian puppy had taken, crossing under the walkway to disappear behind the other building. Then I turned and went inside.

Emily might not think this was a good time to talk, but I didn't plan on giving her a choice.

Chapter 9

I walked to the end of the building's center hallway and found Emily in the kitchen. She was up on a low stepladder scrubbing smoke stains off the wall behind a big, black stove. I had no idea if she heard me enter the room, but she didn't turn around or acknowledge my presence.

"Want some help?" I asked.

Emily's hands stilled. She rolled her shoulders from side to side. I was betting her arms hurt. And the wall still looked pretty bad.

She glanced back at me. "I should have known it would be you."

"I've had more pleasant greetings," I said. "Any particular reason you were expecting me?"

"Oh, I don't know." Emily turned around. "Maybe because whenever there's trouble, you always seem to be right in the middle of it."

"Not this time," I pointed out. "I didn't arrive until after the fact. I'll help you clean that up if you want. Although I think it would probably be easier just to repaint the wall."

"You could be right." She grimaced, then looked back at her handiwork. "I've been working for half an hour, and it hardly looks any better than when I started."

"At least the smell is mostly gone," I said. All the windows in the room were open. A nice breeze had created a cross draft. "That's something."

Emily looked at me balefully. "You're kidding, right?"

I hadn't been. But maybe Emily wasn't in a glass-half-full kind of mood at the moment. In her place, maybe I wouldn't be either.

"Listen," I said. "Can we talk?"

"Isn't that what we're doing?"

"I mean sit down and have a conversation. You know, like adults."

"That sounds ominous." When I didn't correct her, Emily tossed her scrub brush into a bucket of soapy water that was sitting on top of the old, cast-iron stove. "I guess I'm ready to take a break, anyway."

She hopped off the step stool and crossed the kitchen to an industrial-sized refrigerator. Emily opened the door and took a look inside. "Is it too early for beer?"

I peered over her shoulder. "You keep beer in a nursery school refrigerator?"

"No." She sighed. "That was just wishful thinking. I can offer you iced tea, fruit punch, lemonade, or ginger ale."

We both settled on lemonade, poured into tall glasses

from an ice-cold pitcher. The drink was super sweet. I guessed that was how the kids liked it.

"Let's go sit in my office," Emily said. "That way, I don't have to stare at this mess while we talk."

Last time I was in her office, Emily had taken a seat behind the desk. This time, she and I sat down in two up-holstered chairs that faced each other across a low table. She had to lift a batch of file folders off one of the chairs to make room. Emily plopped the folders on the table and dropped onto the cushioned seat with another sigh.

"Some morning," she said, taking a long cold drink of lemonade.

"Some week," I replied.

She gazed at me over the rim of her glass. "That too. First week of school, first week of camp . . . there's always an adjustment period."

I stared at Emily across the tabletop. The things that had been happening here weren't part of any normal adjustment period. She had to know that.

"Emily, what's going on?"

"What do you mean?"

Seriously? Did she really have to ask?

"Ever since camp opened, there's been crazy stuff happening here almost every day," I said.

"That's not true." Emily offered the protest without much conviction.

"How did this morning's fire get started?" I asked.

"I don't know. It was an accident."

"How did your ex-husband's truck end up in the pond?"

Emily opened her mouth to speak. Then she shut it again.

"I know," I said. "Another accident, right?"

Her head dipped in a small nod.

"What about Poppy, Posey, and Pansy?"

Emily looked up in surprise. "What about them?"

"How did they get loose from their pen last week?"

"Umm, it was . . ."

I set my glass down on the table with a thump. That got her attention.

"Don't try to tell me that was an accident too," I said.

Emily ran her own business. She dealt with dozens of small children every day. But I'd never seen her flustered before. Now she was very close to losing her cool. She also looked bewildered.

"I guess I am having a run of bad luck," she said slowly.

"Bad luck?" I repeated.

"Surely you don't think that all those things are connected?"

"I don't know how you can *not* think that," I replied.

She stopped to consider. Then she frowned. "I guess I didn't put it all together like you did."

Either that or she hadn't wanted to think about the fact that she had a real problem.

"I see a pattern emerging," I said. "Maybe you hadn't noticed, or maybe you're willfully ignoring it. But either way, I can't overlook the fact that the children—your campers—are being put at risk."

"I would never—" Emily snapped.

"What? Expose the kids to a runaway truck? Or a kitchen fire?" I narrowed my gaze. "Has it occurred to you they're not the only ones at risk? If this keeps up, you could lose your whole business. Everything you've worked so hard to build could be gone, and your reputation along with it."

"But nobody's gotten hurt . . ." Emily stammered.

"Not yet," I retorted. "But it looks to me like the threat level of the incidents is increasing. So I'm going to ask again, and I hope this time you will give me a truthful answer. What the hell is going on?"

Emily moaned, then leaned down and buried her face in her hands. I gave her a minute to think about everything I'd said. She drew in several deep, shuddering breaths. When she finally lifted her head, her cheeks were pale, and her jaw was set in a rigid line.

"I don't know," Emily said bleakly. Before I could protest, she raised a hand to stop me. "I don't understand any of this."

"You must have thought about it."

"Honestly? I've tried not to. Because none of it makes any sense."

I agreed with her about that. "You told Davey he was overreacting."

"I know." She sighed. "I guess I'll have to apologize to him for that."

"He told me there was a message written on one of the classroom blackboards."

Emily squirmed in her seat. "I wouldn't call it a message exactly."

I lifted a brow. "A warning, then?"

"No, not that either. I thought maybe some of the counselors had been playing around. Maybe trying to scare one another. You know what teenagers are like."

Sure I did. And most of the teenagers I knew tried to stay out of classrooms.

"Had they ever done anything like that before?" I asked her.

"No," Emily replied in a small voice. "But that doesn't mean they couldn't start."

"I don't think denial is the best way to deal with this."

"Neither is browbeating me," she shot back. "I can't explain to you what I don't understand myself."

"I get that," I said. "So rather than acting like adversaries, maybe we should talk this out together and see if we can come up with any ideas."

I'd hoped Emily would agree. Instead she remained silent.

"I'm not blaming you," I told her. "But whatever is going on needs to stop. Otherwise, I'm going to have to decide whether or not it's safe for Davey and Kevin to remain in this environment. And I'm going to recommend that you shut down the camp until you get things figured out."

"You know that's not an option," Emily snapped.

I didn't know any such thing.

"Yes, there have been a few unexplained incidents," she said. "But no one has been hurt. Not even close. In fact, the campers have enjoyed the excitement."

"Right." I frowned. "Like that's a good thing. So now we're allowing the judgment of six-year-olds to guide our reactions?"

"That's not what I meant, and you know it."

"Actually, I don't," I said. "I have no idea what you're thinking, because you refuse to talk about it."

"You have no right to lecture me." Emily lifted her glass and drained the rest of the lemonade. I suspected she was about to bring our conversation to a close.

"Emily, you need help. If you don't want to talk to me, then you should think about consulting the Stamford police. I can give you a name if you want."

She looked at me incredulously. "That's the last thing I'd do. Having the police running around here really would close down my school."

"Okay, no police," I agreed. "For now."

Emily started to rise.

"Wait." I paused, then added, "Please?"

She stopped mid-move.

"Give me five more minutes."

"To do what?"

I gave her the look. The one every teacher has perfected. I knew Emily would recognize what the expression meant. I wasn't going to budge until I was satisfied that we were finished.

"Fine." She sank back into her seat. "Five minutes."

"Have there been any other incidents besides the ones I'm aware of?"

"No," she replied quickly.

Too quickly. So I was guessing that meant yes. I sat quietly and waited for her to speak.

"Okay, maybe a couple of small things. Stuff I didn't think twice about at the time."

"Like what?"

"Last week, the school mailbox at the end of the driveway got smashed. I figured a careless driver must have hit it with his car. You know?"

I did. In her place, I'd have thought the same thing. Mailboxes were an endangered species in Fairfield County.

"Then my electricity went out one night. Again, no biggie. It does that sometimes."

I nodded. "But?"

"I assumed it was a neighborhood outage. But when it wasn't back by morning, I checked with the power company. Nobody else had a problem. I was the only one. They sent out a guy who found that the line to this property had been severed. He said maybe a squirrel had done it."

"A squirrel," I repeated. Considering everything else, that didn't sound like a likely explanation to me.

"He repaired the wire, and that was the end of it," Emily said.

Except it hadn't been, had it?

"Is there any reason why someone would want to harass you?" I asked.

"Me?" Even after all the things we'd talked about, Emily still managed to sound surprised. "Of course not. I'm a normal person. It's not like I have any enemies."

"How about a disgruntled friend?"

"Just you," Emily said with a small smile.

That didn't help.

I briefly thought about everything she'd said. I would have spent more time pondering the problem, but I was on the clock. Soon camp would be letting out for the day.

No doubt about it, I was well and truly stumped. Whenever Aunt Peg was in a similar spot, her first thought was always about the dogs. That didn't seem to apply here, but you never knew. The notion that someone would have given Emily three rowdy puppies at once still struck me as curious. And besides, it wasn't as if I had any other bright ideas.

"The Dalmatians," I said. "Last week you told me you'd received them as a gift. Who gave them to you?"

"I can't see why that matters." Emily was on the defensive again.

"Humor me."

She closed her eyes briefly. Maybe she was praying for patience. If so, I knew how she felt.

"The puppies came from my ex-husband."

"You never talk about him," I said. "I didn't even know you'd been married until you mentioned it the other day."

"Why would I want to talk about him? He's not my favorite person. As you can probably imagine, since we're divorced."

I was divorced too. My first husband, Bob, was Davey's father. Our marriage had ended when he'd abandoned us when Davey was just a baby. Years later, Bob and I had managed to become friends again, but I was well aware that everyone wasn't that lucky.

"Your ex gave you the puppies," I said thoughtfully. A tenuous connection was beginning to form in my brain.

"That's right."

"And the red truck that rolled down the hill belongs to him too?"

"Yes."

"Don't tell me the stove that caught fire was his, too?"

"No." Emily issued a small snort. The question sounded absurd to me too, but I had to ask. "That old thing was here when we moved in years ago."

"And you and your ex aren't on friendly terms?"

She shrugged. "We don't hate each other, if that's what you're asking. Mostly we just ignore one another."

Except when he was giving her presents of dubious worth, I thought.

"Is there a possibility he could be involved in what's been happening around here?"

"Will? I highly doubt it."

"Why?"

"Precisely," she retorted. "Why? What would he have to gain?"

Good question.

"Besides," said Emily, "Will loves that old truck. Probably more than he ever loved me. He'd never do anything to damage it."

She picked up her glass and stood. "I've got to get back to work. Look, Melanie, I know this is what you do. You find problems, and then you leap in and try to solve them. But I don't need your help. There's nothing suspicious going on here. It's just a run of bad luck. You'll see, soon everything will turn around and be just fine."

For all our sakes, I hoped she was right.

Chapter 10

The next morning I awoke to the sound of my phone buzzing on the table beside the bed. I had a new text. I opened one eye and reached out a hand toward the device.

Faith watched the maneuver from her position on the floor. She probably figured I had an equal chance of snagging the phone in my fingers and of knocking it on her head. Unfortunately, she was right.

I sighed, turned over, and gazed at my clock. It was six-thirty a.m. Who needed me at this hour?

"It's probably Peg," Sam muttered sleepily from the other side of the bed. "At least she didn't call and wake everybody up."

Except . . . I could hear the sound of movement in the

hallway outside our bedroom. We weren't the only ones who were stirring. What was going on?

I sat up, grabbed the phone, and took a look. Emily Grace had sent a mass text. The message read, GRACE-LAND CAMP IS CLOSED TODAY. I APOLOGIZE FOR THE INCONVENIENCE.

Before I could process the news, Augie came trotting into the room and jumped on the bed. He just missed landing on top of Sam. Davey was right behind the big Poodle. His hair was mussed from sleep, and his pajamas looked about two sizes too small for him. One more thing I needed to remedy when I had the time.

Davey had his phone in his hand too. He stared down at it with a frown. "Did you see this?"

"Yes," I said. "Just now."

"What do you think it means?"

"What does what mean?" Kevin joined the parade heading into our bedroom.

Eve and Bud were with him. The two dogs took one look at Augie and leapt up beside him. The bed bounced up and down from the impact. Sam put his pillow over his head. I wished I could do the same.

"Your camp is closed today," I told Kev.

He stood on his toes and looked at the message on Davey's phone. He knew his letters, but he couldn't read yet. He liked sending people emojis, though. "How come?"

"We don't know," said Davey.

Kevin shook his head. "No, I mean how come no one told me?"

"We just found out," I said.

"I need my own phone," he announced, "so people can text me things too."

I heard Sam groan from beneath the pillow. I agreed. It was much too early to have to deal with this.

"How about breakfast instead?" I asked Kev.

"Nope." My younger son crossed his arms over his skinny chest. "It's not the same thing."

"If I don't have to drive you to camp, I'll have time to make pancakes."

Kev considered that. "With butter and maple syrup?"

I nodded.

"As many as I want?"

"Within reason," I told him. "No more than twenty."

"Twenty pancakes." Kevin giggled. "Can I share them with Bud?"

"No!" Sam, Davey, and I all said simultaneously. "No sharing food with Bud."

As if anyone ever obeyed that rule. Bud had perfected the art of shameless begging. Even though he was already shaped like a zeppelin.

Hearing his name, the little dog popped out from beneath the covers. Lord knew what he'd been doing under there. When he scrambled down off the bed and ran to the bedroom door, I knew what he wanted. Having just gotten up, Bud needed to go outside.

"Who's letting the dogs out?" I asked.

"I guess I am," Davey grumbled.

"Look on the bright side." Sam had given up on going back to sleep. "You have a day off from work. Maybe we should go to the beach."

"I'm in," I said.

"I didn't want a day off," Davey was still grumbling. "Do you think I'll get paid anyway?"

"I don't see why not," I told him. "Since camp being closed wasn't your fault."

"Whose fault was it?" Kev piped up.

Good question. I was wondering about that myself.

We spent the day at Tod's Point, a busy beach on Long Island Sound just south of Old Greenwich. We weren't Greenwich residents, but earlier in the summer I'd absconded with Aunt Peg's shore pass. As far as I could tell, she hadn't set foot on a beach since the 1970s.

We packed a picnic lunch, a couple of beach chairs, and plenty of sunblock. The boys spent most of the afternoon fooling around in the water. Sam and I relaxed in the shade of a big umbrella, read our books, and went for the occasional swim. The weather, the setting, and the company were all perfect. So I tried not to waste any of it by worrying about Emily Grace and the cryptic message she'd sent out that morning.

Still, I couldn't help but wonder.

Twenty-four hours earlier, Emily had been determined not to shut down the camp. She'd insisted that the campers were not at risk. So what could have happened to change her mind?

"You haven't turned a page in ten minutes," Sam said, glancing over at me. "I know you read faster than that."

I slapped the book shut. "I was just thinking."

"Worrying, you mean." The man is entirely too perceptive.

"Yes."

"About Emily Grace?"

I nodded. The previous evening, I'd told him about my conversation with Emily. Sam shared my concerns. But he'd also advised me to take a wait-and-see approach while Emily worked on solving the problems herself.

We both knew that patience wasn't my strong suit.

"Something else must have gone wrong," I said. "Why else would she cancel today's session at the last minute?"

"I assume there hasn't been a follow-up message?"

Usually I ignore my phone. This afternoon, Sam had been watching me check it every ten minutes.

"Nothing," I told him. "I hope Emily's not in trouble."

"She'll have to get in touch at some point," Sam said. "If only to let everyone know whether or not the camp will be open tomorrow."

"What if it isn't?" I asked.

"Then I suspect you'll probably drive over there to find out why."

"You, recommending that I get involved?" I said with a smile. "That's a switch."

"That wasn't a recommendation," Sam said. "It was a prediction."

"Emily is my friend."

"I know." Now he looked resigned.

"She might need my help."

"Let's hope it's nothing too bad," said Sam.

A second text arrived that evening. Camp was back in session the next day.

"Yay!" cried Kevin.

Davey looked similarly pleased. While Kev and the Poodles were dancing around the living room to celebrate, I pulled my older son aside.

"I want you to do something for me," I told him.

"Sure. What's up?"

"When you're at Graceland, I need you to keep an eye on your brother."

Davey paused. "You know Kev's not in my group, right?"

"I know. Just do the best you can, okay?"

"Sure. No problem." He started to walk away, then stopped. "I know you talked to Ms. Grace yesterday after we spoke. So I figure you're on top of things. But . . . is everything okay?"

"That's what I intend to find out," I told him.

This was beginning to feel like a habit. The next morning, I let both boys out of the car at the drop-off point, then once again pulled out of line to park in front of the admin building. Mia glanced my way as I got out of the car, but she was too busy to comment. It looked as though every parent in the long line wanted to know what had caused the previous day's unexpected closure. I doubted they were having any more luck getting information from Emily's assistant than I had.

I waited until Davey and Kevin had disappeared into the other building before going inside myself. Emily wasn't in her office. Nor was she in the kitchen. Only two days had passed since I'd last been in that room, but someone had been hard at work in the meantime. The soot-stained wall now sported a fresh coat of paint.

A stairway off the kitchen led to Emily's apartment on the second floor. It occurred to me that if she was still holed up in there now—when the camp day was about to begin—there was probably a good reason. Like maybe she didn't want to see anyone.

That thought made me pause at the foot of the steps. I decided against going up to knock on her door. Instead I remained below and sent Emily a text. I had to wait a full three minutes for a reply.

I'M HERE. COME ON UP. I GUESS.

It wasn't the most effusive welcome I'd ever received, but it was good enough. I slipped my phone in my pocket and ran up the stairs before Emily could change her mind. She opened her door as I reached the top step.

Immediately, the words I'd been about to say died in my throat.

Emily was a smart, savvy, pulled-together woman. I'd never seen her look anything less than professional. But right now she was a mess. Emily's face was blotchy, and her hair was snarled. Both eyes were puffy. She didn't look as though she'd slept recently. And maybe she'd been crying as well.

Rather than speaking, I simply stepped forward and wrapped my arms around Emily's shoulders. I thought she might resist the embrace. Instead she laid her head on my shoulder. After a moment, she exhaled with a long sigh.

"That bad, huh?" I said.

She lifted her head and stepped back. "Worse."

"Do you want to talk about it?"

Her lips quirked in a half-smile. "Are you going to give me any choice?"

I shrugged. It was up to her. Yes, I was curious. But I didn't need answers right this minute. I wasn't going to intrude unless she wanted me to.

"You might as well come in," Emily said. "Maybe I'll feel better if I talk to someone."

As I closed the door behind us, I smelled coffee brewing. A coffee maker sat on a counter next to the stove. Emily followed the direction of my gaze and went to pour me a cup.

The apartment consisted of just two rooms. The space in which we stood was a combination living room and dining area, with the kitchen appliances lined up along one wall. A small bedroom, its door half-open, its bed unmade, was visible on the far side of the room.

Two of the Dalmatian puppies were asleep on the rumpled bed. The third one was nearby, its lithe body lying draped over the cushions of a tweed couch whose taupe color matched the curtains on the windows. None of the puppies had reacted when Emily opened the door. Nor had they run to greet me when I came inside. Oddly, even now, they didn't lift their heads. The puppies' mood was just as subdued as their owner's.

"Milk and sugar?" Emily held up a heavy stoneware mug.

"Just a splash of milk please."

She opened her fridge, added the milk, then passed the mug my way. "Thanks," I said, taking it from her. "You look like you need this more than I do."

Emily frowned. "Any more coffee and I'll be spinning like a top. I just finished my third cup."

"This morning?"

"Yeah, I guess." She lifted a hand and raked it through her tangled hair. "What time is it, anyway?"

"Eight-thirty."

Emily should have known that. Her campers were outside arriving for the day. She had a camp to run. All of this was very much out of character for the woman I'd thought I knew. And before Emily did anything else, what she really needed was a shower and a change of clothing.

I watched in dismay as Emily sank down on the couch, narrowly missing the puppy who made no attempt to move out of her way. Emily lifted her bare feet and plunked them down on a vintage trunk that served as a coffee table.

"Sit," she invited.

There was a low, lattice-back chair nearby. I pulled it over and took a seat.

"What's going on?" I asked.

Emily blinked in my direction. "You don't know?"

"No. I have no idea."

"Oh." She seemed to find that mildly interesting. "I just assumed you would have heard about it on the news."

"Heard about what?" I asked, with new urgency. I'd just left both my boys downstairs. "What was on the news?"

"That's a surprise," she murmured. "I guess I was wrong then. I was sure you'd come to gloat."

I still had no clue what she was talking about.

Emily straightened fractionally in her seat. Even that small move looked like it took more effort than she wanted to expend. "It turns out you were right. I should have been more concerned about those things that were going on around here."

A sense of dread settled over me. "Did something else happen?"

"You might say that." She paused as if she needed to find enough energy just to say the words. "Early yesterday morning, the police found a body in the woods." Her fingers flicked a wave toward the rear of her property.

"A body?" I gasped.

Emily nodded. "He'd been shot."

"Do they know who it was?"

"His name was Will Grace," she told me in a small voice. "He was my ex-husband."

Chapter 11

Emily's first revelation came as a shock. Her second one left me speechless.

Unexpectedly, her expression lightened. "What?" she inquired. "You finally have nothing to say?"

I took a moment to recover. Then there was only one thing I *could* say. "Tell me everything."

"Early yesterday morning, I woke up to someone pounding on the door downstairs. When I looked out my window, there were two police cruisers outside."

"How did the police find the body?" I leaned forward and set my mug down on the trunk between us. "Did someone tell them it was there? What were they doing in the woods at that time of day?"

"Slow down," Emily said. "I can only deal with one question at a time. According to the officers, Will was found by one of the residents in the development next door."

When Graceland School was founded, the area had consisted of mostly open, rolling land. Over the years, however, houses had replaced grassy fields as a neighborhood grew up around it. More recently, a developer had purchased a sizable piece of property bordering the school land. He'd built an upscale residential community that had twenty-five homes, a clubhouse, and a swimming pool.

"Apparently the guy had just gotten up," Emily continued. "When he let his dog outside, it ran into the woods and started barking. He was afraid it would wake up his neighbors, so he followed it to see what was wrong. That's when . . ." Emily stopped before finishing her thought.

That was all right. I already knew what came next.

"Why did the police come to you first?" I asked. "Was he found on your property?"

'No." She quickly shook her head. "Actually, it's all state-owned land back there because the state controls the reservoir that's on the other side of the trees. All the properties along this road back up to that same band of woods."

I thought about that. Then I repeated my question. "It sounds as though the police had options. What made them come here?"

"They seemed to think I might know something," Emily said in a small voice.

"About your ex-husband's death?"

"Yes."

"So they knew right away who he was?"

"Will had his wallet on him. There was ID. They ran a background check, and this address came up."

I frowned. I'd known Emily for more than a decade, and I'd certainly never run into her ex. "It has to have been years since he lived here. If he ever did?"

"No, he and I had a little apartment in Norwalk," Emily told me. "I didn't move in here until after the divorce. But Will wasn't the most reliable person. He moved around a lot. And he wasn't above fudging details if he thought it might gain him something. He must have used this as his address for some reason when he applied for his license."

The man sounded like a real prize. No wonder their relationship had soured. Emily might have divorced the man, but apparently she hadn't entirely succeeded in getting rid of him.

"So the police came to you," I said. "What did they want to know?"

"Everything." She grimaced. "Where I'd been the previous night and what I'd been doing. What was the state of my relationship with Will? Did I have any reason to want to harm him?"

"Did they question you before or after they told you about finding his body in the woods?"

"Mostly before," Emily replied. "In the beginning, I had no idea why the police were even here. There was a detective who kept glaring at me like he was trying to trip me up. Finally I told him he could either tell me what was going on or get out of my house."

"So he did," I said quietly.

Emily sighed. "I might have become a little hysterical at that point." She looked to me for understanding. "But then the first thing I thought about was the camp. I couldn't have parents driving in here to find the place swarming with police."

It was interesting that Emily's first response to the news had been to protect the school. She was clearly more concerned about her livelihood than she was about her ex-husband's murder.

"Before he left, the detective said he might want to talk to me again. He even asked if I had an alibi."

"Did you?" I asked. That would certainly be useful.

"Of course not. I was here, asleep. The only ones who can vouch for me are these guys." Emily gazed around at the three spotted dogs.

The puppies on the bed were looking more alert. They hopped down and came padding in to join us. Posey and Pansy, I decided. I was starting to be able to tell them apart.

Pansy came over to sniff my legs and say hello. Posey joined her sister and Emily on the couch. Even now that they were up and moving around, the Dalmatians still seemed remarkably quiet to me. The previous times I'd seen them, the trio had been racing around and playing with each other.

"Don't look at me like that," Emily grumbled.

"Like what?" My gaze lifted.

"It was only a little Valium."

"You took Valium?" I had no idea why she was telling me that.

"No, I gave it to them." Emily indicated the three Dals. "I needed them to leave me alone so I could think."

Yikes. No wonder the dogs were so mellow.

"Is that something you usually do?"

"Of course not," she said shortly. "Obviously, this was a special circumstance. Don't worry, they'll be back to normal soon."

I certainly hoped so. "So what happens next?"

Emily pulled up her knees and tucked herself into a small ball on the couch. "I guess the police will investigate."

"And what do you do next?" I asked.

"Reopen the camp."

"You already did that," I pointed out. "Under the circumstances, are you sure it's safe for the kids and counselors to be here?"

"Absolutely. It's safer than it ever was. There are police all over the neighborhood now. The detective said they'll be around for a while."

"Is that Detective Sturgill, by any chance?"

"Yes." Emily peered at me curiously. "Do you know him?"

"I do." Sturgill and I had crossed paths several times in the past. We weren't exactly friends, but we'd occasionally made pretty good allies.

"Did you tell him about the other strange things that had been going on around here recently?"

Emily feigned a look of surprise. As if the thought hadn't even occurred to her. I wasn't buying it for a minute.

"No," she said.

"Why not?"

"Because how would that make me look?"

"Like a concerned citizen who wanted to do everything she could to aid the authorities in their investigation?"

"Wrong," she shot back. "It would make them think I must have had something to do with Will's murder. And the police are already treating me like they think I'm a suspect."

Which, no doubt, they did.

I pursed my lips in annoyance. Maybe Emily was still in shock. Or maybe she'd dosed herself with a sedative too. Because I knew she was an intelligent woman. And now she clearly wasn't thinking straight.

"That's precisely why you don't want to appear to be hiding anything. How do you think Detective Sturgill is going to react when he finds out?"

She considered that for a minute. "Maybe he won't find out."

Of course he would. This was a murder investigation. And if he didn't uncover those other facts on his own, I'd be sure to tell him. Like a concerned citizen who wanted to do everything she could to aid the authorities in their investigation.

"That's not going to happen, Em."

She trailed her fingers down Poppy's silky back. "See? You think of stuff like that, and I don't. You were right before when you said that I needed your help. I never should have turned you down."

It was a little late for her to be reconsidering now. I wondered if it had occurred to her that if she had taken my concerns more seriously, her ex-husband might still be alive. And if Emily expected me to run interference between her and Detective Sturgill, that was going to be a hard no.

"What are you trying to say?" I really needed her to spell it out.

"I want you to figure out who killed Will." She frowned as if the answer had been perfectly obvious. "In fact, it's a good thing you came by this morning. Now you can get right to work."

"When I offered my help before, things were different," I pointed out. "Now someone has died, and the police are investigating a murder."

"Yes, and they're also investigating *me*," Emily snapped. "I need someone who's going to be on my side. Someone who's smart enough to figure things out. Like you."

I picked up my mug and finished my coffee, stalling for a few seconds while I considered the request. In the end, my answer had to be the same. Emily was my friend. Graceland was my sons' school. Of course I would try to help if I could.

"I suppose I could ask some questions," I said.

"Good." She smiled.

Having gotten what she wanted, Emily looked pleased. That wasn't going to last.

"Let's start now," I said. "With you."

"Me?"

"Yes. You don't appear to be devastated by your ex-husband's death." More like inconvenienced, if I had to assign an emotional reaction to her current state of mind. "You said before that the two of you weren't close."

"No. Not at all."

"And yet you let him keep his truck here."

Emily shrugged. "That doesn't mean anything. I had extra space to store it. Will didn't."

"There has to have been a reason why Will was here the other night. Did he come to see you?"

"Of course not."

"You're sure about that? This is your property. *Something* brought him here."

"It wasn't me," Emily said. "I hadn't spoken to Will in months."

"When was the last time you saw him?"

She had that answer ready. I knew the police would have asked her the same question. "In April. When he showed up with the puppies."

I zeroed in on her phrasing. "So he just *showed up* then too? You weren't expecting him to visit?"

"No. Once Will and I were divorced, I was ready to move on." Emily stopped and sighed. "Not that he believed that. Will was quite the charmer when he wanted to be. He was convinced everyone loved him. He popped in and out of people's lives all the time. I never knew what he was going to do next."

"Like show up on your doorstep with three young Dalmatians?" I asked.

"Precisely. That was *so* Will. He was always either down on his luck or riding high. When he was broke, he'd hit up everyone he knew for money. When he was flush, he'd buy people crazy presents." Emily glanced at the puppies dozing around us. "Whether we wanted them or not."

"That sounds exhausting," I said honestly.

"Tell me about it," she replied.

"So you hadn't had any communication with him at all since April?"

Emily shook her head. "I didn't even know where he was."

"How about before that? When was the last time you'd seen him?"

"I have no idea," she replied. "At least several years. Will came by to ask for a loan. I knew perfectly well that if I gave him something, I'd never see it again. Money flowed through his fingers like water. Anyway, it was a moot point because I didn't have any cash to spare."

I stared at her. "So, having been out of contact for years, didn't it seem odd to you when Will showed up out of the blue with a present?"

"I can see how you might think that," Emily admitted. "But you didn't know Will. The guy was always working some kind of angle. I think he figured the puppies would soften me up. He told me that he missed me. And that he wanted us to give things another try."

I almost laughed at that. Emily looked similarly amused.

"I'm guessing you weren't tempted to take him back."

"Not even close." She snorted. "I knew what the offer really meant. Will was broke again, and he was hoping I'd be enough of a sucker to put a roof over his head while he devised his next grand scheme. I shut that idea down in a hurry."

I pulled in a deep breath and slowly let it out. None of this made any sense. Nor did it shed any light on why Emily's ex-husband had been killed, virtually in her backyard.

Poppy lifted her head and took a look around. That prompted my next question.

"These puppies are clearly purebreds," I said.

"I guess. So what?"

"If Will was broke, where did he get the money to buy them?"

"Knowing my ex, they could have come from any-where," Emily said without interest. "Maybe he picked them up at a dog pound."

That didn't seem likely to me. Thanks to Walt Disney, Dalmatians were hugely popular. These pretty puppies weren't the sort that would have been found languishing in a pound.

Abruptly, Emily glanced at a clock on the wall. Her eyes widened. She nudged Poppy aside and jumped up off the couch.

"Oh my God, is that the right time? I've got to go. I should be outside, reassuring parents that what happened won't impact the camp in any way."

Emily definitely shouldn't be talking to parents looking like that, I thought. Especially if she wanted them to be reassured by what she had to say. She'd obviously forgotten she was still wearing what looked like yesterday's clothes.

"Em," I said gently. "You need to shower first."

"What?" She glanced down at her rumpled outfit as if seeing it for the first time. "Oh, right. Dammit."

Emily spun around and disappeared into the bedroom. I stood up and carried my mug to the sink. Then I headed for the door.

I'd told Emily I would help. But I was already wondering whether that was a good idea. The events of the past thirty-six hours were puzzling from just about every angle. And there were gaps in Emily's story big enough to drive a shiny red truck through.

Emily was sure I was on her side, and yet I suspected she hadn't told me the whole truth. She had to be assuming that I wouldn't uncover anything that might cause my alliance to shift. But what if she was wrong about that?

Chapter 12

At the end of the Graceland driveway, I paused the car and looked both ways. A left turn would take me home. Turning right would send me in the direction of Aunt Peg's house in Greenwich.

I didn't have to think very long about that. I turned right and took out my phone. Aunt Peg's number was on speed dial.

"Are you home?" I asked when she picked up.

"Of course I'm at home," she replied. "Where else would I be?"

Knowing Aunt Peg, I could think of about a million other places. Age hadn't slowed her down a bit. In fact, I was pretty sure it was causing her to gain momentum.

"Glad to hear it," I said. "I'll be there in ten minutes."

I ended the connection before she could ask any questions. Let her stew on that until I arrived.

Aunt Peg lived in an old, restored farmhouse on a quiet lane in back-country Greenwich. Five acres of fenced land surrounded the house, and at one time there had been a kennel out back. That building was gone now, and her five remaining Standard Poodles lived in the house with her.

All of Aunt Peg's Poodles were black. They were also all interrelated with Sam's and my dogs. So every time I arrived at Aunt Peg's house, I was greeted by a bevy of familiar-looking faces.

Four Standard Poodles came cascading down the front steps as I got out of the Volvo. The fifth dog, thirteen-year-old Beau, remained in the open doorway at Aunt Peg's side. His days of running up and down stairs for fun were behind him. Beau preferred to stand on his dignity and wait for visitors to come to him.

I was happy to oblige the older dog. Years earlier, Beau's disappearance had persuaded Aunt Peg and me to heal a long-standing family rift. We'd worked together to track the dog down and bring him home. Nothing about my life had been the same since.

Now I leaned down to Beau's level and cupped his gray muzzle in my hands. "How are you, old man? Are you feeling good today?"

Beau's tail wagged slowly back and forth. I took that as a yes.

Faith's sister, Hope, came skidding past me. Eve's brother, Zeke, was right behind her. The two of them went flying into the house. Willow, carrying her second litter, followed that pair more sedately. Coral was on her dam's heels.

I stood back up, ready to follow them inside. Aunt Peg was blocking my way. Her hands were propped on her hips.

"Well?" she demanded.

"Yesterday morning, a man's body was found in the woods near Laurel Reservoir," I told her.

"I know that." Her eyes narrowed. Obviously she'd expected something better. "I heard about it on the news."

"Graceland School backs up to those woods."

Now she looked interested. "Nobody mentioned that."

"There's more. The dead man was Emily Grace's ex-husband."

Aunt Peg's brow lifted. I finally had her full attention.

"You'd better come inside," she said. Aunt Peg quickly counted canine noses, then shut the front door behind us.

The Poodles and I automatically headed toward the kitchen. That was where Aunt Peg usually hosted visitors. Her sweet tooth was legendary, and frequent guests knew they could count on two things: first, that Aunt Peg would expect them to be both entertaining and enlightening, and second, that she would ply them with sugar-laden calories until they fulfilled those duties.

But hey, no pressure.

"I have pie." Aunt Peg glanced at her watch. "It's early, but I'm game if you are."

I was always game. Before Aunt Peg and I became a team, I weighed ten pounds less and had half as many wrinkles. But at least my life was never boring now.

"You usually have cake," I said.

"That's precisely why I'm branching out." She removed the pie from a bakery box on the counter. "Heaven forbid I become predictable."

Yes, I thought. We certainly wouldn't want that.

"It's blueberry. Fair warning, it might stain your teeth."

"I'm willing to risk it," I told her.

Aunt Peg cut two thick wedges oozing with blueberries and placed them on plates. I opened a drawer and got out two forks. We sat down across from each other at the butcher block table in the middle of the room. Sunshine slanted through a picture window overlooking the wide lawn behind the house. The light in the room had a golden glow.

"So," Aunt Peg said. "Emily Grace's husband. That's a surprise."

"Ex-husband," I corrected her.

She took a big bite of pie and savored it slowly. "Divorced for how long?"

"Many years. I got the impression she married him before she was old enough to know better."

"Amicable?"

"Not particularly."

"Interesting."

She mulled that over, which gave me a chance to sample my own pie. No surprise, it was sublime. Before Aunt Peg could speak again, I went back for a second bite.

"Is the camp closed?" she asked.

"Just for one day," I told her. "It reopened this morning."

"Is Emily sure that's wise?"

"She seems to be."

Aunt Peg glanced my way. "You don't sound as though you agree."

"At the moment, the authorities are still around, so I know the property is safe. But before this happened, several other worrisome incidents took place at the camp."

She nodded. "You told me about the three Dalmatian puppies running loose in the road."

Of course Aunt Peg would remember the part that involved dogs.

"That was one," I told her. "There was also a runaway truck."

She swallowed abruptly and set down her fork. Aunt Peg folded her hands on the table between us and prepared to listen. It was somewhat daunting to be the focal point of her scrutiny.

"The truck was supposed to be parked in its carport," I said. "Somehow it ended up at the top of a nearby incline—with no one at the controls. It went lumbering down the hill and landed in Emily's pond."

"That's not good. I take it nobody was hurt?"

"Luckily, no. But the campers who saw it happen were vastly entertained."

"Also not a good thing," she retorted. "Is that all?"

"No." I snuck in another bite of pie, then said, "There was a fire too."

"A fire," Aunt Peg echoed faintly. No doubt she was remembering the fire—deliberately set—that had demolished her kennel building two summers earlier. "Arson?"

"It's unclear. The blaze started in a very old stove in the school's kitchen. The head counselor saw smoke and quickly alerted everyone. By the time the firetrucks got there, Emily and her assistant, Mia, had already put it out. Emily insisted it was just an accident."

Aunt Peg looked skeptical. I knew the feeling.

"What about the ex-husband's death?" she said drily. "Does she think that was an accident too?"

I shook my head. "The police told her he'd been shot. Murdered. She's really upset about that."

"I should hope so," Aunt Peg muttered. "Does she have any thoughts about how it happened?"

"None. Emily said she hadn't seen Will in years when he suddenly showed in April. It turns out he was the one who gave her the puppies. He dropped them off, and they haven't been in contact since. Emily had no idea what he might have been doing in the woods behind her school."

"Perhaps he was spying on her," Aunt Peg mused. There's nothing she enjoys more than the possibility of intrigue.

I shrugged. I didn't know. That seemed like a good reason to eat more pie.

"The police are treating Emily as if she's a suspect in Will's death," I said around a mouthful of blueberries.

"Of course they are," Aunt Peg retorted. "The man is her ex-husband, and he died behind her school." She reclaimed her fork and cut off a piece of buttery crust. "Does Emily own a gun?"

"How would I know that?"

"You might have thought to ask." She looked down her nose at me. "*I* would have."

Nobody in the room doubted that. Not even the Poodles. My first piece of pie was finished. Now my plate looked naked. So I went back for seconds.

"Let's return to the Dalmatians," Aunt Peg said after a minute that both of us devoted mostly to chewing and swallowing.

Why not? I thought. Aunt Peg was always happiest when she was talking about dogs.

"What about them?"

"The last time Emily saw her ex, he had the puppies with him. He gave them to her—all three at once. A very odd gift, if you ask me. Maybe that means something."

"What?"

"I don't know. I was hoping you would tell me. You're the one who's seen them. What do the Dals look like?"

"They have spots."

Aunt Peg stopped just short of rolling her eyes. "Of course they have spots. But what is their lineage? Do they come from common, puppy mill stock, or are they good representatives of their breed?"

I suspected the latter, but there was no way I was going to tell her that. If I did, she would immediately begin to quiz me about why I thought so. The conversation would then quickly devolve into a whole bunch of questions I wouldn't be able to answer.

"I'm not sure," I said instead.

"Melanie, dear." Coming from Aunt Peg, the word didn't sound like an endearment. "It's been a decade since you started going to dog shows. Have you learned nothing?"

I stared at her mulishly. "I've learned about Poodles."

"Yes. But along with that, you should have also learned about correct structure and movement. And you must have picked some knowledge about breed type."

One could only hope. But still. That didn't make me an expert on Dalmatians.

"Poodles," I said again. Learning one breed had been hard enough.

Aunt Peg reached across the table and helped herself to another piece of pie. "Now you're just trying to be difficult. And I dare say you're succeeding."

I sighed. It was always a shame when Aunt Peg was right. Because it happened so darn frequently.

"They're nice puppies," I told her. "Definitely pure-bred. What difference does it make beyond that?"

"It could make a great deal of difference," Aunt Peg said. "Think about it. Their appearance points to where they came from. And that might turn out to be something we care about very much indeed."

"Will picked them up somewhere," I said. "That's all Emily knew."

Aunt Peg frowned in annoyance. "Jack Berglund's neighbors might have said the same thing about the new Standard Poodle that he showed up with. A dog improbably named Scotty, as I recall."

She looked down at the kitchen floor where Beau was lying contentedly beside her chair. His eyes were closed, and his muzzle was nestled between his two front paws. In his youth, the elderly Poodle had been spirited out of Aunt Peg's kennel in the middle of the night by a rival breeder. The dog had been used as a pawn in a scheme to defraud both the American Kennel Club and a former family business associate. And for a brief period of time, he'd been known as Scotty.

Aunt Peg and I had both cared a great deal about Beau's whereabouts. We'd devoted an entire summer to finding him.

"What a minute," I sputtered. "Are you saying you think those three Dalmatians might have been stolen?"

"Don't look so surprised. Surely you must realize how improbable the current story is. No one in their right mind would simply appear out of the blue to hand over three young puppies to an ex-wife he hadn't seen in years—"

"Emily had an explanation," I said.

Aunt Peg stared at me. "Then perhaps you should have started with that."

"She said Will gave her the puppies as a gesture of

goodwill. He was hoping the two of them could get back together."

"Oh pish." She snorted. "If that was the case, he should have bought her a bouquet of flowers. Or a new stove. Three lively, untrained puppies is no one's idea of goodwill. Those babies were obviously going to run Emily ragged. And what working woman—much less one who owns and operates her own business—has time for that?"

I nodded. She was right. Again.

"That explanation makes me even more skeptical about the veracity of the entire scenario. It's utterly nonsensical." Her point made, Aunt Peg slivered off a bite of pie and put it in her mouth.

I still had questions, however. "Suppose a good Dalmatian breeder did have three nice puppies stolen from him. Don't you think we'd have heard about the theft?"

"Maybe," Aunt Peg replied. "But maybe not. Don't forget, I didn't tell anyone when Beau was missing."

Well, she'd told the local police and the FBI, but since both had declined to investigate, I supposed she figured they didn't count. She'd also told me. But at the time, I'd had no connections to the dog show community. So I supposed that meant I hadn't counted either.

"People have their reasons for keeping things secret," she mused. "And sometimes those reasons can be every bit as important as the information they've withheld. I think I shall have to do a little snooping around."

Aunt Peg looked enormously pleased by the thought.

"But first I'm going to need to see those puppies for myself," she announced. "That will tell me if we're even on the right track. I've judged Dalmatians in the area numerous times. A look might be enough to nudge me in the right direction."

"You're kidding," I said. She could really do that?

"Certainly not. I never joke about important things." Aunt Peg pushed back her chair and rose from the table.

Apparently we were finished talking. I quickly shoved the rest of my pie in my mouth.

"Plus there's another reason I need to meet with Emily," she told me. "If I'm going to arrange a benefit on her behalf, I'll need to get some input from her. Have you spoken with her about it?"

Of course not. With everything that had happened in the meantime, I'd forgotten all about that.

"Not yet," I said.

"It figures," she said. "Will you set up a meeting for me? Sometime in the near future, please. We need to get this ball rolling."

Unexpectedly a picture came to mind—Indiana Jones swiping a gold idol, then being chased from a cave by a giant rolling ball. At times like this, I knew just how Indy felt.

Chapter 13

My phone rang that night when we'd just finished dinner. I was clearing the dining room table, but Sam picked up the device from the sideboard, glanced at the caller, and handed it to me.

"It's Emily," he said, shooing me away.

I grabbed the phone, blew him a quick kiss, and crossed the hall to the living room. Faith and Eve came with me. I connected the call as the Poodles and I were getting situated on the couch.

"I want you to know I'm nearly back to normal," she said.

"Thank goodness for that." I laughed.

"It's a good thing you told me to take a shower before going downstairs. Imagine if I'd gone outside to talk to parents looking like that."

"You might have caused a precipitous drop in enrollment."

I'd thought the two dogs and I were settled, but apparently not. Faith and Eve were now both jockeying for the best position on my lap. Since each of them weighed around fifty pounds, I was getting pummeled.

"Hang on one sec," I said to Emily.

"You, over here," I told Faith, draping the big Poodle over my left leg.

"You, this way." I wedged her daughter against my right hip.

The two Poodles grudgingly complied. Then they made faces at each other across my lap. Was that *really* necessary?

"Okay." I replaced the phone against my ear. "I'm back."

"Who were you talking to?"

"Faith and Eve," I said. Emily had met Faith on numerous occasions. "They're mother and daughter. Occasionally they like to squabble. And I get to play referee."

"Families." Emily sighed. "Sometimes they're the pits."

I assumed she was talking about her ex-husband.

"Tell me about it." I glared first one way, then the other, making sure both bitches had gotten the message that I was the alpha dog in the room.

"I had an idea," she said. "I think you should talk to Owen Grace."

"Okay." I was all in favor of good ideas. "Who's he?"

"Owen is my former brother-in-law. He is . . ." She gulped, then corrected herself. ". . . *was* Will's older brother. The two of them were pretty close. If anyone knows what Will has been up to recently, it would probably be Owen.

I'm sure he can tell you a lot more about his brother's life than I can."

There was a pad of paper and a pen on the end table beside the couch. It required cooperation from all three of us for me to get to it. The bitches made more stink-faces as I negotiated my way around them, but I persevered. "Okay," I said, when I'd written down Owen Grace's name. "Do you have a phone number?"

Emily supplied one and told me that he lived in Southbury. I added the information to my note.

"Have you spoken with him since Will died?" I asked.

"I called him yesterday as soon as the police left," she said. "Owen was totally shocked by the news. He's a decent guy. I'm sure he'll make time to talk to you. I'll send him a text and tell him to expect you. How does tomorrow morning sound?"

"That works," I said. Once I dropped the boys off at camp, I didn't have anything else scheduled. "Listen, on a different topic, my Aunt Peg would like to come and see you."

Emily made a strangled sound.

I frowned at the phone. "What's the matter?"

"That can't be good."

"Why not?"

"You've told me about her. She sounds like some kind of gorgon. Is she going to come and yell at me?"

Offhand, I didn't remember what I might have told Emily about Aunt Peg. Apparently I hadn't painted her in a flattering light.

"I hope not," I said. Knowing Aunt Peg, she might want to have a conversation about Emily's dog-management skills.

"You *hope* not?" Emily squeaked. "That doesn't sound reassuring."

"I never reassure people when it comes to Aunt Peg," I admitted. "But in this case, she just wants to meet your puppies and talk to you about an idea she had for a fundraiser."

"A fundraiser?" Several seconds ticked by before she spoke again. "For the school?"

"Yes. If it's okay with you, I'll let Aunt Peg explain everything in person when we stop by."

"Sure." Emily still didn't sound enthused. "Maybe Saturday morning? I'll be busy tomorrow. My brother, Miles, is arriving at some point. I don't know when, so I don't want to schedule anything."

"Of course," I said. "Will your brother be staying for a while?"

"At least a week. With everything that's been happening around here, Miles wanted to come and lend support. Under the circumstances, I certainly don't mind having a big, strong man staying on the property."

"Good idea," I agreed. "Where's he coming from?"

"New Hampshire. Hanover, actually. Miles is a school administrator, so he has free time during the summer months."

"Interesting that you both went into education."

"I know." Emily laughed. "You never would have guessed that would happen if you'd known us as kids. We were wild back then."

"Is Miles older or younger than you?"

"He's my little brother, three years younger. But that's never stopped him from thinking he should look out for me."

"He sounds like a nice guy," I said.

"He is." Emily replied. "I'm looking forward to having the chance to spend time with him."

I ended the call and carefully maneuvered myself out from underneath the two Poodles. Eve and Faith were both asleep now. They were lying side by side on the cushions, their bodies rising and falling in unison. Dogs don't know how to hold a grudge. They'd probably already forgotten that they'd had a disagreement.

As I left the room to go find my family, I was struck by a sudden thought. Emily had asked for my help that morning because she'd said she needed someone on her side. Had that comment been merely a ploy to arouse my sympathy? Or was Emily's relationship with her brother not nearly as close as she'd made it seem?

"Make sure you take all your stuff when you get out of the car," I said to Kevin the next morning. "If you forget something, I can't come back later and drop it off."

Davey had opened the back door, and he was unfastening the straps on Kev's seat. "You'll probably still be here later," he said with a smirk. "You're just going to go park in front of the other building anyway."

I had been stopping in to see Emily a lot since camp started. But that wouldn't be happening this morning.

"Very funny," I said. "But today I have places to go and people to see."

"Are you going to the supermarket?" Kevin asked as he hopped out of the car. "Because I need raisins."

"Raisins?" I swiveled around to look at him. "What for?"

"Because they taste good." As if the answer was perfectly obvious.

Far be it from me to deny a request for fruit. Even dried fruit. "Okay," I told him. "I'll get raisins. Anything else?"

"Chocolate chip ice cream!" Kevin crowed.

I would take that suggestion under advisement.

"And Oreos," Davey added. "We're out."

"Again? I just bought some."

Davey shrugged. He gave me a sheepish grin. So I guessed I knew where the Oreos had gone. It was a good thing he was a growing boy.

Kevin grabbed his backpack from the floor of the car. He slung it over his shoulder and began to run toward the sidewalk. "Hurry up," he called back to Davey. "It's time for camp!"

"Goodbye," I said to their retreating backs. "Have fun at camp. Eat all your lunch. Don't forget to use your sunblock."

Of course they didn't answer. My two sons weren't even listening. It wasn't nearly as much fun being a mom when no one was paying attention.

The drive to Southbury took just over an hour. After I'd gotten off the phone with Emily the night before, I'd gone on the internet and found out that Owen Grace was an attorney with his own practice. He had an office that was located in the town's picturesque historic district.

According to his website, Owen specialized in accidents, personal injury, and wrongful death cases. He promised that potential clients would pay nothing up front to discuss their problems. I hoped the same would hold true for me. Mostly what I knew about lawyers was that even when you were only having a conversation, they liked to bill by the hour.

Owen's office was located in a handsome red brick building with square proportions and a small cupola in the middle of its roofline. There were several empty parking spaces out front. Inside, the building had been broken up into three small businesses. Owen's office shared its residence with a general contractor and a company that bought and sold rare books.

The center hallway that bisected the building was dimly lit. A bowl of fake flowers sat on an ornate oak credenza that needed dusting. Outside, it was pleasantly warm. Inside, the air wasn't moving at all.

Owen's office was at the end of the hallway. I opened the door and walked into a small reception room. Directly in front of me, a college-age girl was sitting behind a desk, staring down at her phone. Her fingers were busy, tapping on the screen. It looked like this summer job hadn't been her first choice.

The girl didn't look up right away. Instead she finished what she was doing, then cast me a bored glance. "Can I help you?"

"I'm here to see Owen Grace," I told her. "I believe he's expecting me."

She pulled an appointment book toward her across the desktop. "Name?"

"Melanie Travis."

Her finger ran slowly down the page. From where I was standing, it looked mostly empty. "You don't have an appointment," she said.

"Do I need one?"

"I don't know." She stood up. "I guess I could check."

"Please do," I said.

When she walked to the door in the back wall of the room, I was right behind her. She knocked, then waited a moment before opening the door a crack and sticking her head inside. I stepped around her and pushed the door the rest of the way open.

"There's a lady here to see you," the girl started to say.

Owen Grace could already see that for himself since I was standing framed in his office doorway. The attorney rose from his desk, grabbed the sports coat that was hanging over the back of his chair, and quickly pulled it on.

"Thank you, Randy," he said with a wide, practiced, smile. "I'll take it from here."

"Sure." Randy withdrew. "Whatever."

As I stepped into the room, she closed the door behind me. Owen's clients must value their privacy.

In contrast to the hallway and the waiting room, Owen's office was cool, bright, and cheerful. A wide, multi-paned window filled most of the wall behind his desk and let in plenty of light. A colorful collection of framed travel posters covered his walls, hanging beside his college and law-school diplomas. I noted that Owen had graduated from the University of Pennsylvania. Good for him.

He came around his desk to meet me, his hand already extended to shake mine. Owen was in his forties and over six feet tall. He had the trim body of a man who still played pick-up basketball on weekends. Or maybe tennis. His teeth were so white that his smile was almost blinding. His grip was firm enough to be reassuring, but not so strong as to be uncomfortable.

"Owen Grace," he said. "It's a pleasure to meet you."

That remained to be seen, I thought. I hoped he hadn't mistaken me for a potential client.

"I'm Melanie Travis. I believe Emily contacted you about me? I'm very sorry for your loss."

Owen had started to wave me to a plush leather chair that was situated in front of his desk. "Emily?" He stopped and frowned slightly. "Are you talking about Will's ex-wife?"

Damn. She'd told me she would get in touch with Owen and smooth my way. It sounded as though she hadn't done so.

"Yes," I said as I sat down. "She and I are friends. I never had a chance to meet your brother, however."

"Emily sent you?" Owen sounded confused. "And this has something to do with Will?"

"And with his unexpected death," I said gently.

"Are you Emily's attorney?" He moved around to take his own seat behind the desk. "Because you should know that Will named me executor of his estate, such as it is. Frankly, I'm still trying to process what happened. I was planning to get in touch with her next week regarding the will. There was no need for her to send someone here to hassle me."

This wasn't going well at all.

"I didn't come to hassle you," I said quickly. "And I'm not Emily's attorney."

"Then who—?" Owen began, then abruptly stopped. He held up a hand to forestall my response. "No, never mind. It doesn't matter. Whoever you are, you should know there's nothing you can say that will convince me that woman didn't shoot Will herself."

Chapter 14

"**I** think we've gotten started on the wrong foot," I said.

"Is there a right one?" Owen arched a brow in my direction.

Apparently his earlier Mr. Affable act was only for paying customers. Good to know.

"I was just hoping to ask you a few questions," I said.

"Why?"

I went with the truth. "Emily is my friend—"

"You already told me that."

"She's afraid the police view her as a suspect in Will's death—"

"And you don't?"

"No, I—"

"Interesting. Go on." Owen braced his elbows on the desktop and steepled his fingers in front of his lower face.

Now his expression was hidden. Only his dark eyes were visible. And they were staring at me with more than a hint of antipathy. I could feel a palpable challenge shimmering in the space between us.

Abruptly I realized this wasn't a man I would want to confront in a courtroom. Or across a poker table.

"I've known Emily for a long time," I began.

"As have I," Owen interjected smoothly.

His interruptions were really beginning to annoy me. I sat back in my chair and gazed at him in stony silence.

"Are you waiting for something?" he inquired.

"Apparently I'm waiting for my turn to talk."

Owen frowned. "Please proceed."

"Until this week, I had no idea that Emily had ever been married. She and I talk about a lot of things. But in all the years I've known her, she's never mentioned Will. Not even once. He wasn't part of her life anymore." I leaned forward to emphasize my point. "Emily didn't talk about Will because he wasn't important to her."

Owen nodded, but didn't comment. Maybe he'd taken my censure to heart.

"You don't kill someone who means nothing to you," I said. "Indifference is a horrible motive for murder."

Owen continued to remain silent.

"Now it's your turn," I said.

"I would argue that the opposite was true," he replied. "That Emily wasn't indifferent to Will at all. Maybe the depth of her feelings was so great that she couldn't bring herself to speak about it."

That came as a surprise. "You think Emily was still in love with her ex-husband?"

"On the contrary, I suspect that she despised him. You said Emily hadn't previously talked to you about her marriage. Have you discussed it since my brother's untimely death?"

Owen placed a particular emphasis on the last few words. As if he'd wanted to say something else entirely. Perhaps something like "*since Will was shot dead virtually in Emily's backyard?*"

"We talked about it a bit," I told him. "Emily described your brother as impulsive and unreliable. She said that they hadn't parted on the best of terms."

"That's putting it mildly," Owen retorted.

"But their divorce took place years ago. Emily said that she and Will were barely even in touch anymore."

"She probably made it seem as though that was her choice." It was a statement, not a question.

I answered it anyway. "Yes. She did." I stopped, then added, "Of course she did."

Because it was true, I thought. Wasn't it?

"I take it she didn't mention Vanessa Morris?"

"No." I frowned. "Who's she?"

"The woman Will left Emily for. Will drained their joint savings account and ran off to Las Vega with Vanessa. My brother believed he had the golden touch. He intended to double his money at the craps table. As was true of so many of his dubious ventures, Will turned out to be wrong about that."

My mouth was hanging open. I snapped it shut. "Wait a minute. Emily divorced Will because he ran off with another woman?"

That was news. Why was I only hearing about it now?

"No," Owen replied slowly. "*Will* divorced *Emily* because of another woman. While he and Vanessa were in

Las Vegas, he applied for a quickie divorce. At the time, Emily had no idea where he was or what he was doing. She thought he was out of town on a business trip."

My breath seemed to be lodged in my throat. I considered how this new information changed everything I'd thought I knew.

"How did Emily find out the truth?" I asked.

"I gather that came about when she realized that their savings were missing from their account. She called Will in a panic, and Vanessa answered his phone."

"Ouch," I said.

"Indeed. Vanessa was only too happy to tell Emily what she and Will had been up to. Including the divorce proceedings he'd initiated."

"How horrible," I murmured.

Owen nodded. "Will was my brother and I loved him, but we were very different people. I didn't agree with the way he conducted himself in his personal life. Or in his business dealings, for that matter. There were good reasons I made sure that our professional lives were never intertwined."

I sat up straight in my seat. "So then you don't blame Emily for their divorce."

"Certainly not."

"And you think she was justifiably angry about the money Will stole from her?"

"Half of it was his money," Owen pointed out. "But otherwise, yes."

"And you would agree that after she and Will parted ways, Emily went on to build a wonderful life for herself, running her own school and rarely giving her ex-husband more than a passing thought?"

"If you say so," Owen replied.

"Then why did you say earlier that you thought Emily might have shot Will?"

"Because that's what she said."

"Excuse me?" I squeaked.

"It was a while ago, granted. And maybe Emily had had a drink or two at the time. But that was no excuse. Emily told me she would never forgive Will for what he'd done to her. And that one day, she would hunt him down and make him pay."

Well, that gave me plenty to think about on my way home.

Emily and I had been friends for years. But now, after listening to what Owen had to say, I couldn't help but wonder how well I'd ever really known her.

Was it possible that our relationship had been built on a foundation of half-truths and omissions? Or was Owen Grace the person whose words I should be doubting? The man had sounded convincing—but persuasion was his stock-in-trade. Maybe he was the one who was bending the facts to suit his own agenda.

By the time I got home, my head was pounding. Apparently too much thinking in circles wasn't good for me. Fortunately, I knew a cure for that. It was time to take the dogs for a long walk around the neighborhood.

I walked into the house and popped my head into Sam's office. His eyes were on his computer screen and he had his phone pressed to his ear. He sketched me a quick wave with his free hand.

The gesture was equal parts greeting and dismissal. *Ahh, romance.*

I closed Sam's office door and turned to the Poodles

who were crowded around my legs. Bud was there too. He was trying to make himself scarce in that forest of furry black legs. I wondered what the little dog had been up to now.

Whatever it was, it could wait. Instead, I announced to the canine crew that we were going for a walk. Immediately, six sets of paws went scrambling toward the front door.

"Just a minute," I told them. "I have to find Bud's leash first."

The Poodles had been trained since birth to listen and behave. Bud, on the other hand, had his own ideas, most of which didn't involve paying attention to me when the siren call of freedom beckoned. Where he was concerned, I subscribed to the theory that safe was better than sorry.

I checked all the usual places first: the hook near the back door where the lead should have been hanging; the side table in the front hall where everybody tossed stuff when they came in the house; even under the couch where Bud stashed all his valuables.

Still no leash.

Bud followed me from room to room. His stubby tail wagged energetically. *The leash is gone! I don't need a leash!*

"Yes, you do," I told him.

Aside from his other quirks, Bud was also a kleptomaniac. Items he'd pilfered from our neighbors' yards included everything from a garden hose to a decorative flag. Bud was supposed to be Kevin's dog. But when he misbehaved, it always fell to me to make things right again.

As I got up off my hands and knees, I heard something

scratching the hardwood floor in the hall. Bud came with me to have a look.

The front half of Faith's body was lowered so she could wedge her paws and nose under the side table. The Poodle's hindquarter was in the air. Her pomponed tail was waving back and forth. As I approached, she began to whine under her breath.

Slowly Faith inched backward from beneath the table. The end of the lead was in her mouth, the rest dragged along behind. The narrow leather strip must have slithered down behind the table the last time someone used it.

"Good girl!" I said.

She grinned at me happily. *I know!*

By the time we returned from our walk, Sam had emerged from his office. The dogs headed straight to the kitchen to get some cold water. Sam was there, staring into the pantry.

"I'm thinking about lunch," he said.

"Good. Me too." I picked the bowl up off the floor and refilled it. "What are you making?"

"Tuna salad?"

"Sounds perfect. I think we have celery."

"I know we have onions." Sam plucked two cans of tuna off the shelf.

I wrinkled my nose.

"Okay, no onions."

I had no idea how he knew. "You weren't even looking at me."

Sam grinned. "I felt the energy in the room shift."

"Because of onions?"

He was still grinning. "Was I right, or was I right?"

There was no way I was winning this argument. Instead, I went to the refrigerator and got out the mayo and celery. Then I refilled the dogs' water bowl again. And mopped up the floor. While I hadn't been paying attention, Bud must have been swimming.

Over lunch, I brought Sam up to date on everything. He didn't share my predilection for solving mysteries, but he did make a thoughtful and engaged listener.

"This is probably my fault," Sam said at the end.

"What is?" I asked.

"That you've become so involved in Emily's problems. You've been at camp every day, dropping the kids off and picking them up. If I'd been doing my share of driving, you wouldn't have another mystery on your hands."

I'm not sure either one of us really believed that.

"How about if you take a break and I pick up the boys this afternoon?" Sam offered.

"Umm . . . no, thank you."

"You're sure?" His blue eyes twinkled. Now I knew he was teasing. "Because it's no problem."

"Actually, there are a couple of things I need to talk to Emily about."

Sam nodded. He'd seen that coming.

"But if you're offering me a break, how about if you do the shopping and cook dinner tonight?"

His gaze flickered in the direction of the outside deck. Sam's grill was out there. The one that stoked his primitive urges. *Man build fire. Man cook meat for family.*

"It's a deal," he agreed.

Excellent. This way we both got what we wanted.

* * *

That afternoon, the pickup line hadn't yet begun to form when I pulled in the Graceland School driveway. The camp session wouldn't end for half an hour. I expected I would find Emily either in her office or in one of the classrooms. What I hadn't expected was to see two people in front of the school buildings, engaged in a loud argument.

One of those people was Emily. The other was a man I'd never seen before. He was middle-aged, and had a squat body and a shiny bald head. Wearing acid green pants and a bright yellow polo shirt, he was dressed for a game of country club golf. A large pair of aviator sunglasses covered the top half of his face.

The man was standing much too close to Emily. I watched as he lifted his hand and shook his finger in her face. She didn't even flinch. Nor did she reply. Her lips were drawn in a thin line of annoyance.

I quickly pulled the Volvo over and got out. Emily glanced my way. She didn't look happy to see me. The man was oblivious to my approach.

"I'm telling you, this is the last straw," he yelled. "I knew this was a mistake from the beginning, and now I've been proven right!"

"Excuse me," I said loudly.

The man's gaze swung my way. "Who the hell are you?"

"Melanie Travis," I told him. "Who are you?"

"Steve Lambert," he spat out.

"Steve lives in the Greenfields community next door," Emily said.

"I don't just live there." Lambert's tone was smug. "I'm the head of the Homeowners Association."

"Big deal," I said.

"It is a big deal," he ground out. "It means that I'm the person in charge of seeing that proper rules are made and followed. The HOA exists to ensure that no one resident is allowed to adversely impact the quality of life for the group."

"You're not in Greenfields now," I pointed out. "You don't get to make the rules here."

He started to reply, but I cut him off. "I'm sure the other members of the HOA would frown on the idea of you coming over here to browbeat your neighbor."

Emily reached over and placed a gentle hand on my arm. "That's enough, Melanie."

"Are you sure?" Steve Lambert's behavior had gotten my hackles up, and I was just getting started.

"Yes, I'm sure. Steve was just leaving."

"No, I wasn't."

"Yes, you were," she said firmly.

Steve gazed back and forth between the two of us. His face was mottled an ugly shade of red. It wasn't a good look with the green pants.

"All right, then I'll go. But you'd better watch out, missy." He sneered at Emily. "You haven't heard the last of this. And that's a promise."

Chapter 15

"Nice guy," I commented.

We both watched as Lambert got into his car—a bright yellow Corvette—and peeled out of the driveway. I guessed he didn't care that this was a school zone.

Emily sighed. "Steve's usually not that awful. He's just having a bad week."

"I'm sure you know the feeling. So don't think you have to make excuses for him on my account." I paused, then added, "It sounded like he was threatening you."

She nodded. Like she thought that was okay. Which it most definitely was not.

"Want to tell me about it?" I asked.

Emily frowned, but didn't reply.

"I assume it has something to do with Will's murder? Was that the last straw he was referring to?"

"Come on." She gestured toward a pair of Adirondack chairs, placed in the shade beneath a leafy maple tree. "Let's sit for a minute."

When we were both seated, Emily said, "Greenfields bills itself as a premium residential community with luxury amenities to please even the most discerning homeowner."

"That sound posh."

"That's exactly what you're supposed to think. The prices are pretty posh too. Even for Fairfield County. People who buy homes there are told they'll experience pastoral suburban living at its finest."

"Pastoral," I repeated. "As in peaceful?"

Emily nodded.

"Except that Greenfields has a school—albeit a small one—right next door."

"Yes." She frowned. "That's been an issue ever since the place opened."

"But your school was here first," I pointed out.

I wondered if that was the mistake Steve Lambert had referred to. Although he'd seemed to imply that the problem was Emily's fault.

"Not only were we here first," she said, "but we have a zoning variance that gives us every right to continue to be here. But that doesn't matter to Steve and his HOA. As far as they're concerned, we're a commercial business operating in what they think should be solely a residential neighborhood."

"They can't shut you down," I asked. "Can they?"

"No, but they can sure complain a lot. The Greenfields residents grumble about the extra traffic coming to the school. And they bitch and moan about the noise. Dogs, kids, everything bothers them." She paused to roll her eyes. "They've actually asked if there's some way I can keep the campers from laughing and shrieking as they run around the playground."

"Good luck with that," I said.

"Once when we were working on a particularly stinky science project, we took it outside behind the school. I guess the wind must have been blowing the wrong way because next thing I knew, we got a complaint about odor pollution. I didn't even know there was such a thing."

I tried not to laugh. I didn't entirely succeed.

Emily wasn't amused. "Last year on parents' night, they called the police, hoping they'd come and disrupt the event. That time their gripe was that the wattage of our outdoor lights was too bright."

"Holy moly," I said. "I had no idea. They must drive you nuts."

"Usually, when one of the residents comes over here, I just smile and nod until they get tired of talking and go away. Then I go right back to what I was doing. But Steve Lambert? He's a whole new kind of crazy."

"In what way?"

"The previous head of the HOA was a guy in his seventies. I don't think he heard half the complaints the homeowners were making. He certainly didn't bother to respond to most of them. And when he did, he was kind of apologetic about it."

"Steve didn't sound apologetic," I said. "More like apoplectic."

"Yeah, that's more his style. I'm betting he was a drill sergeant in his former life." Emily grimaced. "Steve wants everything his own way. Immediately, if not sooner. He's convinced that my school has a negative impact on their property values. He's even been down to the town hall, to look up ordinances he can use against us. He's demanding that we cease and desist."

"Cease what?" My brow furrowed. "Existing?"

"Pretty much."

"That's not going to happen."

"I know that, and you know that," Emily said. "But Steve is convinced that eventually he'll be able to force the zoning board to do what he wants. Now he's using the fact that my ex-husband's body was found on the land behind us to bolster his case that our existence is a hazard to the neighborhood."

Unfortunately, that might be the kind of complaint that the zoning board would pay attention to. Maybe Emily couldn't afford to keep ignoring Lambert. Maybe she needed to start fighting back.

"His parting words sounded a lot like the warning that was written on your blackboard," I said. "Do you think Lambert could be the person behind all the things that have been going wrong around here?"

Emily stared at me as if the thought had never occurred to her. "I always thought Steve was just full of hot air," she said after a minute. "But now I don't know. I'll have to think about that."

We both paused as a bell chimed inside the school building. The sound signaled that camp had ended for the day. The kids would be heading to their lockers to pick up their belongings. Only a few more minutes remained before both of us would need to be moving along.

"I talked to Owen Grace this morning," I said.

Emily stiffened, suddenly wary. Or maybe she felt

guilty. Considering the way she'd set me up, either one would do.

"Oh?" Her gaze skittered away. "How did that go?"

"Not nearly as well as I'd hoped. For one thing, Owen had no idea who I was, or why I was there. It was your idea that I should talk to him. You were supposed to tell him about me, remember?"

"You're right," she admitted. "And I meant to contact him. I knew Owen would have useful information for you. I just wasn't sure if he'd be willing to share it— especially if the request came from me."

"You should have told me that ahead of time. Then maybe he wouldn't have mistaken me for your attorney."

"You?" Emily sputtered out a laugh. "My attorney?"

Excuse me if I didn't find the notion as funny as she did.

"We got past that quickly enough," I said. "And then we talked about Vanessa Morris. It's odd that you didn't think to mention her."

"Vanessa? Why would I want to talk about her?"

I would have thought the answer to that was obvious. "Maybe because she's the woman who ran off with your husband?"

"That happened a long time ago." Emily shrugged to indicate her indifference. "Will and Vanessa didn't stay together. They were probably tired of each other before his divorce from me even came through. I have no idea whatever happened to her."

"And yet, sometime after that, you were still angry enough about it to threaten Will. You promised to make him pay for what he'd done to you."

"Owen told you that?"

I nodded.

"Did he also tell you that I was drunk at the time?"

"He said you sounded pretty serious."

"Right," Emily scoffed. "At that moment, I was as serious as five or six shots of tequila could inspire me to be. Think about it, Melanie. I didn't have to kill Will to be rid of him. The divorce had already accomplished that."

Abruptly, she looked past me toward the school. Mia was striding across the lawn in our direction. The assistant's regulation polo shirt was coming untucked. Frizzy tendrils of chestnut hair had escaped from her braid to curl wildly around her ears.

Emily and I both stood up as she approached. A line of cars was beginning to form in the driveway. Any minute now, campers would come pouring out of the school building. Three counselors were out front getting everything organized. Kevin and Davey would be along shortly too.

"I've been looking all over for you," Mia said to Emily. "Brian needs to talk to you. He's in the gym."

"Is everything all right?"

Mia shot me a quick glance. "Sure. No problem."

"Good." Emily's tight smile didn't fool either one of us. "I'll be right there." She turned to me quickly before leaving. "Melanie, you and your aunt are stopping by tomorrow morning, right?"

"Right," I said. "See you then. And good luck with . . . whatever that is."

I expected Mia to follow Emily back to the school. Instead, she remained beside me until Emily was out of earshot. When she spoke, there was a sharp edge to her voice. "You must not trust us very much."

I looked at her in surprise. "What are you talking about?"

"Most parents drop their kids off, then leave for the day. But you're always around here, checking up on us." She waved a hand in the direction of Greenfields. "I hope you're not affiliated with *those* people."

"Of course not," I said. "And I'm not checking up on you. Emily is my friend. I'm here because I'm trying to help her."

"Oh." Mia's expression cleared. "Then I guess that's okay. Right now Emily needs all the friends she can get."

I got back to the Volvo just as Davey and Kevin were exiting the school building together. When I waved, Davey spotted me. He looked annoyed as he steered his little brother over to our parked car.

"Why aren't you ever in the car line like the normal mothers?" Davey asked as he threw his lanky frame into the front seat.

It was left to me to get Kevin buckled into his booster seat. "Maybe because I'm not a normal mother?"

Seriously? Did I even have to point that out?

"You say that as if it's a good thing," Davey grumbled.

"Isn't it?" I slid in behind the wheel and started the engine. "Different is interesting."

"Not when you're my age."

He was right. I'd forgotten that being a teenager was all about fitting in.

"Don't worry," I said as I joined the line of cars leaving the school. "Nobody notices but you."

"Yes, they do," Davey told me. "Everybody notices."

I hadn't expected that. "Like who?"

"The other counselors. And Brian. Even Mia said something about it."

I frowned. Mia had felt the need to talk to both of us? That seemed like overkill. Not to mention that she was butting into something that was really none of her business.

"Don't worry about Mia," I told him, inching the Volvo forward. "She and I talked. We're good."

"Did you buy me raisins?" Kevin asked.

"Not yet," I admitted.

"How about chocolate chip ice cream?"

"Nope." Our turn came, and I pulled out onto the road.

"I guess that means no Oreos either?" Davey asked.

"Sorry," I told him.

"Oh, man." Kevin groaned. He slumped in his seat. "That sucks."

"Hey!" I gazed at him in the rear-view mirror. "Watch your language."

Davey looked over at me and grinned. "What Kevin meant to say was that our lack of sweets was an unfortunate development."

"You're a fresh kid," I told him.

He was still grinning. "I'm my mother's son. How about if we make a stop at the supermarket?"

"We're on our way there now," I said.

Aunt Peg picked me up the next morning in her minivan. I buckled myself in and prepared for a hairy ride. Aunt Peg thinks speed limits are for sissies. And since she has a gift for talking herself out of speeding tickets, nothing I say has ever been able to change her mind.

"I need you to be on your best behavior today," I said as scenery went whizzing past my window.

She cast me a glance. "What are you talking about? I'm always well-behaved."

"Yes, but your idea of good behavior isn't the same as

everyone else's. Emily's been through a lot lately. I don't want you doing anything to add to her problems."

"Don't be silly. I'm just going to look at some puppies. Emily will barely even notice I'm there."

"You also want to talk to her about the benefit," I reminded her.

Aunt Peg nodded. "I've started making calls. Everyone thinks it's a splendid idea. I've already lined up several dozen breeders who want to take part."

That was fast.

"Really?" I said. "Those people don't even know Emily."

"No, but they do understand that the purebred dog community is in need of some good PR. Plus, we're offering breeders the opportunity to show off their dogs and promote their breeding programs. Who wouldn't be excited about that?"

Not anyone I'd ever met through Aunt Peg. That was for sure.

"I've also spoken to the editor of the *Stamford Advocate*. He'd said he'd be delighted to give us some coverage."

I turned to face her. "You've made all these arrangements without talking to Emily first?"

"Well, whose fault is that?" Aunt Peg asked. "I've been waiting for you to introduce us. Time's passing, Melanie. Of course I went ahead and got to work. Do you think Emily will agree to hold the benefit on school property?"

"Probably," I said. "Assuming we can get a permit. Although her neighbors may not think much of the idea."

"Oh?"

"It turns out some of them aren't happy that Emily is

running a business in their midst." I recalled that there'd also been objections to noise and dogs. "And they don't sound like dog lovers."

"Pish." Aunt Peg snorted. "That's hardly a deterrent. We'll just have to change their minds."

In her world, things were just that easy.

But who was I to disagree? Today, Aunt Peg was in charge of the proceedings. I was just along for the ride.

Chapter 16

"This is lovely," Aunt Peg said as we turned in the gate and drove down the long, tree-lined driveway. "What a beautiful setting for a school."

"Before Emily took over the property, it was used as an artists' retreat," I told her. "She had to make some changes, of course. But she worked hard to retain the site's rustic appeal."

I had texted Emily when we were three minutes away. When we reached the head of the driveway, she was outside waiting for us. Poppy, Posey, and Pansy were racing around the yard behind her.

Aunt Peg kept a careful eye on the puppies' whereabouts as she brought the minivan to a stop. I knew she wouldn't approve of Emily allowing three untrained puppies to run around loose. I hoped she didn't begin our conversation with a complaint.

Aunt Peg surprised me, however.

She strode straight over to Emily, extended her hand, and said, "You must be Emily Grace. I've heard so many nice things about you, from both Melanie and the boys. Your nursery school has been wonderful for our whole family. I'm Margaret Turnbull. My friends call me Peg."

I gaped at Aunt Peg from behind her back. Who was this unfamiliar woman—and why had I never met her before? Yes, I'd made a plea for civility. But I hadn't actually thought she'd honor it.

"Thank you." For a moment, Emily looked similarly taken aback. After the stories she'd heard, this effusive greeting wasn't what she'd been expecting. Then she relaxed and returned Aunt Peg's smile. "It's nice to meet you. Melanie talks about you all the time."

"Don't listen to a word she says," Aunt Peg replied. "Melanie exaggerates everything."

I cleared my throat. Loudly. In case they'd forgotten that I was standing right there.

The three Dalmatians had been distracted from their game by our arrival. They came galloping over together to check us out.

"What pretty puppies," Aunt Peg said as Pansy attempted to jump up on her. She deftly sidestepped the puppy's charge. "Three Dalmatian bitches, all the same age. How unusual."

"I thought the same thing when Will gave them to me," Emily agreed. "I suppose they might have come from the same litter."

Aunt Peg was watching as the trio tumbled and played on the ground around us. "They did."

Emily slanted me a look. I just shrugged.

I knew what she was thinking. We'd barely been there two minutes. And already Aunt Peg thought she possessed more information about the puppies than their owner did. Emily looked skeptical, but I knew better.

When it came to dogs, Aunt Peg was never wrong.

"How do you know that?" Emily asked.

"Look at them," Aunt Peg replied, as though the answer was perfectly obvious. Which, to her, it was.

Pansy joined her sisters, and the puppies ran off again. They raced in big, looping circles around the yard. At this distance, I could barely tell the three Dalmatians apart, much less form an opinion about their ancestry.

Aunt Peg hunkered down into a low squat. She clapped her hands loudly. The puppies stopped what they were doing and turned to look at her. When she beckoned with her fingers, they came trotting over. More Aunt Peg magic.

"The one in front is Poppy," Emily told us. "She's the bravest, and usually the first to leap into anything new."

Aunt Peg nodded. Her gaze was still fastened on the puppies. For all I knew, they might be engaged in some kind of subliminal messaging.

"Pansy is next," Emily continued. "You just met her. She's the tomboy of the group. Posey is bringing up the rear. She's a real sweetheart. If you want a dog to cuddle with, Posey is your girl."

"Posey is your favorite," Aunt Peg commented.

Emily's chin lifted. "I like them all. Puppies are like children. You can't pick a favorite."

"Really?" Aunt Peg gazed up at Emily as the puppies swarmed around her. Her hands were in constant motion. They slid over the Dals' bodies. They lifted paws and checked teeth. "I've always thought having a favorite was a good thing. Then everybody knows where they stand."

Go ahead. Ask me if I'm the favorite.

"It's a good thing you're not a teacher," Emily replied. "Favoritism keeps you from addressing each child's needs equally and individually."

"I can see why Melanie speaks so highly of your nursery school." Aunt Peg braced her hands on her thighs and stood. "In that context, I commend your theory. May we sit down?"

Since the day before, when Emily and I had sat and talked under the maple tree, a third Adirondack chair had joined the other two. Assuming our acquiescence, Aunt Peg headed that way. The Dalmatians fell in line behind her, following along as though she was the Pied Piper.

"The puppies like you," Emily commented as we took our seats. "They don't usually take to strangers so quickly."

"All dogs like Aunt Peg," I said. "She has a gift."

"Dogs like me because I like them back," Aunt Peg said simply. "We're drawn to each other by mutual appreciation. You asked me how I could tell these puppies came from the same litter."

"Yes." Emily nodded eagerly.

"Mostly it's due to a similarity in type. These three all share a certain make and shape. Their bodies, their angulation, and their expressions are remarkably similar. Small details—the arch of their feet and the set of their ears, for example—are virtually the same. All of which points to the probability that they were produced by the set of same parents."

Emily and I stared at the puppies, both of us trying to

see the same things Aunt Peg did. Her hands moved as she spoke, indicating where we should be looking.

"That's not to say that there aren't differences between them," Aunt Peg continued. "Poppy has the prettiest eyes and the best markings. Pansy has a beautiful topline, but she's slightly cow hocked. And Posey is missing two teeth."

"How do you know all that?" Emily asked in amazement.

Aunt Peg blinked, surprised by the question. "It's my job to know that."

"Aunt Peg is a dog show judge," I said. "And Dalmatians are one of her breeds."

"I thought you had Standard Poodles."

"I do. But I'm also a student of the whole canine cornucopia." She paused for a small frown. "These puppies are fine representatives of their breed. Under the circumstances, that seems rather odd."

"What circumstances?" Emily asked.

"The unusual way they came to be in your possession," Aunt Peg said. "Melanie told me they were an unexpected gift from your ex-husband."

"That's right."

"During the course of your marriage, had he ever given you live animals before?"

"Well . . . no," Emily admitted.

"But now—years after the two of you had parted—he suddenly showed up with three lovely Dalmatian puppies?"

"It came as a surprise to me too," Emily said.

"Did he tell you where the puppies had come from?"

"No. And I didn't ask. At the time, I had more important things on my mind. Like making sure that Will didn't succeed in worming his way back into my life."

Aunt Peg nodded as if that made perfect sense. "So the gift of three puppies wasn't enough to soften your resolve?"

"If anything, it hardened it," Emily retorted. "I didn't realize it soon enough—not until after we were married—but Will wasn't a trustworthy person. He never held a normal job. And he always kept his business dealings private. Money came in and went out again without my ever knowing how or why. All I knew was that Will usually seemed to have some kind of deal in the works."

"You're saying your ex-husband was a con man," Aunt Peg summed up.

"No, I'm not." Emily winced. "I would have called him an entrepreneur. Or perhaps an opportunist. Will was always on the hunt for his next big score."

Aunt Peg and I shared a glance. He sounded like a con man to us.

Emily looked at the Dalmatians, who were now lying in the shade at our feet. "Will believed in the deals he put together. He was always sure they'd work out well for everyone involved. But . . ."

"That didn't turn out to be the case?" I said.

Her gaze lifted. "I didn't ask where the puppies had come from because I thought Will probably got them as some kind of payoff."

"For what?" I asked.

"I don't know. It was just a thought I had at the time. Like if a deal Will was mixed up in had fallen through, maybe one of his partners ended up owing him money he didn't have. So the guy gave him the Dalmatians instead."

"Except that Will apparently didn't want the puppies." I made no attempt to hide my skepticism. "Because he gave them away to you."

"Will wasn't the brightest guy," Emily admitted. "If someone told him these dogs could be sold for a lot of money, he would have believed it. You know, because of the movie." Her eyes drifted Aunt Peg's way. "And because of you."

"What about me?" Aunt Peg asked.

"Emily knows about Beau," I told her. "I was a substitute counselor at Graceland camp that summer."

"I told Will that story once," Emily said. "About how the dog was worth a lot of money, and you were desperate to get him back."

The reasons Aunt Peg wanted to find Beau had little to do with money, I thought. But Will probably wasn't the kind of person who would worry about nuance in a tale that involved a large sum of cash.

"So you think he accepted the puppies as a payment of some kind," Aunt Peg said. "And then found out they weren't worth anything to him?"

Emily nodded.

"Did they come with papers?"

"Papers?" She looked blank.

"Pedigrees," I told her. "AKC registrations?"

"No, it was just the dogs themselves. Will presented them to me like he thought he'd come up with a great idea. 'Dalmatian puppies!' he said. 'Just like in the movies. The kids will go nuts for them!'" Emily looked at me. "And they do. You know that."

I nodded. Meanwhile, Aunt Peg was frowning again. That reminded me of another question she'd prodded me to ask.

"Do you own a gun?" I said to Emily.

"Me?" She looked shocked. "Of course not. What would I do with a gun?"

The obvious answer to that hung in the air between us.

"Even if I wanted a gun—which I don't," Emily said pointedly, "it wouldn't be safe to have one here with all the kids around."

"Certainly not," Aunt Peg agreed. "I can't imagine what Melanie was thinking to even ask such a thing."

I glared at Aunt Peg. She slipped me a quick wink.

Then she leaned toward Emily as if the two of them were well on their way to becoming best friends. "Listen now, we need to move along. You and I have a fundraiser to discuss."

"Okay." Emily sounded doubtful. "Melanie mentioned something about that. I've been wondering what she was talking about."

"Let me explain."

I'd never met anyone who could resist Aunt Peg when she had an objective in mind, and Emily proved to be no exception. Her initial uncertainty melted away as Aunt Peg outlined her vision for the event. Within minutes, the two women had formed a team. With the benefit barely in the planning stages, both were eager to get started. I listened in silence as they discussed everything from scheduling, to marketing and logistics.

Nobody asked for my input, which was fine with me. I'd previously been involved in plenty of Aunt Peg's pet projects. This time, all I had to do was sit in the grass and play with the puppies. It definitely felt as though I'd gotten the better deal.

The sound of an approaching vehicle made me glance around, then stand up. A silver Lexus was coming up the school driveway. I wondered if Emily was expecting more visitors. Aunt Peg and I quickly gathered up the puppies so they couldn't run toward the car.

"That's my brother, Miles," said Emily, standing up too. "He went into town to talk to the mechanic about Will's truck. Don't worry, he knows he needs to be careful."

Miles parked beside Aunt Peg's minivan and got out. Emily had told me a few things about her brother—but one thing she'd neglected to mention was how handsome Miles was. Like movie star handsome.

Maybe that wasn't the kind of thing older sisters paid attention to. But Aunt Peg and I certainly did. We were both staring as Miles approached our group. His graceful, lengthy stride ate up the ground between us.

Emily's brother had the body of an action hero, with broad shoulders that tapered to a narrow waist above long legs. His features were classically handsome, his eyes a deep shade of green. The slight breeze artfully tousled his rich brown hair. When he smiled, his whole face lit up.

"Hi, you must be Melanie," he said, holding out a hand to me. "I'm Miles Harlan. I appreciate all the help you've given my sister."

"I haven't accomplished much yet," I told him, before turning to introduce Aunt Peg.

"You've been a good friend," Miles said seriously. Even his voice was swoon-worthy. "And that means a lot to both of us."

"It's lovely to meet you, Miles," Aunt Peg cut in. "But Melanie and I must be going. We've taken up enough of Emily's morning." She turned to Emily. "Thank you for allowing me to meet your puppies."

"They enjoyed meeting you too," Emily replied. "Melanie, I'll call you later, okay? I have a couple more ideas for you. People you might want to talk to."

"Sure," I said. "That would be great."

What I'd told Miles was unfortunately true. I hadn't really accomplished anything yet. It was time for me to get to work.

Chapter 17

"You certainly rushed us out of there in a hurry," I said to Aunt Peg when we were in her minivan on our way home.

"What's the matter?" She spared me a glance. "Did you want to stay and continue making calf-eyes at Miles?"

"I have no idea what you're talking about." I muttered. "And what are calf-eyes anyway?"

"They're big and googly, and they convey an element of longing. It wasn't an attractive look on you."

"It doesn't sound like an attractive look on anyone," I said. "And I wasn't longing for anything."

"Then you should be happy to be heading home," she retorted.

I stared at her suspiciously. "You know something."

"I know a great many things. Which one would you like to hear about?"

"The one that pertains to Emily's problems—" I started, then abruptly stopped. This was Aunt Peg I was talking to, after all. "No, the one that pertains to Emily's *Dalmatians*. You learned something, didn't you?"

Aunt Peg snorted under her breath. "It look you long enough to figure that out."

"Tell me," I said.

"First of all, those puppies that your friend has been letting run loose all over creation aren't just run-of-the-mill Dalmatians. They are well-bred, well-made dogs, most likely produced from champion stock. A reasonably competent handler could finish two of them in the show ring without even drawing a deep breath."

"Wow."

That earned me another look. "That's all you have to say? Wow?"

"I'm surprised?"

"Frankly," Aunt Peg sniffed, "I'm surprised you couldn't tell that much yourself. How many Non-Sporting groups have you watched in the last decade?"

Too many to count, I thought. But I was pretty sure that was a rhetorical question.

"Usually the Dalmatian stands near the head of the line, right beside the Standard Poodle. Have you never bothered to take a look?"

Of course I'd seen my share of champion Dalmatians. Usually out of the corner of my eye while I'd been watching the Poodles.

"Apparently not closely enough," I said.

"I see. I expect you to remedy that deficit at the show next weekend."

"Yes ma'am."

"You needn't be rude," Aunt Peg said. "I went to Graceland today as a favor to you."

"No, you went to Graceland because you wanted to see three Dalmatian puppies who'd piqued your curiosity," I corrected. "I was the one who came along as a favor. Now tell me what else you learned."

"What makes you think there was more?"

I sighed under my breath. Now she was just being difficult. And possibly waiting for an apology.

"With you, there's always more," I said instead.

"Indeed there is." Aunt Peg sounded pleased with herself. I hadn't meant it as a compliment. "Those puppies aren't just quality Dalmatians. They also have the look of a dog I've judged several times. One who's currently standing at stud in Westchester County."

That got my attention. I swiveled in my seat to look at her. "Are you saying you might know who the puppies' sire is?"

"At the risk of repeating myself, yes."

"And with that information, you can probably figure out who their breeder was?"

"Again, yes."

"Then I'll be able to find out how Will got possession of them."

"Indeed." Aunt Peg nodded happily. "Once I've called around and asked a few questions, I may be able to solve this whole mystery for you."

That came as a surprise. "You'll know who killed Will Grace and why?"

"Oh that." She dismissed the question as if its answer wasn't important. "I was talking about the mystery of the puppies."

I should have known.

"I guess that's a start," I said.

That afternoon, I was out on the deck, watering the marigolds in the flower boxes. I'm not much of a gardener. Keeping hardy flowers alive during their natural growing season is about the best that I can manage. Faith and Eve were lying nearby supervising.

Davey came walking out the back door. One of his hands was extended in my direction. "It's for you," he said.

I glanced over at him. "That's my phone."

Davey shrugged. He already knew that. "That's why it's for you."

"Who is it?"

"Ms. Grace. She says she has some info for you."

"Cool." I put down the watering pot.

"You know people stopped using that word years ago, right?"

"Neat-o," I replied. "Do you like that better?"

"Not really," my teenager grumbled. He handed over the phone and left.

"Neat-o?" Emily said when I'd lifted the device to my ear. "Really?"

"You're a teacher," I told her. "You should know it's a parent's sworn duty to embarrass their children. Is everything okay?"

"Yes, fine. I feel much better—more secure—now that Miles is here."

"That's good," I said. "Even better, there hasn't been another incident in the past few days."

"I should hope not," Emily replied. "The authorities have been all over the place. And now my brother is here to help keep an eye on things. Hopefully the worst is behind us."

"Amen to that," I said.

"I called to give you a couple more names."

"Great." I walked inside the kitchen to get a pen and paper. "Shoot."

"The first one is Jeff Earley. He and his wife, Linda, are neighbors."

"They live in the subdivision?"

"No, on the other side. They're an older couple who've been in their house for years. Both of them are retired, so they're around a lot. Maybe they saw something—or heard something—that could be useful for you."

Emily gave me the couple's phone number. I was sure the police would have already interviewed the Earleys, but hopefully they wouldn't mind talking to me too.

"The next guy is Bradley Luft." She also supplied his contact info.

I wrote both things down. "Who's he?"

"Bradley was Will's best friend. They grew up together in Darien, so they were lifelong buddies. Even when I was married to Will, I suspected Bradley knew him better than I did. And I was probably right."

"Thanks. I'll see about talking to both of them," I said. "Have you been in touch with Detective Sturgill about how his investigation is going?"

"Definitely not," Emily replied. "I don't intend to talk to him again if I don't have to. I don't even want my name to be on his radar."

She'd shut that topic down in a hurry, I thought. On the other hand, if I was a suspect in a murder case, maybe I'd feel the same way.

"There are a couple of other people I'd like to see," I told her. "Maybe you know how to contact them?"

"Who?" Emily asked.

"Vanessa Morris—"

"You don't need to talk to her," she interrupted. "She has nothing pertinent to say."

"Maybe not," I allowed. "But I won't know that until I try. Do you know how I can reach her?"

"No, I don't. Like I told you the other day, Vanessa's old news. I have no idea where she is."

"Okay." I let her think I was capitulating. "I'd also like to talk to whichever of Malcolm Hancock's heirs you've been dealing with."

"Why?" Once again, Emily didn't sound happy.

"Because if anyone has a vested interest in making trouble for you—trouble that could lead to your closing the school and leaving the property—it's the Hancock family."

"No," she said firmly. "I refuse to believe that. Peyton's a respected businessman. He wouldn't do anything underhanded."

I scribbled the name Peyton Hancock on my pad. "How can you be so sure?"

"For one thing, his family has plenty of money. This property is merely a minor asset of theirs. I doubt the Hancocks are even aware of my problems. And I have every intention of keeping it that way."

"But—"

"Listen to me, Melanie. The Hancocks didn't have

anything to do with Will's murder. They're important people, and I don't want you bothering them."

I ended the connection and stared at my phone thoughtfully. Was it my imagination or was Emily trying to limit, perhaps even control, the scope of my inquiries? I'd assumed that she and I were both searching for the truth. So why was she trying to get in my way?

Some days, it seemed as though Google was my best friend. Before the afternoon was over, I knew how to get in touch with both Peyton Hancock and Vanessa Morris. Peyton was easy to find. When I put his name into the search engine, several dozen references immediately popped up. I could read about everything from his finance company, to his charitable causes, to his social life.

Vanessa Morris took longer to locate. Not because I couldn't find anyone by that name, but because the opposite was true. The name was common enough to be shared by multiple women. It wasn't until it occurred to me to take a shot in the dark and type in the name "Vanessa Morris Grace" that I was finally able to narrow down my search.

Emily had told me that Vanessa and Will hadn't stayed together. She'd certainly never mentioned anything about a marriage. I wondered if she'd been misinformed. Or was that another attempt at misdirection on her part?

That question immediately shot Vanessa to the top of the list of people I was anxious to meet. My luck continued to hold. When I called ahead, Vanessa agreed to see me.

Sunday morning, Sam proposed another outing to the beach. I thought that sounded like a wonderful idea—as long as I didn't have to go.

"You have other plans?" Sam cocked a brow in my direction. That was no mean feat since he was shaving at the time.

"Umm . . . yes. " I caught his eye in the mirror that spanned the double sinks in our bathroom.

"Does this have anything to do with Emily Grace?"

"Maybe."

Sam didn't look surprised. We'd been down this road so many times before that now all he did was shrug. "Will you be home in time for dinner?"

"Of course," I replied brightly. I'd gotten in touch with Vanessa, and she'd agreed to meet with me. But that wouldn't take all day. "I'll even cook dinner."

"I'm holding you to that," Sam said. "And it better be something good. No hot dogs."

I gave him a snappy salute to seal the deal.

It took me longer than that to take my leave from Faith. The big Poodle had been left behind a lot lately. This morning, she was convinced that wherever I was going, she should be coming along.

I stooped down in front of her and cupped her muzzle in my palms. We looked into each other's eyes. Faith's tail wagged slowly back and forth. She liked this part of the conversation. We both did.

"I'm sorry," I told her. "But I've never met this woman, and I don't know anything about her. I'd have to leave you in the car, and it's too hot for that."

I'll lie down and wait for you.

"I can't let you do that. It wouldn't be safe."

Faith sighed unhappily. Her tail drooped downward. She stepped back to disengage from my hands.

"I'll make it up to you later," I said.

She looked up. *Promise?*

"I promise," I told her.

Vows made to dogs and children were inviolable. Now I'd have to figure out how to make that happen.

Vanessa Grace lived in Ridgefield, twenty miles from North Stamford. Her address led me to a town house community so new that the signage on the road still announced its grand opening. The rows of attached homes were classic in style, with peaked roofs, matching front doors, and plenty of windows. I parked against the curb out front.

When I pressed the doorbell, the chimes that rang out were loud enough to be heard two houses away. Several seconds later, the door drew open. If I had that level of noise alerting me to visitors, I'd be quick to respond too.

Vanessa Grace was younger than I'd expected, probably in her early thirties. Dark auburn hair curled halfway down her back, and there was a sprinkling of freckles across her nose. She was dressed in bright pink cropped pants and a T-shirt tight enough to advertise a voluptuous figure. The nails on her fingers and toes were painted in a matching shade of electric blue.

For a moment, I simply stood and stared. Nothing about Vanessa—or her pristine home—was what I'd imagined. Perhaps because of the dismissive way Emily had spoken about the woman who'd run off with her husband, I'd pictured Vanessa as a tawdry, middle-aged gold digger.

Not that Will had had much gold to dig. But still.

Looking at the attractive young woman in front of me, I realized I couldn't have been more wrong.

"You must be Melanie," Vanessa said with a smile.

She pulled the door open wide. "Please come in. I have the air-conditioning on full blast. I'll get you a sweater if you're too cold."

"Thanks, but I'm sure that won't be a problem." I stepped inside and was met by a blast of frigid air. "You have a lovely home."

From the entryway, I could see through to a bright living room that was furnished in pastel colors. A couch and two chairs were grouped around a glass coffee table with stainless steel legs. Several large pieces of modern art hung on the walls.

"I'm glad you like it," Vanessa replied cheerfully. "I haven't been here long. The place is still a work in progress, but it's beginning to feel like home."

She waved toward the couch. "Have a seat. Can I get you something to drink? I just made a pitcher of iced tea."

"That sounds great." I watched over the wide counter that separated the kitchen from the living room as she filled two tall glasses with ice cubes, then poured the tea over them. Vanessa then added a plate of sugar cookies to a small tray and came back to join me.

"This should hold us for a while," she said, sinking down into a chair opposite the couch. "Now, what can I do for you?"

Over the years, I'd found myself interviewing numerous people I didn't know. Some had been helpful, others were recalcitrant. But I'd never run across someone like Vanessa, who seemed genuinely delighted to see me.

"Thank you for agreeing to meet with me." I paused for a sip of tea. It was cold and tart, and tasted delicious. "But if you don't mind my asking, why did you?"

Vanessa's eyes twinkled. "When you called, you said you wanted to talk about romance gone wrong. That's right up my alley. I figured it couldn't hurt to talk. And who knows? Maybe I'll get lucky and you'll give me something I can use in my next book."

Chapter 18

"Your next book?" I sputtered.

"Yes." Vanessa was amused by my response. "I write romance novels. Mostly contemporaries, but the occasional historical romance too."

My jaw dropped. How had my internet search missed that?

"Really?"

She nodded.

"I'm impressed. I've never met an author before."

Vanessa shrugged. "Mostly we're not that interesting."

"That's not true." I found her chosen career fascinating. "Are you successful at it?"

She glanced around the beautifully appointed room. "I make a living."

I took that to mean yes. It seemed a shame I had to change the subject.

"I wanted to ask you about Will Grace," I said.

"Go ahead," Vanessa replied. "I've already spoken to the police, and I'll tell you the same things I told them. Unless you manage to come up with better questions than they did—which you might, considering you told me over the phone that you're a friend of Emily's. How's she doing, by the way? Please don't tell me she's playing the role of the grieving widow."

"No, she's very clear about the status of their relationship," I said, surprised Vanessa would care enough to ask about her predecessor. "Although Will's death has been problematic for her."

"I'm guessing Emily portrayed me as the Jezebel that stole her husband?"

"Actually, she referred to you as old news."

That made Vanessa laugh. "Well, I guess that puts me in my place. Sugar cookie?" She lifted the plate and offered them to me. "They're homemade."

"Thank you." I slid a cookie off the plate and popped it into my mouth. "*Are* you the Jezebel who stole Emily's husband?"

"No way. My going to Las Vegas with Will was all his idea. And let me be perfectly clear—at the time, I had no idea he was married."

That was a point in Vanessa's favor.

"You must have been quite young then," I said. "How did you and Will meet?"

"In a bar, how else?" She stopped just short of rolling her eyes. "I'd just graduated from college with no idea about what I wanted to do with my life. So yes, I was young and probably stupid. When I met Will, he seemed like a sophisticated older man. Someone who knew things I didn't. Will bought me a drink, and things developed from there."

She frowned, thinking back. "Three months later, Will asked me to elope with him. It all sounded incredibly romantic and exciting—until we arrived in Las Vegas and I found out that he had to get a divorce first."

"Once you found out about Emily, why didn't you leave?"

"I thought about it. But I'd given up the room I was renting and spent all the money I had on my plane ticket. So where would I have gone? Besides, at that point, Will still seemed like a decent guy. I decided to stay and see things through—like maybe I'd turn out to be the only person in the world for whom two wrongs would turn out to make a right."

Vanessa paused to chuckle at the naïveté of her younger self. That made me smile too. Before meeting her, I'd been prepared to disparage the woman and her actions. Now I was seeing both in a new light. But as I helped myself to another sugar cookie, a sobering thought crossed my mind. Vanessa wouldn't be the first murder suspect whose company I'd enjoyed. And several of those suspects had turned out to be murderers.

"So I guess you did end up marrying Will," I said. "Emily wasn't sure about that."

"Oh, we got married all right. And Emily knew all about it. She's probably just in denial," Vanessa scoffed. "Will always said Emily buried her head in the sand whenever something happened that she didn't want to think about."

"Are you still married?" I asked. "I found you by Googling your married name."

"No, divorced the guy, kept the name. Vanessa Grace sounds pretty. And it looks just right on the cover of a romance novel. His name is about the only useful thing Will ever gave me."

"Was there something in particular that led to your divorce?" I asked.

Vanessa thought a moment before replying. "Short answer, I grew up. But you probably want to hear more than that?"

I nodded.

"Like I said earlier, when I met Will I didn't know what I wanted out of life. But after he and I had been married a year, I knew exactly what I *didn't* want. And that was to be saddled with a hustler like him. I knew I had to move on . . . before somebody got hurt."

I'd been reaching for another cookie. Now my hand stilled. "You were afraid Will might hurt you?"

"No, but some of the people Will associated with weren't very nice. He lived to gamble. Cards, dice, whatever anyone was playing, Will wanted in. He always thought he couldn't lose."

I guessed that explained Will's fondness for Las Vegas.

"There were other things too—stuff he didn't want to talk about. After a while, I stopped asking questions. I figured I was better off not knowing. Life with Will was like a roller coaster. It didn't take me long to realize that I couldn't live like that."

"It sounds as though you and Will have been divorced for a while," I said. "Did you stay in touch with him afterward?"

"Yes, but not by choice." Vanessa frowned. "Whenever Will needed money, he looked me up. He even tried to convince me that I owed it to him. He said it was his influence that made me the success I've become."

Vanessa and I both shook our heads. *Men.*

"That's just stupid," I said. "Not to mention offensive."

"I know. Right? One time he even tried to dump some puppies on me. Three of them, if you can believe that. He'd picked them up somewhere and needed a place for them to stay."

"Puppies?" I sat up in my seat. "Dalmatian puppies?"

"Yeah, I guess. Anyway, they had spots. I was getting ready to move in here at the time. I told him to take a look around. Where in this town house did he see enough room for me to manage three growing puppies?"

"Wait a minute," I said. "Will only wanted you to *keep* the puppies for him? He didn't offer them to you as a gift?"

"A gift? No way." Vanessa snorted. "What kind of stupid gift is that?"

Point taken.

"Did he tell you where the puppies came from?" I asked.

"Don't know. Didn't care," she replied. "Like I said, sometimes it was better not to ask too many questions. I figured they were probably part of some crazy scheme. Which meant I didn't want anything to do with them."

"Now your ex-husband is dead," I said. "Does that worry you?"

"What? Like someone might come after me too?" Vanessa considered the question. "No, not at all. It would worry me a lot more if I was Emily."

'Why is that?"

"Because it happened at her school. I'm betting she was right there at the time. In fact, it wouldn't surprise me to find out that she's the one who pulled the trigger."

"Emily?" My voice squeaked. "Why?"

Vanessa shrugged. "After what Will did to her, she hated him. Isn't that reason enough?"

Vanessa was a writer, I reminded myself on the way home. By definition, that meant she had a flair for the dramatic. I wondered if she was right about Emily's feelings toward Will. If she was, then Emily had been lying to me. Or maybe Vanessa had been lying to me. Or maybe Will had lied to Vanessa about Emily's feelings for him.

This whole thing felt like a hopeless muddle. Maybe I'd have been better off opting for a day at the beach.

Faith was waiting for me when I opened the door to the house. That was no surprise. We both knew it was time for me to make good on my promise. I handed out dog biscuits all around, then put the rest of the pack out in the backyard. While they amused themselves, I took Faith for a long walk—just the two of us. No interruptions, no distractions. It was perfect.

After that, I spent the rest of the afternoon making myself useful. I clipped, bathed, and blow-dried Tar. When my family arrived home after a long day at Tod's Point—sunburned, sticky, and covered with sand—I was the one who was cool and calm for a change. I'd even started preparing the lemon chicken I was making for dinner.

"You look like you had a good day," said Sam.

I stood up on my toes and gave him a kiss. "I did. I had the kind of day that reminds me how lucky I am."

"You're not lucky," Kevin informed me. He'd dragged his beach towel into the house. Now Bud was hanging on the other end and being pulled across the floor. "You even lose at checkers."

"That's a matter of skill, not luck," Davey said. "Mom's just not good at playing games."

"Oh yeah?" I propped my hands on my hips. "Says who?"

My whole family stared at me. Even the Poodles.

"Pretty much everybody," Sam told me gently.

"Maybe I'm letting you guys win. Has that ever occurred to you?"

"Good one, Mom." Davey laughed.

"Yeah," said Kevin. "Good one!"

He tried to high-five his brother, but their hands missed. Instead Kevin smacked Augie on the head. The Poodle yowled in protest, which made Kevin drop his end of the towel.

Immediately, Bud took off with it. Tar went flying after him. A few seconds later, we heard something crash in the living room.

Sam and I exchanged glances. Neither one of us moved.

Davey sighed. "I'll get it."

Sam and I watched him go. Kevin went running after his big brother. Hopefully the dogs hadn't broken something useful. Like the television.

"Tar looks great," Sam mentioned. "Good work."

"Thank you." I wrapped my arms around his waist.

Sam's blond hair was crusted with salt and sticking straight up in spots. He smelled like fresh air and the ocean, and when he gazed down at me and smiled, there was nowhere else in the world I wanted to be. We shared another kiss before the boys could come back and stop us.

The lemon chicken dinner was a big success. Even better, the television hadn't been smashed, though we did lose a vase no one really liked. That night, I hustled the boys off to bed early, then Sam and I followed suit.

Monday morning, Davey, Kevin, and I were once again in the car on our way to Graceland camp. And again I had a game plan for after I'd dropped off the boys. Hopefully, this would be a good time for me to call on Jeff and Linda Earley.

Like Graceland School, the Earleys' house was set back from the road at the end of a long driveway. Colonial in style, it was painted white with pine green shutters and looked as though it probably dated from the middle of the previous century. By Connecticut standards, that meant it was relatively new construction.

A low stone wall bordered a narrow band of woods between the Earleys' property and the school. As I neared the house, I saw an older man bending over a gap where the wall had crumbled and the rocks had fallen to the ground. I got out of my car and went over to say hello.

The man straightened as I walked across the wide lawn between us. He reached around to brace a fisted hand at the base of his back, before stretching his shoulders up and back. His other hand pulled a kerchief out of the pocket of his workpants. He used it to wipe his brow.

It wasn't even nine o'clock yet, but the temperature was already in the eighties. Luckily, the stone wall was shaded by the trees beside it.

"That looks like hot work," I said as I approached.

"It is," the man agreed. His head was mostly bald, and the hands that had now dropped to his sides were gnarled with age. "I've been out here an hour already, and it isn't getting any cooler. Can I help you with something?"

"I hope so. Are you Jeff Earley?"

"In the flesh. And you are?"

"Melanie Travis. I'm a friend of your neighbor, Emily Grace."

Jeff nodded. "That poor lady. She's had nothing but trouble lately over there at that school."

"That's what I wanted to ask you about, if you don't mind?"

"No, I guess not," he replied. "As long as you don't mind if I work while we talk. I want to get this section of wall rebuilt before the sun's overhead."

"Sure," I said. "Can I help?"

He looked at me appraisingly. I was wearing a T-shirt, khaki shorts, and sneakers. And I was at least several decades younger than he was. I figured all that had to count in my favor.

"You know anything about building stone walls?" Jeff asked.

"No. I just enjoy looking at them." In Connecticut, stone walls were everywhere.

Jeff pointed at a large rock near my feet. I picked it up and handed it to him. "What caused your wall to fall down?"

"I dunno." He shrugged as he set the stone on top of those he'd already placed in the gap. "Old age, probably. If I had to guess, I'd say this wall must be at least a hundred years old."

"Really?" I was surprised.

"That's right. Nearly all the walls around here date back to when Connecticut was a farming state. Settlers cut down trees to plant their crops, then discovered how rocky the soil was. Building walls was more of a disposal system than anything else. They piled up all the rocks in a row to get rid of them. These days, there are more than a hundred thousand miles of old, unused stone walls in the New England area."

"I had no idea," I said as I handed Jeff another sizable rock.

"That's a two-hander," he told me. "We're almost finished with those. The smaller ones go near the top."

I nodded. Looking around, I saw plenty of small stones waiting to be picked up. "How come you know so much about these walls?"

"Probably because I live right next to one." Jeff's gaze lifted to run the length of the low barrier. Out behind his house, the stone wall disappeared into the dense woods that abutted the reservoir. "Now that I'm retired, I've got time on my hands. Take it from me, it doesn't pay to let your brain stagnate after you stop working. I'm trying to educate myself about at least one new thing every week."

"Good for you," I said.

"I know you didn't come here to listen to me ramble on about stone walls." Jeff turned to face me again. I'd picked two smaller rocks, which I placed into his outstretched hands. "I'm guessing what you really want to talk about is Will Grace's murder."

Chapter 19

"Yes," I replied.

Jeff stared off in the direction of the school. "You wondering who did it?"

I nodded.

"Me too," he said. "It doesn't make the wife and me feel very safe knowing that someone could get himself shot just a couple hundred yards from our back door. Especially after we found out that the victim was related to our neighbor."

"How long have you known Emily?" I asked as I cast around on the ground for more small rocks to hand him.

"A long time," Jeff replied. "Could be almost twenty years."

I looked in the direction of the school. Now, in the

middle of summer, its buildings were just barely visible through the leafy trees. "Have you or your wife noticed anything suspicious happening over there recently?"

Jeff thought for a moment, then shrugged. "Well, you know, it's a school. So people are coming and going all the time. Nothing suspicious about that. Mostly, Linda and I just try to tune it out, you know?"

I nodded again.

"I'll tell you what though. The artists—that place used to be an artists' retreat, did you know that?"

"I did."

"They were quieter. Not so much screaming and running around like you have over there now."

"He's talking about the children," a woman's voice said from behind us. I hadn't heard her approach.

Linda Earley, I presumed. She was a slender woman, probably in her seventies, whose gray hair was cropped short around her head. Big, red-framed glasses circled her eyes. Bright yellow feathers dangled from both ear lobes. She was carrying three bottles of cold water in her hands.

"This is Melanie Travis," Jeff told her. "She's a friend of Emily's. Wants to talk about what happened next door."

He removed two of the water bottles from her hands. Keeping one for himself, he handed the other to me. "Melanie, this is my wife, Linda. You can probably tell that, since the minute she showed up she started correcting me."

"I wasn't correcting you." Linda opened her bottle with a practiced twist of the cap. "Merely elaborating on what you'd said. But here's another thought. Maybe it seemed quieter to us back then because we both had jobs and weren't at home during the day. Could be the artists were every bit as noisy as those children, but we weren't around to hear them."

"See?" Jeff asked with a grin. "There she goes again."

I couldn't help but smile with him. The two clearly enjoyed goading each other. "It's nice to meet you," I said to Linda. "Thank you for the cold water."

"It was the least I could do." She gazed at her husband and shook her head. "Especially after I looked out the window and saw that he'd roped you into helping him move those big rocks around."

"I offered," I said.

"She did," Jeff confirmed.

Linda still looked exasperated. "You know that wall is only going to fall down again."

"Probably," Jeff agreed. It sounded like an argument they'd had numerous times before. "But now that I've fixed this spot, next time it will happen somewhere else. In fact, I might even get Melanie's phone number so I can call her to come and help when it does."

Linda laid a hand on my arm. "Don't listen to him. He's just an old man who likes to hear himself talk."

I opened my water bottle and took a swallow. "That's a good thing. Because I came here to ask questions."

"How's that working out for you?" Linda asked with a laugh. "Have you managed to ask any yet?"

"One or two," I told her. "Probably not the important ones."

"Then you go ahead now." She propped her hands on her hips. "I'll stand here and try to keep Mr. Motor Mouth on track."

"Actually, I wouldn't mind hearing from both of you

about your impressions of what's been going on next door."

"Most of what I know I learned from the police," Linda said. "They came over here right away to talk to us. I've been trying to follow the story in the media since then—but nobody's saying much. So I doubt I'd have anything to tell you that you don't already know."

"You mentioned that you can hear kids playing at the school," I said. "The night that Will Grace was killed, did you hear the gunshot?"

Jeff and Linda looked at each other. They both shook their heads.

"The detective told us it happened around midnight," Jeff said. "If that's the case, we would have been asleep by then."

That didn't help.

"The man who was killed was Emily's ex-husband. Had you ever met him before, or ever seen him around the school?"

This time it was Linda who answered. "To tell the truth, we didn't even know Emily had an ex-husband. For most of the time we've lived in this house, Jeff and I were both working. And it's not like we have a reason to spend time next door at the school anyway. If I hadn't seen Will Grace's picture in the newspaper, I wouldn't even know what he looked like."

"Me either," Jeff added.

Another dead end. At this rate, I'd be out of questions in no time. I took a sip of water, then tried again.

"What's the best way to access the woods behind your property and the school?" I asked. "How would someone get there?"

"Easiest way is to go straight up Emily's driveway, walk around the buildings, and keep going until you hit the trees," Jeff said.

I probably could have phrased that question better. "Suppose you didn't want to do that? Could you get into the woods from the opposite direction?"

He shook his head. "Not unless you wanted to swim across the reservoir, which—since it's against the law—I wouldn't recommend."

I huffed out a frustrated breath. "The properties on either side of the school also back up to those woods, right?"

Linda suddenly went pale. "You mean, like *our* land? Are you saying that a murderer might have walked right past our house on his way to shoot someone?"

"Not necessarily," I said quickly. "Don't forget, the school has a neighbor on the other side, too. I'm just trying to figure out why someone would have been back there in the first place. What could have drawn them there in the middle of the night?"

"Maybe it was a secret meeting place," Linda guessed. "I loved Nancy Drew when I was a child. I bet that's what she would have said."

"Speaking of the school's other neighbor," Jeff said, "that's the Greenfields development. From what I hear, some people in that place don't much like the idea of living next to Emily's school."

"I've met Steve Lambert," I told him.

"That man's the worst." Linda frowned. "He comes by a couple of times a year, trying to whip us up into a frenzy over the issue. He's got a petition that he's been taking all over the neighborhood. He wants everyone to sign it."

"Our motto is 'live and let live,'" Jeff said. "Last time

Steve was here, I told him where he could stuff his petition. He hasn't been back since."

"Now that you mention it, though, anyone could access those woods from Greenfields," Linda said. "Isn't that how the body was found in the first place?"

"I believe it is," I agreed. "Were either of you aware that Emily had been having other problems at her school in the days before her ex-husband was killed?"

Linda and Jeff exchanged another look. It seemed to be a habit of theirs.

"What kinds of problems?" Jeff asked.

"Someone released her puppies from their pen, and they nearly caused an accident out on the road."

"You're talking about the Dalmatians?" Jeff asked.

I nodded.

"Those darn dogs being loose isn't anything unusual. They come over here and pee in Linda's garden at least once a week. If Emily's telling you a different story, she's been pulling your leg."

I frowned. That wasn't the answer I'd expected to hear.

"That's not the only thing," I said. "Someone took her truck out of the shed behind the school and sent it rolling down the hill into the pond."

Linda snorted under her breath.

"What?" I asked.

"That old truck was a heap of junk long before it ever landed in the water. The only good thing about it was its paint job."

Jeff nodded. "We borrowed it once to haul some stuff. That was a few years ago, and it was barely drivable then." He paused, then added speculatively, "Before you waste any time worrying about Emily losing her truck, maybe you should ask her how much she had it insured for."

I gulped. Again, not the answer I'd expected.

"What do you know about her stove catching fire last week?" I asked.

"This is the first we're hearing about it," Linda replied. "Did the fire do much damage?"

"No, fortunately it was discovered quickly. Emily and Mia managed to get the blaze put out before the fire truck even arrived."

"Well, then, there you go," Jeff said. "It sounds as though Emily has everything under control."

Except for the fact that her ex-husband had been murdered, I thought.

I thanked the Earleys for their time. Linda went back inside the house. Then I helped Jeff finish repairing his stone wall.

It seemed like the least I could do.

Half an hour later, I was on my way. I paused at the end of the Earleys' driveway. There weren't any cars coming, but I did see a runner heading swiftly down the road in my direction. It was Emily's brother, Miles.

I'd thought the man looked good in street clothes. That was nothing compared to his appeal in a sweaty T-shirt and lightweight athletic shorts. His damp hair was slicked back off his forehead, and his face was a study in concentration. Miles's legs pumped up and down in a steady rhythm, sneaker-clad feet hitting the macadam with precision. He clearly took his running seriously.

I remained stopped until he'd gone by, waving as he passed in front of the car. Miles didn't return the gesture.

I figured he probably hadn't even noticed it, until he made an abrupt U-turn and came running back.

I rolled down my window as Miles slowed his stride. Lifting his arm, he fiddled with some settings on a sports watch that looked complex enough to train Olympians. He stopped beside the car, but continued to jog in place.

"Hey, Melanie," he said. "I thought that was you. How's your morning going?"

"Just fine. I was visiting Emily's neighbors."

He nodded up the driveway. "The Earleys, right? Em told me about them. She said they're nice people."

"They are." I leaned my arm on the open sill. "You look like a real runner out there. How far did you go?"

Miles shrugged. "Just five miles."

Just, I thought.

"Are you training for a race?"

"No, my racing days are behind me. Now I just try to keep in shape."

Again with the *just*, I thought.

"How's Emily doing?" I asked.

"Better, now that I'm here." Miles's steps slowed. "At least I hope that's true. Anyway, things appear to have calmed down. So that helps. Em told me you were helping her try to figure things out. Are you some kind of detective?"

"No," I said. "I'm just a friend who's trying to be useful. You must have known Will when he and Emily were married."

Miles nodded. Then frowned. "He wasn't the guy I would have picked to marry my sister. But nobody asked my opinion."

The sun was high above us. I squinted as I looked up at him. "So you didn't like Will much."

"Truthfully, I never got to know him very well. I lived in Boston back then. He and Em were down here. So I probably only saw him a couple of times a year. Then they got divorced, and he was gone."

Miles shrugged. It wasn't hard to read that unspoken sentiment. *Good riddance.*

"Do you have any thoughts about why someone would have wanted to shoot him?"

"No, because it's not my problem," he replied. "That's for the police to worry about. The only thing I wish is that it had happened anywhere else but here."

Chapter 20

After Miles left to continue his run, I took out my phone and called Bradley Luft. Thankfully, this time Emily had already spoken to him and explained who I was. Will's best friend said he would be happy to meet with me.

He proposed that we meet over lunch. Bradley knew of a small café just north of the Merritt Parkway that served good food. It was called The Bean Counter. Would that suit?

I almost laughed at his choice. Then I told him it would suit me just fine. We agreed to meet at noon.

The Bean Counter belonged to my brother, Frank, and my ex-husband, Bob. It was a joint venture that had come about by chance, then turned into a terrific partnership. Bob was an accountant. He did the books and oversaw all the practical matters that kept the café running. My gregarious brother, Frank, managed the front of the house. He greeted guests, served up food, and was always on the hunt for new items to feature on the menu board.

The café was housed in a small clapboard building on old Long Ridge Road, well north of Stamford's main business district. Bradley and I were having an early lunch, so the compact parking lot out front wasn't yet full. That meant my chances of getting a table were pretty good too.

Frank was behind the counter at the back of the room when I entered the café. He looked up as the door opened, saw it was me, and gave me a cheery wave.

My brother and I share certain physical similarities, like tawny brown hair and strong jawlines. But beyond those visible attributes, we have little in common. I'd always been the slow and steady ant to Frank's flighty grasshopper. It wasn't until we were in our thirties that we'd finally managed to put aside our differences and become friends.

"You should have told me you were coming," he said. "I'd have fixed you something special."

"You can try to make that sound like a treat, but I'm not buying it," I said with a laugh. Relatives who dropped by the café were often made to sample Frank's culinary works in progress—whether they wanted to or not.

My brother placed both hands over his heart and pretended to be wounded. I wasn't buying that either.

"How about something from the menu?" I studied the board on the wall behind him. "Maybe a chicken salad platter?"

"Coming right up," Frank said. "Go grab a drink and a booth. I'll send it over when it's ready. Are you on your own today, or are you meeting someone?"

"Meeting someone." I fished out my wallet and offered him a credit card.

Frank waved my hand away. "I know it's not Bertie. She and the kids are visiting her family in Michigan."

"Which is why I'm not having lunch with your wife," I pointed out unnecessarily. "Now don't be nosey. It's no one you know."

The door to the café opened behind us. Frank gazed at the newcomer over my shoulder. "That guy?"

I turned and had a look too. The man who'd entered the café was the right age to be Bradley Luft. In his mid-forties, he wore a madras shirt that he'd left untucked to cover an expanding waistline. His sandy hair was thinning in front and long in the back. The topsiders on his feet weren't just scuffed, they were battered to near oblivion.

"Possibly," I told Frank.

His brow shot upward. "You don't know?"

Brothers. Why do they always think they're in charge?

"I'll find out in a few seconds," I told him. I crossed the room and smiled. "Bradley Luft? I'm Melanie."

"Call me Brad," he said. "I see you've already ordered. Find us a place to sit, and I'll be right over."

While Brad placed his order, I poured myself an iced tea and slid into a booth near the café's front window. He joined me there a few minutes later.

"Is it my imagination, or is the guy behind the counter looking at me funny?" he asked in an undertone.

"It's probably not your imagination." I sighed. Then I turned around and glared at Frank—a clear signal to knock it off. "He's my brother."

"Your brother works at The Bean Counter?"

"My brother owns The Bean Counter," I corrected

him. "But try not to hold that against it. It's still a great place to eat."

"Easy for you to say," Brad muttered. "He's not staring at you."

I slid out of my seat and gestured for him to do the same. Then I reached into the booth and switched the position of our two drinks. "There." I pointed him back to where I'd been sitting. "Now he can't see you. And he won't dare stare at me because he knows I'll go over there and smack him."

Brad smirked as he took his new seat. "Much better. Now I just have to hope he doesn't spit in my food."

"You don't have to worry about that. Frank takes the quality of his food very seriously."

Brad didn't look entirely convinced. He and I made small talk, mostly about the weather, until our food arrived. My chicken salad platter looked wonderful. Brad's Ruben sandwich came with a mound of french fries. Too bad I didn't know Brad better—because then I could have nabbed a few.

The café was quickly filling up with customers. The line to order at the counter now stretched nearly all the way back to the door. Once Frank was too busy to pay any more attention to us, Brad and I both relaxed.

He wolfed down half his sandwich in three quick bites, then said, "Since Emily's the one who got us together, I'm assuming you want to talk about Will?"

"Yes." I swallowed, then continued. "Emily told me you and Will grew up together. And that you've been best friends for years?"

Brad nodded. "He and I met in kindergarten. We bonded over our mutual loves for red licorice and kickball."

"So you must have known him better than anyone."

Brad put three fries in his mouth at once, then chewed slowly as he considered. "I guess you might say that. At any rate, our relationship lasted longer than either of his marriages."

"Do you have any idea what he might have done to get himself killed?"

This time, Brad didn't hesitate. Not only that, but his quick answer came as a surprise. "I have lots of ideas about that."

"You do?"

"Sure. The police detective asked me the same question, so I've had plenty of time to think about it. Did you ever meet Will?"

"No." I popped a cherry tomato in my mouth. "By the time I got to know Emily, the two of them were already divorced."

"Will was a great guy. Easygoing, fun to be around. The kind of guy who wants to be everybody's friend. You know?"

I nodded.

"But there was another side to him too. Once Will was your buddy, the wheels in his brain would start turning. He'd be trying to come up with ways that you could be useful to him. That was Will's sharpest skill actually. He was great at convincing other people to do stuff for him."

"Like what?" I asked.

"Pretty much anything that would put money in his pocket. Will always had something running on the side. When we were in grade school, he was convincing kids to shoplift candy for him. In high school, he was the guy you went to if you wanted to buy a term paper instead of writing your own."

Brad grinned appreciatively. "I have to hand it to him, Will was clever. I wish I had the gift of being able to profit from other people's work."

I put my fork down on the side of my plate. My lunch was good, but the conversation was even better. I wanted to concentrate on it fully.

"Did he ever get caught?" I asked.

"Oh sure. Will talked himself out of more tight spots that most people ever even get into. He was a master at letting someone else take the fall. One of his frat brothers got kicked out of college for a scheme that Will was behind. At least that's the way he told the story."

Brad sounded full of admiration as he recounted Will's exploits. As if he was proud of the things Will had been able to achieve. And more than a little envious.

"He must have been a hard person to be friends with," I said.

"Yeah, for most people." Brad shrugged. "But Will and I went way back. I knew him for who he was. I also knew better than to let him take advantage of me. Whenever I got mixed up in one of his deals, I made sure to do it on my terms, not his."

"Because you didn't trust him."

"Hell no," he said with a laugh. "Only an idiot would have done that."

"But you did do business with him."

Brad's amusement suddenly vanished. Now he looked wary. "Yeah, maybe once or twice. No more than that."

"Recently?"

"No," he replied quickly. "The stuff Will was mixed up in, that's a young man's game. He liked living on the edge and never knowing where the next big score might come from. After a while, all that did was make me nervous."

I let Brad think about that for a minute. While he did, I resumed eating. Slices of hardboiled egg were fanned around the rim of the plate. I ate them one by one.

"It turned out you were right to be nervous," I said eventually.

"What do you mean?"

I would have thought the answer to that was obvious.

"Will is dead," I said. "Somebody shot him. Probably someone he'd taken advantage of."

"I wouldn't know anything about that."

Brad had finished his sandwich. And no wonder. He'd been shoveling food in his mouth almost faster than he could chew. It looked as though maybe my questions had been making him nervous too.

"You'd be the perfect person to know something about that," I said mildly. "Since you were Will's closest friend."

Brad blinked, then swallowed heavily. He grabbed his diet soda and drank it down, then slid out of the booth. "We're done here," he said.

I watched as Brad quickly made his way through the crowded room. Seconds later, the door slammed behind him. He ran down the outside steps and got in his car.

When I turned back to the table, Frank was standing in front of me. He shook his head sadly. "You always did have that effect on men."

"Oh stuff it," I said.

The next morning, I took Sam up on his offer to drive the boys to camp. I wanted to talk to Detective Sturgill of the Stamford PD, which meant I would need to head in the opposite direction. While I'd been poking around on my own, I knew the detective's official investigation would have been proceeding in a more orderly fashion.

Sturgill and I had met the previous summer when a member of my book club had been murdered. At the time, the detective had made it very clear that he neither needed nor wanted my assistance. But in the end, I'd been able to provide him with some useful information. Maybe I could do so again. And if I was lucky, maybe he would share some of what he'd learned with me.

The Stamford Police Department was situated in a brick and glass building whose imposing exterior was probably meant to intimidate. It succeeded brilliantly on that score. Just climbing the wide concrete steps and walking inside gave me the willies. And I'm usually not guilty of anything.

A woman officer was behind the reception counter. I gave her my name and told her I was there to see Detective Sturgill. She wasn't impressed.

"Is he expecting you?"

"Not exactly," I said.

She waited for me to elaborate.

I didn't.

After a standoff that seemed to last at least a minute, the officer picked up a nearby phone and made a call. Then she motioned me toward a row of uncomfortable-looking chairs lined up against a wall. It looked like a place where people who'd been arrested would sit while they waited to be processed. I moved away from the counter and opted to stand instead.

Eventually, Detective Sturgill came striding down a hallway from the back of the building. He was at least a decade older than me—and judging by the lines on his face, they'd been hard years. The detective's body was thick all over, but he moved with an air of authority that commanded attention. Dark, bushy eyebrows lowered in a scowl when he saw me.

"I should have known you'd show up again sooner or later." Sturgill's voice was deep and gravelly. "To what do I owe the pleasure this time?"

"Will Grace's murder," I said in a low tone. The woman officer was trying to eavesdrop on our conversation. There was no point in making it easy for her.

"How'd you get mixed up in that?"

"Emily Grace is a friend of mine. She asked for my help."

"Help," he repeated. He didn't sound happy. "If she wanted help pertaining to her ex's murder, she should have come to me."

I shrugged. It hadn't been my call.

"And now you want to talk?"

"Maybe we can compare notes," I said.

A sharp spurt of laughter erupted behind me. The woman quickly turned it into a not very convincing cough. Sturgill didn't look happy about that either.

"Come on," he said. "We'll go to my office. And you can tell me everything you know."

Chapter 21

I followed Detective Sturgill down the hall.

If he expected me to tell him everything I knew, I decided, then he'd better be prepared to offer me something in exchange. Either that or threaten to arrest me. But I wasn't about to spill my guts for nothing.

"Here we are." Sturgill stopped and pushed open a door.

It led to a small, square room with a minimal amount of furniture, all of which appeared to have been chosen for practicality rather than comfort. At least there was a window, which was now firmly shut. Icy air blasting through vents near the floor had lowered the temperature in the space to somewhere just north of arctic.

Maybe Detective Sturgill was cold-blooded, I thought. That would explain a lot.

"Take a seat," he said.

Aside from the chair behind his desk, there was only one other chair in the room. It was made of metal and had a hard seat. That was freezing too. The thin fabric of my summer clothes didn't provide much of a buffer from the chilly surface. I sat down gingerly and tried not to shiver.

"Sorry, I don't have any control over the temperature," Sturgill told me. "The whole building's regulated from a central source." He gazed around. "I guess maybe I could close a vent or two."

"Thank you." I clasped my arms over my chest for warmth. "I'd appreciate that."

Detective Sturgill fiddled with a few levers, then sat down behind his desk. He folded his hands together in front of him and gazed at me across the width of his blotter. His expression was one of resignation.

"So, Emily Grace is a friend of yours?"

"That's right."

"How did you two meet?"

"Both my sons attended her nursery school. And one time, years ago, I was a substitute counselor at her summer camp."

The detective sighed. "You keep unusual company, Ms. Travis. You know that, right?"

I wished I could refute that, but I couldn't. Instead I just nodded.

"Could be that your old friend shot her ex-husband."

"She didn't," I replied.

"How do you know that?"

"Emily doesn't own a gun," I said.

"Sad to say, these days they're not hard to come by," Sturgill replied. "Nor to dispose of."

"Emily had no reason to want to kill Will."

"Did she tell you that?"

"Yes."

"Did she also mention that he cleaned out their bank account and left her for another woman?"

"That happened a long time ago," I told him.

Sturgill shrugged. "Some people carry a grudge."

"Other people divorce their husbands and move on," I retorted. "Are you aware that in the days leading up to Will's death, other strange things were going on at Graceland School?"

Finally, he appeared to be mildly interested. "What kind of strange?"

"An old truck that was parked in a carport went careening down a hill into a pond."

"On its own?"

"No one was driving it." I wiggled my toes to keep the circulation moving in my feet. Of all the days to have worn sandals. "But somebody had to have put the truck in neutral and given it a push."

Sturgill nodded. "Anyone hurt?"

"No, but a few days later, a stove caught fire in the kitchen. No one should have been in there at the time."

The detective frowned. At least he was listening. "Was there a lot of damage?"

"Again, no. A counselor saw smoke and raised the alarm. Emily and Mia were able to put the fire out."

"It sounds like Ms. Grace is having a string of bad luck," he allowed. "Though neither one of those incidents sounds particularly concerning."

Thank goodness I hadn't told him about her smashed mailbox or loose puppies, I thought.

"If Ms. Grace was worried about those things," Sturgill said, "she should have mentioned them to me when we spoke."

"Emily was upset," I told him. "She felt as though you were treating her like a suspect."

"There's a reason for that. She is a suspect. And the fact that she didn't tell me about those other events makes me think that maybe she was involved in them too."

"That's ridiculous," I snapped.

Detective Sturgill shrugged. "Ms. Grace strikes me as a smart woman. Maybe she thought a few distractions would throw us off the scent."

"Or maybe somebody's out to get her."

His gaze narrowed. "Do you have any proof of that?"

"Malcolm Hancock owned the property on which Graceland School sits. He leased it to Emily nearly twenty years ago. The lease is up for renewal in eighteen months, and Malcolm's heirs would rather sell the land for development than continue with the current contract."

"I'm aware of that," Sturgill said.

"Maybe there's someone who doesn't want to wait that long. Someone who's trying to make Emily vacate the land sooner."

"One of the heirs, you mean?"

I gritted my teeth. The man was being deliberately obtuse.

"Yes. Emily's been dealing with Peyton Hancock. Have you spoken with him about Will's murder?"

"I'm not going to divulge that to you," Detective Sturgill said. "Just to be clear, you and I are *not* comparing notes. You may tell me any facts you have that you think might be pertinent to my investigation. In response, I may or may not acknowledge whether I was already in possession of that information. Understand?"

"Yes," I replied grudgingly.

"Now, is there anything else you think I should know?"

I considered standing up and leaving in a huff. But aside from saving me from becoming a human icicle—what would that accomplish? Detective Sturgill and I were both working toward the same goal. Even if I was the only one of us who thought we were on the same team.

I had come to tell him what I'd learned. I might as well get on with it.

I started with everything I'd found out about the kind of man Will Grace had been. Then I mentioned that Will's second ex didn't think any more highly of him than his first wife had. And that his closest friend appeared to know a lot more about Will's shady dealings than he wanted to let on.

I also described the argument I'd witnessed between Emily and Steve Lambert, the head of Greenfields HOA. And I pointed out that the person who'd discovered Will's body was also a Greenfields resident. Like maybe Detective Sturgill would want to make a connection there. He just shook his head about that.

To be fair, he did hear me out. Then, when it was his turn to talk, he offered me . . . nothing. Sturgill wasn't impressed with anything I'd brought him. It was clear he still thought of Emily as a likely suspect in her ex-husband's murder. I could only hope that one of the small nuggets of information I'd passed along might convince him to keep an open mind.

That night, Aunt Peg showed up just before dinner.

"Did we know she was coming?" I asked Sam.

I was guessing no. Because he looked just as surprised as I did.

"I knew!" Kevin cried happily. "I invited her."

That was a pleasant change. Usually Aunt Peg invited herself.

"When did you do that?" I asked Kev.

"This morning before camp. She called on the phone. She wanted to talk to you."

"I was here," I said, thinking back. Of course I'd been here. I lived here. "Why didn't you bring me the phone?"

"Apparently you were in the shower," Aunt Peg said. Davey had let her in the front door, and she'd spent the next five minutes saying hello to the Poodles before moving on to engage the less important (i.e., human) members of her family. "He told me he wasn't allowed to let the phone get wet."

"Smart kid," Davey said.

Kev grinned. He lived for praise from his brother. "I told her she should come to our house for dinner."

"And I agreed that was a splendid plan." Aunt Peg looked around at us. "Except now it appears that nobody was aware of it except Kevin and me."

"No problem," I said quickly. "I'm making pasta with fresh tomatoes, spinach, and mushrooms. I'll just throw some extra stuff in the pot."

"Aunt Peg can have my garlic bread," Kevin said. "Because . . . ewww."

I sighed. That child's tastes changed weekly. "I thought you liked garlic bread. Last time I served it, you ate two pieces."

Davey began to laugh.

I rounded on him. "What?"

"Kevin didn't eat it. Bud's the one who ate two pieces."

"Really?" I glared at my family.

Three heads nodded. Even Sam's. That was a low blow.

"You let Kevin give Bud garlic bread?" I asked my husband.

"Believe me, there was no permission involved," Sam said. "I just happened to catch a glimpse of the handover, and by then it was too late."

"That little dog is a menace," I muttered. "I ought to ban him from the kitchen during meals."

"You can try." Davey looked like he was already calculating the odds of my likely failure.

"Speaking of Bud," Aunt Peg said. "Where is he?"

Oh good lord. She was right. Bud was missing.

I headed straight for the kitchen. With my luck, he was probably swimming in the pot with the pasta.

Fortunately, the pasta did not have to be rescued from Bud. And he hadn't even glanced at the vegetables that were simmering in olive oil and herbs. So dinner proceeded without a hitch—if you didn't count the fact that the boys refused to set the dining room table because Aunt Peg was family, which to them meant that we should eat in the kitchen.

Aunt Peg was no help in that regard. She insisted the boys were correct, that she most definitely was *not* company. Then she set the big round kitchen table herself. Sometimes there's mutiny on all fronts in my house.

After dinner, the boys went into the living room to play a video game. Sam, Aunt Peg, and I lingered at the table with our coffee and tea. Now that we were alone, Aunt Peg could finally broach the topic that had prompted that morning's call. We were all in agreement that any conversation regarding Will Grace's murder was only suitable for adult ears.

"I've been doing a bit of sleuthing," she announced. "And it turned out my guess was correct. The sire of Emily's Dalmatians is a dog named Champion AllSpots Alistair. He belongs to Deborah Munch, who lives in Scarsdale."

"Good work," I said. "Did she tell you how Will Grace ended up with the three puppies?"

"No," Aunt Peg admitted. "And you can't jump ahead. Because after that, I ran into a bit of a snag. Deborah owns the puppies' sire, but she wasn't the breeder of the litter they came from."

"But she must have known who was," Sam pointed out.

Aunt Peg nodded. "That was Mr. Rory Scott from eastern Pennsylvania. Deborah said he had a lovely Dalmatian bitch and was very excited about the breeding. She looked forward to receiving rapturous reports from him about the litter. And in the beginning she did. Then, rather abruptly, all communication from Mr. Scott ceased."

"Did she ask why?"

"Not immediately. Deborah didn't want to be a bother. But she'd been thinking about taking a bitch from the litter herself—and eventually she decided that interest entitled her to exhibit a little nosiness as to how they were doing."

"And?" I prompted when Aunt Peg paused for a sip of tea.

"In the interim, half the litter seemed to have vanished."

"Vanished?" Sam repeated. "Rory Scott told her that?"

"Not in so many words. Indeed, not in many words at all. I gather Mr. Scott was rather curt with her. Whereas earlier, he'd been elated about the quality of the puppies and their future prospects in the show ring, later he would only say that the three bitches were already gone."

"Gone where?" I asked.

"That is the salient question, isn't it?" Aunt Peg gazed at the two of us. "Deborah was quite crushed by the outcome. She was sure she had made her interest clear to Mr. Scott. Indeed, she'd been planning a trip to Pennsylvania to see the litter. And then suddenly the bitches were no longer available."

"We need to talk to Rory Scott," I said.

"Of course we do," Aunt Peg agreed. "And we shall do so on Friday."

"Friday?" I frowned. What was Friday?

"The dog show in Rumson," Sam supplied. "Coral's entered to try to win another major."

Of course. How could I have forgotten that?

"Do we know whether Rory Scott also has an entry?" I asked.

"We do," Aunt Peg told me. "And he does."

There was no point in asking where she'd gotten that information. Aunt Peg always had her ways.

"Now," she said, sounding pleased with herself, "on to the next topic."

There was more? Full credit to Aunt Peg. She might show up unexpectedly, but her visits were never dull.

"That name you mentioned last week, Malcom Hancock? I remembered why it sounded familiar."

"Is that Malcom Hancock of Hancock Finance?" Sam asked. When I'd told him about Emily's financial problems, I must not have mentioned who the leaseholders were.

"Quite so," said Aunt Peg.

"He died last year," Sam said. "I read about it in the paper."

"Yes, and the lease he held on Emily's property transferred to his heirs," I told him.

"It was one of those heirs I remembered hearing about," Aunt Peg said. "Quite a few years ago, one of Hancock's children was arrested after a hit-and-run accident in Greenwich. A pedestrian was mowed down by a driver who immediately left the scene. The pedestrian later died, so it all became rather a big deal."

"It sounds as though it should have been," said Sam.

"Things were very different in those days. We told ourselves that crimes were committed by criminals, and not by teenagers who'd been raised in the lap of luxury and given every advantage."

I snorted under my breath.

Aunt Peg looked at me and nodded. "Indeed. Evidence from the scene proved that Hancock's teenage son was the person responsible. As you can imagine, the media had a field day with that."

"Did he go to jail?" I asked.

"No, he did not. His father hired him an excellent lawyer, who made sure the boy did everything right. He confessed to what he'd done, apologized to the grieving family, vowed to turn his life around, and threw himself on the mercy of the court. In the end, he was given probation and community service."

"He wouldn't get off so leniently now," Sam said.

"No, he would not," Aunt Peg replied crisply. "The tables have turned in that regard, and that's all to the good.

After the deal was struck, the media lost interest in the story. The teen—who, I'm sure, was strongly advised to keep his head down and his hands clean—faded from view. I hadn't thought about him in years. He must be in his mid-thirties by now."

"What was his name?" I asked. "Do you remember?"

"Yes, it stuck in my mind because it was unusual. The boy's name was Peyton. Peyton Hancock."

Chapter 22

"Wow," I said.

Sam and Aunt Peg both turned to look at me.

"Peyton Hancock is the person Emily has been dealing with about her lease renewal. She told me to stay away from him."

"Oh pish," said Aunt Peg. "That's the last thing you should do. Peyton Hancock may well be the key to everything that's gone wrong at Graceland School. Of course you should go see him. What have you been waiting for?"

Good question. The truth was, I'd put off talking to Peyton because I was more than a little intimidated by the idea of bearding the scion of Hancock Finance in his den. And nothing Aunt Peg had said tonight made the idea seem any more appealing.

She was right, however. It was imperative that I find out what Peyton Hancock had to say.

"I'll go tomorrow," I told her.

"Good." Aunt Peg nodded. "Then there's one last thing we need to talk about. The Graceland School benefit."

Oh right. As if I didn't already have enough to do.

"Emily and I have been busy making plans," she told us. "We've chosen a date and a name. We're calling the event 'A Day in the Country.'"

"I like that," said Sam. "Except it doesn't say anything about purebred dogs or responsible breeders."

Aunt Peg was unconcerned. "Don't worry, we explain that part when we describe what the event is about."

"Describe it where?" I asked.

"Emily is a whiz at social media. So far, she has us on Facebook, Instagram, and Twitter. As of this morning, the Facebook page has more than a thousand likes."

I shook my head. The mind boggled.

"When's the date?" asked Sam.

"The first weekend of August."

"That's just three weeks away." Sam sounded just as surprised by that as I was.

"No time like the present," Aunt Peg said cheerfully. "Since we're holding the event at Graceland, it made sense to fit it in between the end of the first camp session and the beginning of the second. I've already lined up nearly sixty tri-state breeders who want to participate. At least a dozen of them will be showcasing new or rare breeds. I expect we'll draw quite a crowd."

"It's great that you've found so many members of the dog community who want to take part," said Sam. "But if the whole point of the benefit is to raise money—"

"We'll be charging admission," Aunt Peg broke in.

"Five dollars for individuals and ten dollars for families. With free parking. Plus, each breeder will be donating a sum that's equal to a single dog show entry."

"That's all good," Sam tried again. "And I can see you bringing in plenty of Graceland parents who are eager to support the cause. But if you want the event to be a real success, you're going to have to find a way to attract a much wider audience."

"Like television coverage, perhaps?"

"If only that were possible." I said.

"It's already lined up," she informed us blithely.

Sam and I both stared at her. "How did you manage that?"

"Local TV stations are always looking for human interest stories. So I presented them with one. I called it, 'Westminster Dog Show Judge Rallies Community to Save Beloved Neighborhood School.'"

I started to laugh. Aunt Peg just kept talking.

"The producer lapped it right up. An angle like that is right up their alley. The day before the benefit, a reporter is going to interview me on the six p.m. news. I'll be sure to have a bevy of adorable dogs with me. Trust me, no one will be able to resist."

"Why didn't you tell us about this earlier?" I asked.

"Why didn't you ask?" she shot back.

"Is there anything else you've lined up for the event that you haven't bothered to mention?" Sam asked.

Aunt Peg's eyes were twinkling. "We also have three food trucks coming. Did I tell you about that?"

Sam and I shook our heads.

"How about the country western band?"

I sputtered out a laugh. "Aunt Peg, where did you find a country western band?"

"At a country western bar, of course. Where else would you look? Such lovely young men. They've agreed to donate their time and play for tips."

"I'm impressed," I said.

"As you should be," Aunt Peg replied. "When I put my mind to something, there's very little I can't accomplish."

As if anybody doubted that.

"The same is true for you," she said into the silence that followed that pronouncement.

"Pardon me?"

"It's time for you to get yourself in gear." Aunt Peg removed Raven's head from her lap and rose from the table. "I'm not the only one who has things to do. You. Peyton Hancock. Tomorrow. Don't take no for an answer."

So I followed Aunt Peg's example and went for it.

That meant stretching the truth a bit when I called Hancock Finance the next morning to make an appointment. I implied that I was representing Graceland School and told Peyton's secretary I needed to discuss options that would be available to us going forward. He put me in the book for one-thirty that afternoon.

After I dropped the boys off at camp and ran some errands, that still left me with several hours to kill. I filled them mostly by giving in to my nerves and pacing around the house. Faith tried to help. She had no idea what I was worried about, but her footsteps followed me quietly from room to room anyway. Faith's unconditional support was always welcome.

When it was finally time to get ready to go, I pulled a cream-colored linen suit out of the back of my closet. I hadn't worn it in several years, but thankfully it still fit. I put a pink camisole underneath the jacket and matching pink sandals on my feet.

When I studied my reflection in the mirror, I almost didn't recognize myself. Sam must have felt the same way.

He stuck his head out of his office as I was leaving and said, "That's what you're wearing?"

"Yes." I stopped in my tracks. "What's wrong with it?"

Sam didn't answer right away. He was still staring.

"It's a suit," I told him. "It makes me look business-like."

"No, not really," he said. "It makes you look like you arrived in a pink Cadillac that you earned by selling cosmetics door-to-door."

That wasn't the first impression I'd been aiming for. Not even close.

"I'll change," I said quickly.

Sam checked his watch. "You don't have time."

"I'll have to make time." I was already heading for the stairs. "You just told me I look like a popsicle."

"A very pretty popsicle," Sam said. I paused again. "Besides, what do I know? I work in a home office and never see anyone. And women's fashion is a mystery to me. I'm sure you look fine."

I turned to face him. "That's not what you said a minute ago."

"A minute ago, I wasn't thinking."

"Or, a minute ago you were being truthful. And now you're just trying to make me feel better."

"I hope it's working," Sam said. "I'd give you a hug, but I'm pretty sure that suit is linen, and I don't want to make things worse than they already are."

I nodded. And looked at my own watch. I was out of time.

"Go," he told me. "You look terrific."

I swept my car keys off the side table, then reached down to give Faith a quick pat. "I should have just worn shorts," I muttered as I let myself out.

Hancock Finance was located in a three story office building a block away from Greenwich Avenue. The building had a square concrete façade and three rows of large windows that sparkled in the summer sun. A directory inside the front door informed me that Hancock Finance's offices were on the top floor.

I exited the elevator directly into the company's reception area. A young man seated behind a desk asked if he could help me. I gave him my name and expected to be asked to wait. Instead, he immediately stood.

"Please come this way," he said. "Mr. Hancock is expecting you."

We walked down a short hallway to a door that was partially open. The receptionist knocked, then motioned for me to step inside the room. When I had, he withdrew and closed the door behind me.

Peyton Hancock's office was large and furnished in a stark, modern motif. A rug with a geometric pattern covered the center of the floor, and a big plexiglass and chrome table served as his desk. Light poured in through the windows that filled one entire wall.

Peyton Hancock looked younger than I'd expected. Tall and trim, he stood up and walked around his desk as the door closed behind me. A suit jacket hung over the back of his chair, and the top two buttons of his dress shirt were undone. His sleeves were rolled back, revealing forearms that were covered with a dusting of blond hairs. Peyton greeted me with the kind of smile that seemed calculated to inspire confidence in potential investors.

We introduced ourselves and sat down in a pair of armchairs that faced each other across a low table. There was a full bar built into a nearby alcove.

"Can I get you something to drink?" Peyton asked. "Beer? Wine? Sparkling water? Or Hal can bring us coffee, if you'd prefer."

"No, thank you." I realized that my fingers were clenched together in my lap. Pulling them apart, I smoothed the wrinkles from my skirt. "I'm fine."

"Good." Peyton sat back, resting his arm along the curved top of his chair. He waited for me to speak first.

"I want to begin by telling you how much Emily Grace appreciates your offering her the opportunity to renew her lease on the property where Graceland School now stands," I said.

Peyton nodded.

"The school has been in operation for nearly twenty years. It's highly regarded in its field. It's a place whose mission your father believed in."

"I'm aware of that," he replied. "That was my father's vision. He felt it was important to help people whose dreams had real merit. And, obviously, Emily made the most of what he was able to offer her."

"She's very grateful for everything your family has done for her," I said.

"And she would like our largesse to continue." Peyton's expression was stern enough to discourage hopes from being harbored on that score.

"You should know that Emily's working to raise the money she'll need to renew the lease at the terms you're currently offering. As you may be aware, however, she's run into a few small difficulties lately."

Peyton lifted a brow. "A dead body seems like more than a small difficulty. I'm wondering how those people who hold her school in such high regard feel about that complication?"

"Of course, everyone knows she wasn't responsible for what happened," I said quickly.

"Do they? It's my impression that the police are investigating Emily as a suspect in her ex-husband's murder."

I leaned back in my seat, affecting what I hoped looked like a casual pose. "I'm sure you have better connections than I do. What else have the police told you?"

Peyton's gaze remained level. "If my resources are better than most, it's only because my family owns the property next to where the shooting took place. Believe me, we don't perceive that as an advantage. A murder is not something the Hancock family wishes to be associated with."

"Even if it turned out to be the impetus for removing Emily from your property before her lease ends?" I asked. "I understand there are developers who are anxious to get their hands on that land. I'm sure you've had some significant offers to sell."

I'd hoped the question wouldn't anger Peyton, and it didn't. Instead he looked amused.

"Let me make sure I understand you," he said. "Are you trying to suggest that a Hancock family member might have been responsible for that man's murder, with profit as the motivating factor?"

I shrugged lightly. That seemed like a safer idea than agreeing outright. Or mentioning that Peyton's character hadn't withstood the temptation to act dishonorably when his own interests were at stake in the past.

"If that's the case, you could not be more wrong," he said. "Even if I were willing to set ethics aside in order to gain control of that land—which I am not—I wouldn't have needed to kill anyone to do so. An under-the-table offer was made to me several months ago that would have accomplished the same thing. I turned it down then, and there's been no reason for me to change my mind since."

I stared at him in surprise. "Who made that offer?"

"It was presented to me by Will Grace."

My surprise turned to shock. "The man who was subsequently murdered behind your property?" I sputtered.

"Precisely," Peyton said.

Chapter 23

"**D**o I look as dumbfounded as I feel?" I asked.

Peyton nodded. It seemed he was trying not to smile.

"Emily isn't aware of that," I said firmly. At least I hoped she wasn't.

"I didn't think so," Peyton agreed. "Grace certainly didn't give me the impression he'd brought me the offer with her endorsement. In fact, quite the opposite."

With everything I'd learned about Will Grace over the past ten days, there was only one thing I could say. "He came to you for money, didn't he?"

"Yes. Grace framed the request as a loan—though I doubt either one of us thought for even a moment that the money would ever be repaid."

"What did Will offer to do for you in return?" I asked.

"He said he still possessed a great deal of influence over his ex-wife. That she would do whatever he told her to."

I snickered at that.

"That was my first thought too," Peyton agreed. "Though I was able to hide my feelings better than you do."

"Sorry," I mumbled. "Please continue."

"Grace informed me that he was aware of the status of Emily's lease. He said when the time came for renewal, Emily planned to raise a fuss about the new terms. She would go to the media and paint the Hancock family as moustache-twirling villains, eager to prey on a poor defenseless woman. Grace offered to help me circumvent that problem. In exchange for a generous sum, he would convince Emily to vacate the property quickly and quietly."

"All of that is wrong," I said. "Emily feels indebted to your family for the opportunity your father gave her. I'm sure she would never turn around and stab you in the back."

"What she might or might not do was a moot point with regard to my response to Will Grace. The man struck me as a shifty character from the outset. Even if I had been interested—which I was not—the man inspired no faith in his ability to deliver what he was offering. I turned him down flat."

"That was a good move," I said.

"That was the only move," Peyton replied sharply. "That's not the way Hancock Finance, or the Hancock family, does business. There's nothing illegal or immoral about our plan to rewrite Emily's contract when it expires at the end of next year. Surely people will understand that."

I nodded, then said, "Does it seem like an odd coincidence to you that Will would try to make a deal concerning that piece of property—and then be found dead there just a few months later?"

"Not necessarily. Considering the dexterity with which he outlined his scheme, I doubt that I'm the first person Will Grace has tried to dupe. Perhaps not even the first he thought he could engage in a deal over that particular property. For whatever reason, he seemed to think he could make a score there. Perhaps it's poetic justice that he discovered in the worst possible way that he was wrong."

"Was that the last time you had any contact with him?" I asked.

"When I showed Grace to the door, I told him I didn't want to hear from him again." Peyton's lips flattened in disgust. "Nevertheless, as he was leaving, he pressed his attorney's business card into my hand. He said if I wished to reconsider his offer, that was who I should call."

"Do you still have that card?"

"I did until last week." Peyton stood up, signaling that he'd given me enough of his time. "I'd tossed it in a drawer and forgotten about it. Then Grace was killed and the police came to see me. I gave the card to the detective."

"Do you remember the name that was on it?" I asked as we walked to the door together.

"I should hope so, since I just saw it. The two men shared the same last name. Owen Grace was the attorney. His office is in Southbury."

"Yes," I said. "I know."

This time I'd managed to surprise him. "You do?"

"Owen is Will's brother."

"Not two peas from the same pod, I hope," Peyton said.

I hadn't thought so. But now I might have to reevaluate.

When we'd spoken, Owen had been clear about the fact that his business dealings weren't intertwined with his brother's. Now it looked as though he'd been lying to me. If he hadn't told the truth about that, what else might he have lied about?

"I guess that remains to be seen," I said.

I considered calling Aunt Peg to tell her that I'd followed her directive and met with Peyton Hancock. But with Coral's next dog show just two days away, I knew she'd be busy grooming the Standard Poodle. Rather than interrupting her, I decided to head back to Graceland School. Camp would still be in session, but hopefully Emily would have time for a chat. I wanted to bring her up to date on what I'd learned.

As soon I turned in the school's driveway, I saw the three Dalmatians running around the grassy field beside the entrance. The puppies shouldn't have been that close to the road without supervision. I quickly stopped my car and started to get out. Then Pansy raced toward the trees before circling back the other way, and I realized that the dogs weren't alone. Miles was in the field with them.

As I continued up the driveway, Miles called the puppies to him. The trio quickly obeyed. When he began to walk back toward the school buildings, they followed along behind him.

When I got out of the Volvo, Miles was just a few steps

away. The puppies came running over to sniff my legs and check my pockets. I patted each of their silky heads in turn.

"That was amazing," I said to Miles. "You need to teach Emily how to do that."

"Do what?" He raked a hand back through his hair. There was a sheen of sweat on his brow. He and the Dalmatians must have been outside for a while.

"How you get those puppies to listen to you. And to follow when you want them to go somewhere."

"It's no big deal."

"Yes," I said, "it is."

Miles shrugged. "I've just been spending time with them, that's all. Actual quality time. No yelling, or chasing, or telling them everything they do is wrong. Emily's problem is that she never bothered to train these guys."

"You're right," I agreed.

"Puppies are like sponges, they absorb whatever you expose them to—the good stuff and the bad. If you don't set expectations for their behavior, they'll decide for themselves what they want to do."

Right again, I thought. Aunt Peg would love this guy.

Miles grinned. "Plus it helps that I'm a big believer in positive reinforcement—and that I always have a pocket full of treats."

"Hey, puppies!" he said, drawing the dogs' attention back to him. "Who wants a biscuit?"

The three Dalmatians immediately spun away from me to line up in front of Miles. He slipped a hand in his pocket, then raised it above the puppies' heads. Three sets of dark eyes followed it.

"Sit!" he told them.

Poppy and Posey quickly lowered their hindquarters to

the ground. Pansy took a little longer, but within seconds she was sitting too.

"Good dogs." Miles slipped a small biscuit into each puppy's mouth. "Well done!"

"Well done to you too. If you keep that up, they'll be solid citizens in no time." I couldn't help but smile. "How long are you going to be staying?"

"Just until Emily gets her problems sorted out," he replied.

That thought had a sobering effect on both of us.

"I'd hoped to be back in New Hampshire by the end of next week. But Emily's been talking about some sort of country fair/school benefit that she and your aunt have cooked up. Now she wants me to be here for that."

"You might enjoy it," I said. "The event is shaping up to be great. Last I heard, they'd hired a country western band."

"Whooheee!" Miles pretended to doff a cowboy hat and twirl it. "I guess that means I'll have to brush up on my line dancing."

The Dalmatians suddenly saw something near the school. All three heads turned. Then they jumped up and took off running.

"Their sit was great," I said with a laugh. "Now you have to work on their stay."

We looked to see where the dogs were going. Emily was standing in the doorway of the smaller building. She lifted her arm over her head and waved.

"It looks like we've been summoned," Miles said. "I hope there isn't more bad news."

"No, we're good," I told him. Emily was smiling.

I hoped she'd still be happy when I finished telling her what I knew.

* * *

By common consensus we ended up in the school kitchen, because that was where the cold drinks were. While Emily got several bottles of green tea out of the refrigerator, I refilled the puppies' bowl with fresh, cool water.

The cafeteria next door—used when school was in session—had neat rows of plastic tables and chairs. In the kitchen, there was just a scarred wooden trestle table that looked as though it had seen several generations of use. We sat down around it. The Dalmatians fanned out on the cool linoleum floor.

Emily gazed at me and Miles across the table. "You guys looked like you had plenty to talk about out there."

"We did," I told her. "We were discussing dog training."

"Oh." She frowned. "I thought it might have been something interesting."

That attitude, in a nutshell, explained why the puppies had been running wild for the past three months.

"It was interesting to us," Miles said.

"He and I were agreeing that the puppies' lives are easier when they understand what's expected of them," I added.

"I know what I expect," Emily retorted. "I want them to come when they're called, behave in the house, and stop barking all the time."

"Those are all tall orders," Miles told his sister. "Especially since you don't appear to have put much effort into training them to do those things."

"I'll get to it," Emily glared his way. "I've been a little busy, okay?"

Miles didn't snap back at her. Instead, he twisted the top off his bottle and took a long swallow of tea.

"Are you aware that before Will gave you those Dalmatians he offered them to Vanessa first?" I asked.

Emily's glare swung my way. "How do you know that?"

"I talked to her a couple of days ago about your mutual ex-husband. That was one of the things she mentioned."

"I told you not to do that," Emily snapped.

"You also asked for my help. That means I get to talk to anyone who might have useful information." Out of the corner of my eye, I saw Miles's head dip in a small nod of approval.

"Vanessa is the woman Will ran off with, right?" he asked.

"That's right."

"What else did she have to say about Will?"

"Mostly good riddance," I told him. I glanced back at Emily. "She and Will were married, by the way. It didn't last long before she kicked him to the curb."

"Which is exactly what he deserved." She snorted. "I guess that means she doesn't have a motive for wanting him dead?"

"Probably not. She said that you were the most likely person to blame."

Emily's outraged expression wasn't entirely convincing. "I have no idea why she would say that."

"Really?" Miles smirked. "It's not like it was a secret how you felt about the guy when he dumped you."

"Why can't anyone ever get past that?" Emily's voice rose enough to make Poppy lift her head to look at us. "All that crap is behind me. Okay?"

Well, sure, I thought. And that was where it would have stayed—if her ex-husband hadn't been murdered virtually in her backyard. Surely Emily had to understand why it was necessary to talk about this.

"Let's change the subject," she said.

"Okay," I replied. "Peyton Hancock."

"Oh lord." Emily moaned. "You went to see him, didn't you?"

"I did."

"If he refuses to renew my lease because you went down to Hancock Finance and annoyed him, I will never forgive you."

"At the moment, it doesn't seem to matter whether he offers you a renewal or not," I pointed out mildly. "Because you can't afford the terms the Hancock family plans to propose. So I hardly think that anything I said or did has any bearing on the matter."

"She has a point," Miles agreed.

Emily frowned. "Whose side are you on, anyway?"

"I assume that's a rhetorical question, but I will answer it anyway. I'm on your side. We both are. So rather than snapping at us, you might try showing a little gratitude."

Bravo, Miles, I thought. As a family member, he could say what I, a friend, could not.

"You're right," Emily admitted after a minute. "Melanie, I apologize. My behavior was uncalled for. I wouldn't tolerate it from a student, so there's no reason either of you should have to tolerate it from me. Please tell us about your conversation with Peyton."

Her small speech cleared the air. The three of us relaxed. For now—because what I was about to say was bound to be disturbing.

"Peyton told me that Will had approached him last spring with a scheme to screw you over and extort money from the Hancocks," I said.

"What?" This time Emily's outraged expression was entirely real. "Damn that man, anyway," she growled. "It's a good thing Will is already dead, or I swear I could murder him myself."

Chapter 24

"That's exactly the kind of talk that gets you in trouble," Miles said.

"Shut up." Emily reached over and gave her brother's arm a sharp slap. "You just told me I'm among friends. That should mean I don't have to watch every word that comes out of my mouth."

She continued to look annoyed, however. "Every time I think Will can't sink any lower, he still manages to surprise me. I can't believe that bastard tried to make a deal with Peyton Hancock behind my back."

Miles muttered something under his breath. I suspected he was lamenting Will Grace's treatment of his sister.

Emily frowned, thinking back. "That must have been

around the same time Will gave the puppies to me. He asked me for money then too. I didn't give it to him," she added unnecessarily.

"Will was never happier than when he had a deal in the works," Miles said. "What did this one entail?"

"He assured Peyton that in exchange for a sum of money, he could convince Emily to give up this property without a fuss."

She shook her head. "As if Will would be able to make me do anything—much less that."

"Your compliance probably didn't matter," Miles pointed out. "Will's success was contingent on selling the idea itself, not on following through. Once he had his money, there'd always be a reason why he couldn't deliver what he'd promised. Luckily, Peyton Hancock was smart enough not to fall for Will's meaningless twaddle."

"Meaningless twaddle," Emily said with a small smile. "I'll have to remember that. It describes Will Grace's life to a tee."

A bell rang in the other building, signaling that the camp day had come to an end. Emily stood up. She gathered our empty plastic bottles to throw in the recycling bin. There was one more thing I wanted to mention before we left.

Detective Sturgill suspected Emily had been responsible for the suspicious incidents that had taken place at the school. I disagreed with his assessment, but I didn't have a better idea. Maybe Emily or Miles did.

"In the days leading up to Will's death, odd things were happening around here," I said. "But now another week has passed, and nothing has gone wrong since. Why do you think that is?"

"For the first few days, the police were all over the place," Emily replied. "And now Miles is here keeping an eye on things."

"It still seems curious," I mused.

"Not to me," Miles said. "I think it makes perfect sense."

"How?" I asked.

"Obviously, those things stopped happening because of Will's death. He must have been the person behind all of it."

"But why would he want to do that?" Emily looked confused. I felt the same way.

Miles shrugged and offered a guess. "Maybe he was trying to get your attention for some reason."

"It would have been easier to call her on the phone," I said shortly.

Miles frowned, then voiced a sentiment we all agreed with.

"I'm just glad it's over," he said.

The next morning, after I dropped the boys off at camp, I drove half a mile down the road and turned in the entrance to the Greenfields subdivision.

When I'd met Steve Lambert the previous week, the man had been red in the face and making threats. Now that he'd had a few days to calm down, I hoped the head of the development's HOA would be more amenable to holding a civil conversation.

Ornate brick walls with GREENFIELDS etched in block lettering flanked both sides of the wide entrance. A profusion of colorful summer flowers decorated the beds in front of them. Just inside was a small, unmanned gatehouse that appeared to be merely decorative. A sign beside it announced that Greenfields was private property, and that no trespassing, soliciting, or skateboarding was allowed.

Feeling duly warned, I entered the development and coasted slowly up a wide, tree-lined avenue. On either side of the road were rows of matching ranch style houses with cross gabled roofs and well-tended lawns. The homes' colors had all been chosen from the same muted palette. Individual landscaping appeared to be limited to a few low bushes and a single tree.

No one had hung up a decorative flag or put a flowered wreath on their front door. There were no toys or bikes scattered around the yards. Garage doors were closed. No cars were parked in driveways or at the curb.

Everything I saw looked perfect. And perfectly sterile. It was like driving through a Stepford neighborhood.

If this was Steve Lambert's preferred way to live, no wonder he hated Graceland School—where children ran and played, people made noise, and sometimes things got messy. Graceland was real life with all its glorious joys and complications displayed in plain view. To me, Greenfields looked bleak and colorless by comparison.

A discreet sign identified a large building as both the subdivision's office and its clubhouse. Not surprisingly, the design of that structure matched all the rest. As I drove past, I saw a swimming pool and cabana behind the clubhouse. A few people were sitting beside the pool on lounge chairs, but otherwise the place was deserted.

GPS directed me to Steve Lambert's address. That was a good thing because now that I was in the subdivision, every lane and byway looked alike to me. A number on the mailbox beside Lambert's driveway assured me I was in the right place. As I parked beside the curb and got out of my car, I saw a curtain twitch in a front window across the street.

One of Lambert's neighbors was checking me out. Discreetly, of course. Maybe that was what passed for entertainment around here.

Lambert's house was painted gray. So was his front door. I didn't see a doorbell. Maybe they were considered too noisy for this quiet neighborhood? The thought nearly made me laugh. Until it occurred to me that maybe that was prohibited here too.

I lifted the cast iron knocker on the door and let it drop. A heavy thud reverberated inside the house. After what seemed like a long time, the door finally cracked opened.

Steve Lambert stood framed in the small space he'd allowed for us to see each other. A pair of reading glasses was perched low on his nose, and he was holding a newspaper in one hand. The expression on his face wasn't friendly.

With not a hint of recognition, he said, "We don't allow soliciting in this neighborhood. You should have seen the sign when you came in. If you don't leave immediately, I will call the police."

"I'm not selling anything," I told him. "My name is Melanie Travis. We met last week."

Lambert stared at me. He blinked several times. It didn't appear to help. Obviously I was still a mystery to him.

"Where did we meet?" he demanded.

"Next door, at Graceland School."

"Next door." He grunted unhappily. "That place is a travesty. Are you a friend of the Grace woman?"

"Yes." Since he was already working on riling himself up, it seemed smarter not to elaborate.

"Too bad for you, then. Any day now she'll be going to jail, and that ramshackle bunch of buildings she calls a school will be closing down."

"I don't think so," I said firmly.

"No?" He squinted at me through the slender opening. It would be much easier to talk if he'd invite me in. Or at least open the door a little wider. "Maybe you didn't hear then. That lady murdered her ex-husband."

"No, she didn't."

"That's not what the paper says. I'm reading about it right here." The pages rattled in his hand as he shook them for emphasis. "The police are hot on her trail."

That was utter garbage. I had nothing to gain by pointing that out, however. And it might cause him to slam the door in my face. So instead, I tried a less direct approach.

"That's actually what I was hoping to talk to you about."

Lambert frowned. "Go ahead. Talk."

"Out here?"

"Well, you're not coming in."

I glanced back in the direction of that twitching curtain. "I guess I don't mind if your neighbors hear what I have to say if you don't."

Abruptly, the door eased open somewhat. Lambert stuck his head out. He took a cautious look around. No one else was outside to be seen.

Maybe they were all dead, I thought cynically.

Lambert's gaze returned to me. Now his body barred the opening. It looked as though we would be holding this conversation on his front step.

"Why would I care about what you have to say?" he asked.

"You should care," I told him. "As you've made clear

to Emily, everything that happens in this neighborhood impacts you. And a man was shot to death not far from here. That has to be a concern."

"He was killed at that damn school," Lambert growled.

"Actually, he was killed on state property," I corrected him. "But his body was found by someone who lives right here in this subdivision. With you."

"Get rid of the school, get rid of the problem," he snapped.

I swallowed a sigh. It was like talking to a brick wall.

"I understand that's been your rallying cry for a while," I said.

"With good reason. Because now I've been proven right. A man is dead. Murdered. Right under our very noses."

"And you think that bolsters your case that the school needs to be shut down?"

"It sure as hell does."

"Then perhaps it also gives you a motive for the murder," I said mildly.

"Me?" Lambert hooted. "You must be joking. I'm an upstanding, law-abiding citizen."

"So is Emily Grace."

"Try telling that to her ex-husband."

"*Ex*," I said, "as in gone from her life. Emily had no reason to want to kill him."

Lambert shrugged. "That will be up to the police to decide. And they already think she did it. Once they arrest her, all us neighbors will finally be that much closer to getting that school shut down."

"You mean you and the other Greenfields residents?"

"Of course. Every time we hold a meeting, the problem is raised for discussion. We're all in agreement."

I doubted that. Lambert seemed like he would be a

hard man to agree with on almost any topic. Still, there didn't seem to be much point in continuing our conversation. It was time for me to go.

"The neighbors on the other side too," Lambert said.

I turned back to him. "The other side?"

"That older couple, Jeff and Linda Earley. They're every bit as mad about the situation as I am."

That certainly wasn't what they'd told me.

"Are you're sure about that?"

"Of course I'm sure. Their property value is suffering just like mine. They signed my petition. Both of them did."

The surprise I felt must have shown on my face, because Lambert suddenly looked quite pleased with himself. That alone was enough to make me reconsider. Obviously the man had a vested interest in making me believe that the entire neighborhood was on his side. Maybe I shouldn't accept everything he told me at face value.

"Can I have a look at your petition?" I asked.

Lambert stepped briefly away from the doorway. When he returned, he thrust two, clipped-together sheets of paper into my hand. "Here. See for yourself."

I only had to skim through the first few lines to know that he'd handed me the right document. After that, I didn't bother to read the whole thing. My gaze dropped to the bottom of the page, where there were several lines of signatures.

Not all of them were legible. I didn't see the Earleys' names.

"Not there." Lambert grabbed the petition back, flipped it to the second page, and pointed to a middle line with a pudgy finger. "Jeff and Linda Early. Signed and dated."

He was right. The Earleys' names had been added to his petition.

Well, damn. I hadn't expected that. And to think I'd helped Jeff rebuild his stone wall.

The sound of the door closing jerked me back to the present. I heard Lambert's lock click into place. That was fine by me. I was ready to be done with him too.

I walked back to my car, my posture stiff with annoyance. Once again, the flicker of a curtain in the window across the street caught my eye. I lifted a hand and aimed a brisk wave in that direction.

This whole eerily quiet place was starting to creep me out. I hoped Lambert and I had given our furtive audience an eyeful.

Chapter 25

"I hate it when people lie to me," I said to Sam later that night.

Kevin was in bed, and Davey was in his room with his door closed, which probably meant he was texting with his friends. Bud, Augie, and Tar were upstairs with the boys.

Sam had wandered into the living room and turned on the TV. When I joined him on the couch, Faith, Eve, and Raven jumped up to fit themselves on and around us. Sam and I each ended up with a big Poodle on our lap, while Eve was wedged into the space between us. Way to kill the romance, guys.

Sam picked up the remote and flipped through the channels. He settled on a game show with lots of flashing lights and clanging bells. Yet another romance deterrent.

That was when I'd decided that I might as well talk instead.

"I hope you're not referring to Peg," Sam replied. His eyes left the screen just long enough to glance my way.

We were both aware that Aunt Peg had been known to shade the truth when it suited her purposes. And occasionally just for fun, because she liked to keep her relatives on their toes.

We were also aware, however, that now was not a good time to take Aunt Peg to task. The next day, we'd all be attending the dog show in northern New Jersey. Considering what was at stake, the outing was bound to be fraught with nerves for everyone involved. It was vital that we at least begin the day in Aunt Peg's good graces.

"No, it wasn't Aunt Peg," I said. "Not this time."

"It better not have been Davey."

"Of course not." I smiled. "He's a really good kid." I considered for a few seconds, then added, "Most of the time, anyway."

"He's a teenager," Sam said easily. "He's allowed a few lapses."

I ran a hand down the length of Faith's back, and she snuggled her body closer. If we weren't in such tight quarters, I knew her tail would be wagging. "The people I'm talking about are a couple I met earlier in the week, Jeff and Linda Earley. They live next door to Graceland School. They seemed like such nice people."

Another glance flicked my way. "Until?"

"Until I talked to Steve Lambert this morning and found out they'd lied to me about signing his petition to get the Graceland property rezoned so Emily can be ousted from the neighborhood."

"Isn't Steve Lambert the HOA guy who's had Emily's school in his sights for a while?"

"Yes, that's him."

"Then maybe he's the one who isn't telling you the truth."

Now Sam was watching cards flip over to reveal the answers. The category on the screen was prehistoric winged creatures. Was he even interested in that stuff?

"I wish," I said. "Because Lambert is a perfectly odious man. Nothing would make me happier than for the police to pin Will Grace's murder on him. But he showed me his petition. Jeff and Linda's names were there."

Sam pressed the PAUSE button on the remote. The screen froze. When he turned to face me, Raven shifted sideways on his lap. Now they were both looking at me.

"The whole reason you're talking to these people is because you're hoping that they'll point you in the direction of a murderer, right?"

I nodded.

"So it's pretty much inevitable that some of them will be lying to you."

He had a point.

"That doesn't mean I have to like it," I grumbled.

Sam reached over Eve's back and gave my knee a comforting pat. If it weren't for the three big black dogs in the way, that might have developed into something more interesting. Instead Sam unpaused the screen. Bells began to ring. Lights began to flash.

"Look," he said happily, "it's an *Ambopteryx*. They had webbed wings, like bats."

I peered at the TV. Apparently, Sam knew more about the subject than I'd thought. "That's a creepy looking animal," I said.

"Reptile," he noted, before returning to our former topic. "Think about it this way. The good guys aren't lying to you. And the bad guys don't matter. In the end, they'll get what they deserve."

I hoped Sam was right about that. Because what concerned me more than anything was the niggling fear that Emily might be the one who wasn't telling me the truth.

At the dog show two weeks earlier, we'd been blessed with a beautiful outdoor location and superb summer weather. This time around, we weren't as lucky. The Branchville Kennel Club had chosen a lovely, park-like setting for its event. But skies that were merely cloudy when we left Connecticut were pouring rain by the time we arrived in northern New Jersey.

Of course we'd all brought our rain gear. The one thing that couldn't be water-proofed, however, was Coral's meticulously blown dry—and soon to be hair-sprayed—coiffure. The Poodle would have to be carefully managed all day to ensure she didn't reach the show ring looking like a wet mop.

The inclement weather meant that the handlers' tent was even more crowded than usual. This time there was no dawdling when we unloaded our supplies. We were as intent on nabbing our own small bit of grooming space as everyone else. When Terry saw us coming, he moved some of Crawford's tables into a closer configuration. Fortunately, there was just enough room for us to wedge our things in beside their larger setup.

Aunt Peg arrived five minutes later with Coral. She carried the Standard Poodle from the unloading area to our spot beneath the tent, so that not even the dog's feet would touch the wet ground. She placed Coral gently on the tabletop.

"Well, this is cozy," she said, surveying the arrangements. "Thank you, Crawford."

The handler, busy brushing a Standard of his own, turned and nodded in our direction. "Any time."

"Just so you know, we intend to repay your largesse by beating you today in the ring," she told him.

This time Crawford flashed us a quick grin. "Maybe. But I'm going to make you work for it."

"Did you hear that?" Aunt Peg poked Davey in the shoulder. "I believe Crawford has thrown down the gauntlet."

Davey, unpacking the tack box, snuck Crawford a glance. "That's nothing new. Crawford makes everybody work for it. We'd be disappointed if he didn't."

"Not me." Sam laughed. "I'd enjoy an easy win every now and then."

Aunt Peg harrumphed under her breath. "With this rain, no one will have an easy time of it today."

Terry shrugged. As always, he was in a good mood. Even bad weather didn't have a dampening effect on that. "At least we all have to deal with the same conditions."

"I'm going to go park the car," Sam said. "I'll take Kevin with me. Davey, you'll get started brushing Coral?"

Davey was lining up his pin brush, greyhound comb, and slicker brush along the edge of the grooming table. "I'm on it."

"I need to park as well," Aunt Peg said. She pointed in my direction. "You're with me."

"I am?"

She rolled her eyes. I guessed that meant I was.

"Where are we going?" I asked after we'd dashed out

from beneath the tent and grabbed dry seats inside her minivan.

"First, to the parking lot."

I knew that. "And then where?"

Aunt Peg maneuvered the van across the grassy field to the asphalt lot. With so many vehicles coming and going, the whole area would probably be a sea of mud by late afternoon. By then, we wouldn't care, however. Our show day would be over, and Coral would have already won or lost.

Aunt Peg shot me a look. "Don't you know?"

"If I did, I wouldn't keep asking. Are we playing twenty questions?"

"No, we're going to introduce ourselves to Mr. Rory Scott and see what he has to say for himself."

Right. The Dalmatian man. I'd been so busy worrying about Davey and Coral's chances that I'd forgotten all about him. "He's here?"

"I told you he would be." Aunt Peg smiled with satisfaction.

"That was before this typhoon blew in."

She just shrugged. "It's much easier to show a smooth-coated breed in the rain than a Standard Poodle. Indeed, my spies have already laid eyes on him. Rory Scott is set up at the other end of the grooming tent."

A laugh bubbled up from deep in my chest. I turned in my seat to stare at her. "Wait a minute. You have spies?"

"In a manner of speaking. Other people might call them useful connections. I prefer the clandestine nomenclature myself."

Of course she did. I'd long suspected Aunt Peg had a secret yearning to become an undercover operative. And now here we were, on a mission of sorts. If we turned up some useful information, this could be wish fulfillment on a couple of levels.

We left the minivan in the parking lot and walked back to the tent. Aunt Peg had an umbrella. I pulled the hood of my raincoat up over my head. We both were wearing rubber boots. This wasn't our first rainy day dog show.

"When do Dalmatians go in the ring?" I asked. I didn't see any Dals out on tabletops. Then again, they didn't require much pre-ring grooming.

"They've already been judged," Aunt Peg said. "I didn't want to bother Mr. Scott beforehand. I assumed he'd be busy then."

That made sense. People who stopped by our setup when we were prepping our Poodles for the ring often got short shrift. Those who came later—after the day's results had been determined and the pressure was off—received our full attention.

"Did your spies tell you whether or not he won?"

"Reserve Winners Bitch," she told me.

"Damn," I muttered.

His result in the ring would do much to determine whether we found the man in a good mood or a bad one. Reserve Winners was the frustrating, second-best award. Winners Bitch got the points. Reserve went home with nothing but a striped ribbon.

"There he is." Aunt Peg nodded toward a middle-aged man who was leaning back against a grooming table and perusing his show catalog. A liver-and-white Dalmatian was snoozing in the ground-level crate behind him.

"How do you know?"

"Easy," she said. "Deborah told me he had red hair and lots of it."

The red hair was just the beginning. With his chubby

cheeks, freckled skin, and bright blue eyes, Rory Scott had the look of a sized-up leprechaun. He was even wearing a green shirt. Apparently it hadn't brought him luck.

Aunt Peg headed his way, skirting deftly through the setups between us. I followed in her wake. Rory looked up as we approached. He smiled tentatively.

"Hello, Mr. Scott." Aunt Peg stopped in front of him and stuck out her hand. "I'm Peg Turnbull, and this is my niece, Melanie. I was wondering if we could have a few minutes of your time?"

"Sure. Of course." He took her hand and pumped it heartily. "I know who you are. In fact, I've shown under you."

"Have you? Did I put you up?"

"Actually, yes." He smiled. "It was a very good day."

"I'm delighted to hear that."

Less than thirty seconds had passed, and they were already on their way to becoming friends. Meanwhile, I had yet to be called upon to say a thing. When Aunt Peg was around, it was hard not to feel superfluous.

"What can I do for you?" Rory asked.

"I was speaking with Deborah Munch the other day about her stud dog, Alistair."

"Handsome dog." He nodded his approval.

"She told me that you'd had a litter by him earlier in the year."

A shadow crossed Rory's face. "I did, yes. The last litter out of the best bitch I've ever bred."

"Deborah mentioned that you had high hopes for the litter. She also said she was hoping to get a bitch puppy from it for herself."

Rory turned away. He set down his catalog on top of

the crate. "Unfortunately, that turned out not to be possible."

"So I understand," Aunt Peg said. "I gather the distribution of that litter did not proceed as planned. It seems several puppies went missing?"

Rory looked up sharply. "I never said anything like that."

"No, you did not. But it was never made clear to Deborah where those bitch puppies ended up."

"You'll have to excuse me," he snapped. "But I don't understand the purpose of this conversation. Why are my dogs any concern of yours?"

I stepped out from behind Aunt Peg. "Because we would like to help you."

"Help me?" Rory frowned. "What are you talking about? Why would I need your help?"

"If the three bitch puppies from that litter are safely home in your kennel, then you're right, you don't need any assistance from us," Aunt Peg said. "If that's not the case, however, then I believe we can be very useful to you."

"How?" he asked suspiciously.

"What if I told you I know where your missing puppies are?"

"Truly?" Now the man looked utterly shocked.

"We think so," I said.

"They're alive and well?"

Aunt Peg nodded.

"Healthy?" Rory paused, then added, "Not spayed?"

"Yes to all those questions." I pulled out my phone and showed him a picture of Poppy, Posey, and Pansy sitting in Emily's yard.

He snatched the device from me and quickly enlarged the picture. His hands shook as he stared at each of the three puppies' faces in turn. Emotion made him blink several times. "These are really my girls?"

"We believe so," I confirmed.

Rory swallowed heavily. "Oh, those sweet babies. I thought they were gone forever. I pictured them sitting in a dog pound. Or somewhere even worse. And now you're telling me that my pups are fine and you know where they are?"

"That's right," Aunt Peg said.

Rory gave me back my phone. He scrubbed his eyes with his hands before regaining his composure. Then he treated Aunt Peg and me to a blinding smile. Like someone had just offered to show him the pot of gold at the end of the rainbow.

"This is the answer to a lot of prayers," he said.

Chapter 26

"I was hoping you would say that." Aunt Peg smiled.

I did too. That made three of us standing there, looking very happy.

"We can reunite you with your puppies," Aunt Peg said. "However, we want something in return from you. Information."

Rory's smile dimmed. He nodded cautiously.

"The woman who currently has your bitches has no idea who bred them, nor where they originally came from."

"How did she get hold of them?" Rory asked.

"Her ex-husband gave them to her three months ago," I said. "A man named Will Grace."

Rory Scott, so talkative a minute earlier, suddenly had nothing to say at all. Rain pounded on the roof of the tent above us while Aunt Peg and I waited for him to comment.

"I'm assuming you know Will," I said finally.

"I know him, all right," Rory spat out. "Bastard stole those puppies right out of my kennel."

"If you knew he'd taken them," Aunt Peg said, "why didn't you go get them back?"

Rory stared past us, his gaze focusing on the show rings in the distance. "It wasn't that simple."

"It never is," I agreed. "Tell us what happened."

"Why should I do that?"

"Because we know where your puppies are and you don't," Aunt Peg told him. "If you prefer, however, we will go away and leave you alone."

"No!" His reply was swift and emphatic. "Not until you tell me where they are."

"We'll share that information after you tell us about your business dealings with Will Grace," I said.

Conflicting emotions played across his face. He didn't want to do as I'd requested—but we hadn't left him much choice. Rory struck me as the kind of man who was well versed in the art of negotiation. He was probably wondering how little he could get away with revealing.

We had access to his puppies, however. That gave us the winning hand.

"The truth, please," I told him.

Rory glared in my direction. He was stuck, and he knew it. "Did you know Will Grace?"

"No," I replied for both of us. "But we know what kind of man he was. There's little you can say about him that will surprise us."

His head dipped in a curt nod. "All right, then. Will and I were running a little hustle together. Nothing where anyone would get hurt, you understand. Just something to earn us a few bucks."

"Go on," said Aunt Peg.

"There was a poker game in Atlantic City. We'd been set up with a couple of whales from suburbia who thought they were card sharps because they were better than their country club cronies. It was all supposed to be easy. Will and I were just going to beat them at their own game."

"I'm guessing things didn't go as planned," I said.

Rory grimaced. "It turned out we were the ones who'd been set up. Will and I were lucky to escape with the shirts on our backs. We left all our cash behind and then some."

"What did that have to do with your puppies?" Aunt Peg asked.

"Will's a real sore loser. And when something goes south, it's never his fault. He blamed me for what had happened. He told me I owed him."

"Money?" I said.

"Of course money. What else?" Rory looked at us as if we were stupid. "But I didn't have any money to give him. And even if I did, I wouldn't have, because the whole screwup was just as much his fault as mine. We argued about it, and he went storming off. I thought that was the end of it."

He sighed heavily. "Except then it wasn't."

"Why did Will decide to target your dogs?" I asked.

Rory frowned. "He knew I showed them, and he was always asking questions about that. One time he told me this crazy story about some lady who had a show dog that was stolen. It was worth thousands of dollars, and she went to great lengths to get it back. I have no idea where he heard that."

Aunt Peg and I shared a look. We knew where. The story sounded very familiar to us.

"My mistake was bragging about that litter and the high hopes I had for them," Rory said. "I shouldn't have let Will know how important those puppies were to me. But it never crossed my mind that he'd think he could use them as a bargaining chip."

"So Will Grace stole your puppies and held them for ransom," I summed up.

Rory nodded. "Pay up or else."

"That's extortion," Aunt Peg said.

"So what?" Rory replied glumly. "It's not like I was going to go to the police."

Aunt Peg had gone to the police when her stud dog, Beau, had been stolen. It hadn't helped at all. They'd directed her to animal control.

"If those puppies were so important to you, why didn't you just swallow your pride and pay him?" I asked.

"I couldn't. Will wanted twenty-five thousand dollars for them."

Aunt Peg and I shared a shocked look.

"I take back what I said before," she said. "That's not just extortion, it's highway robbery."

"I thought that was just his opener," Rory told us. "Will knew I could never come up with that much money. I figured we'd make a deal. I also figured that once he'd been saddled with those three pups for a week, Will might be just as happy to get rid of them as I was to get them back."

"But that didn't happen," I said.

"No, it didn't. Because not long after that, Will disappeared."

"Disappeared?" I repeated. He'd surprised me again. "When? Do you mean recently?"

"No, this was a few months ago. In the spring some-time. The guy just vanished. I couldn't find him any-where. Eventually I gave up on ever getting the puppies back. I figured maybe Will used them to pay off a debt somewhere. For all I know, he's in Mexico now. Or maybe the Caribbean."

Apparently Rory hadn't heard about the news of his former friend's demise.

"There's something you need to know," Aunt Peg said.

"What's that?" His tone was still combative.

"Will Grace is dead."

Those few words had a big impact. Rory's face went pale. His freckles stood out against his suddenly ashen skin. He sagged back against the grooming table. "You know that for sure?"

"Yes." Aunt Peg and I both nodded.

"How did it happen? When?"

"Will was shot a week ago," I told him. "In Connec-ticut."

He stared at us as if he was still hoping that we'd change our minds. When we remained silent, he finally said, "Who did it?"

"No one knows," Aunt Peg replied. "The police are in-vestigating. And we've been asking questions too. In light of recent events, I might guess that Will didn't just disappear several months ago. He went into hiding."

"I could maybe see that." Rory considered the idea. "Will was the kind of guy who only saw the end result he wanted. He refused to think about potential complica-tions. Maybe he vanished because he crossed the wrong person."

"Are you talking about someone you might know?" I asked.

Rory quickly held up his hands in front of him, palms facing outward. It was a gesture of innocence—or maybe denial.

"Not me," he said. "I don't have anything to do with people like that. The poker thing was just a sideline. Will was the one who always needed the next score to keep his head above water. That kind of pressure can make you do things a more prudent person wouldn't touch."

"It looks as though Will's lack of prudence caught up with him last week," I told him. "If you come up with any names you'd like to share, I'm sure Detective Sturgill of the Stamford Police would want to hear them."

Rory suddenly looked wary. When he gave his head a very deliberate shake, I guessed that meant it wasn't going to happen.

"Thank you," Aunt Peg said. "You've been very helpful."

"I told you everything I know," Rory replied. "Now it's your turn. You'll get my puppies back for me, right?"

"We'll start working on it," she agreed. "Had they been microchipped before they left your kennel?"

"No." He frowned. "I hadn't gotten around to it. It's not like I was expecting them to disappear."

We all thought about that for a minute. Circumstantial evidence certainly pointed toward the puppies being his missing Dalmatians. But it would have been better if he'd had proof.

"Just so you know," I said, "the woman who's been taking care of them all this time thinks of the puppies as hers."

"I'm not worried about that," Rory replied with confidence. "I'm sure she and I will be able to come to a suitable arrangement. You said Will gave them to his ex-wife. Is that Vanessa?"

I looked at him in surprise. "You know her?"

"No, but Will talked about her a lot. They'd gotten a divorce, but he was always trying to figure out a way to get back together with her. It turns out that after she left him, she struck it rich writing romance novels. Is that crazy, or what?"

"Vanessa doesn't have your Dalmatians," I told him. "They're with Will's first wife, Emily."

Rory shrugged. "Will never mentioned that one at all. You be sure to tell her I'll be more than happy to pay for the puppies' care and for all the time she's spent on them. How soon do you think I can see my girls?"

"We'll have to find out about that," Aunt Peg said. "But we should be able to let you know in a day or two."

Rory tore a page out of the back of his catalog. He scribbled down his name and phone number twice. Then he ripped the page in half and handed a piece to each of us.

"The sooner, the better," he said. "I'll be waiting to hear from you."

"I hope you'll be able to keep those promises you made," I said to Aunt Peg as we made our way to the other end of the tent. "Emily thinks the puppies belong to her. What if she doesn't want to give them up?"

"Then we'll just have to convince her differently," Aunt Peg replied.

As if it was just that simple.

When we got back to our setup, Coral was standing on her grooming table gazing around the tented area. Davey and Sam had accomplished a lot in our absence. The Poodle had been thoroughly brushed out, her topknot was in, and her hair had been sprayed up. Sam and Kevin had even run over to the ring to pick up Davey's armband. Aunt Peg and I must have been gone longer than I'd thought.

"It's like running through soup out there," Sam said with a grimace.

"Like soup," Kev agreed with a happy nod. At his age, mud was something to be savored.

"All we can hope is that Coral looks terrific when she steps into the ring, because as soon as the judge sends the class outside, everything's going to fall flat. At least all the other bitches will get soaked at the same time."

I used a spare towel to dry Kev's hair. For some reason, the child hadn't put his hood up when they'd run across the grassy expanse to the other tent.

"Unless Mr. Connelly doesn't send them around the ring," I said.

In bad weather, judges sometimes evaluated their entries in the small section of the ring covered by the tent. Showing a big breed in that reduced amount of space meant that the judge would never have a chance to see how the dogs really moved. His decision, therefore, would be based mostly on what they looked like standing still.

Now that she was fully mature and sporting a glorious coat, Coral looked impressive when she was stacked. But it was her fluid, ground covering movement that really made her stand out. Without that to set her apart, Davey would have to work twice as hard to draw the judge's eye to his bitch.

"Don't worry, he'll send them around the ring," Aunt Peg said firmly.

I wondered if she was planning to stand near the in-gate and glare at Mr. Connelly until he complied with her wishes. Aunt Peg had little patience for fellow judges who didn't come prepared for adverse weather conditions. Rain boots, waterproof hats, and slickers were mandatory on a day like this. And woe to anyone who didn't plan appropriately.

"Frankly, I'm more concerned about the major holding." Aunt Peg lifted her head and gazed around the large tent as if she was counting Standard Poodle noses. "There better not be any wimps who looked at this ugly weather and decided to stay home."

Today the major was in dogs. The six Standard bitches that had been entered would only earn the Winners Bitch two points. That bitch would then need to be awarded Best of Winners over the Winners Dog in order to win the four point major.

"All the dogs are here," Sam told us. "I checked when I was at the ring."

"Of course they're here," Terry said from two tables away. He was putting the finishing touches on Crawford's Open bitch. "Majors have been scarce this year. Everyone needs this one just as badly as you do."

I assessed the Standard Poodle Terry was working on with a critical eye. A white bitch with dark skin and a beautiful expression, she was dainty and ultra-feminine. Davey and Coral had beaten her two weeks earlier, but that was no guarantee of success today.

Judging dogs was a subjective exercise. Each judge weighed a breed's faults and virtues differently. And a dog who'd given a sparkling performance one day could be unaccountably dull the next. Often a handler's skill became the deciding factor that made the difference between winning and losing.

Davey was just fourteen, a talented amateur who still had a lot to learn. While Crawford was . . . well, what most other handlers aspired to be.

No sooner had the thought crossed my mind than Crawford came ducking under the tent. He had a silver Toy Poodle sheltered beneath his waterproof jacket. It was a good day to be showing a portable dog.

Terry glanced at his partner and raised a brow.

"Best of Variety," Crawford replied. "But he now looks like a drowned rat. The wet grass in the ring was almost up to his stomach."

At least we wouldn't have that problem with our Standard Poodles.

"We'll have time before the groups," Terry said calmly. "I'll be able to fix that."

Crawford put the Toy dog down on a tabletop. He quickly rolled up the dog's leash, then banded the wet hair on his ears. Crawford nodded toward his Open bitch. "The judge is moving right along. Is she good to go?"

"Ready as she'll ever be." Terry grinned.

Aunt Peg was standing beside Coral's grooming table. Davey was just a few steps away. He'd already put on his slicker and stuffed his pockets with liver. Now he was attaching his numbered armband and checking to be sure he had a comb.

"How about you?" Aunt Peg asked him. "Are you good to go, too?"

Davey slipped Terry a wink. "Ready as I'll ever be," he said.

Chapter 27

Getting Coral from the handlers' tent to the covered area between the show rings was a production. Carrying her would crush her towering topknot. So the only option was for her to make the trip on foot—and quickly. That meant dashing across the grassy expanse with Davey on one side of her and Sam on the other. Aunt Peg would run along behind the trio holding a very large umbrella over the big Poodle.

Nobody cared if Sam and Davey got wet. Or me either, for that matter.

Once the important jobs had been delegated, I was tasked merely with bringing a dry towel, a pin brush, and a spare can of hair spray to the ring. I was also keeping a close eye on Kevin, who had a tendency to wander off whenever something interesting caught his eye.

"That was fun," Kevin said when we'd all scooted under the long tent that ran between the two rows of rings. "Let's do it again!"

"Not just yet," I told him. "First, we're going to watch Davey show Coral."

Kev's cheeks were glowing. He hopped up and down, enjoying the way his red rubber boots squelched in the soggy ground. Before I could stop him, he tossed back the hood of his slicker and shook in place like a puppy.

That earned us some well-deserved dirty looks.

"Sorry!" I aimed a general apology in the direction of . . . well, pretty much everyone. Then I took Kev's hand and guided him over to the Poodle ring.

The rest of our group was already there. Sam and Aunt Peg were standing with Coral cocooned protectively between them, while Davey made minor repairs to her coat. Despite the mad dash across the field, the Poodle still looked great.

Terry and Crawford were nearby with their Open bitch. Crawford didn't have a Standard Poodle dog entered today. Nor was he showing his special. Which meant his only opportunity to do well in the variety would be with his lovely white bitch. That didn't help our chances at all.

"Why doesn't Crawford have his special here?" I asked Aunt Peg quietly. He'd been winning with the big, white dog all summer.

"Last time Mr. Connelly had the dog in a group, he didn't use him," she replied. "There was no point in bringing him if the judge doesn't like him."

"Maybe Mr. Connelly doesn't like white Poodles," I said hopefully. It wasn't unusual for a judge to have a color preference.

Aunt Peg slanted me a look. "No, that's not it."

I waited for her to tell me what *was* it.

Aunt Peg didn't oblige me. She was too busy watching the Standard Open Dog class.

When I realized she was counting the numbers for the third time, I elbowed her in the side and said, "There were two dogs in the Puppy class. Now there are four Open dogs. That's six. It held."

"That's six," Kevin repeated. I had a death grip on his hand. He used it to tug me down to his level. "What held?"

"The major did."

Kev's eyes widened. "Davey won the major?"

"No!" I quickly shushed him before Aunt Peg could hear us and decide that we'd jinxed her entry. "Davey hasn't even gone in the ring yet. See?" I gestured toward Coral. The Poodle was standing quietly while Davey combed through her ears. "He's waiting for their turn to come."

"It better come soon," Kevin told me. "We've been standing here for*ever*."

Actually, more like ten minutes. The child lived his life in dog years.

Our judge, Mr. Connelly, was wearing both a raincoat and a hat. We were all happy to see that he was using the entire ring to judge his Standard Poodle entry. The dogs were lined up in the covered area for his initial perusal. But then the judge wanted to see them move—and he sent them out in the deluge to do so.

Winners Dog went to a handsome cream-colored dog in puppy trim. So much for my color bias hopes. I gulped when I realized that Coral—or whoever was awarded Winners Bitch—would also have to beat that striking puppy to secure the major.

With only a single puppy entered, the Puppy Bitch class went by in a flash. There were five bitches in Open. When the steward called the class to the ring, Crawford deftly maneuvered his bitch to the head of the line. Davey held back, waiting until the others had filed in. He and Coral would bring up the rear.

The judge took his time making a first pass down the short line. He paused to take a long look at each bitch, obviously aware that this would be his only chance to see them with their stylized outlines intact. When Mr. Connelly reached Coral, he stopped beside her, then sent a swift glance back to Crawford's bitch at the front of the line.

Aunt Peg drew in a sharp breath. Her reaction confirmed what I'd already suspected. Our judge two weeks earlier had made the Open class into a duel between Coral and Crawford's bitch. Based on what we'd seen, Mr. Connelly appeared to be thinking along the same lines.

He lifted his hands, indicating that it was time for the class to gait around the perimeter of the ring. My gaze was focused on Davey and Coral, so it took me a moment to realize that nobody was moving. A chuckle from the middle of the group—quickly silenced—alerted me to the fact that something unexpected had happened. There was a delay at the head of the line.

When I looked to see what was the matter, I almost laughed myself.

Crawford's white bitch had her feet planted determinedly in place. She was staring out at the rain-soaked ring with an expression of utter disdain on her face. Crawford and Terry must have figured out a way to get the Poodle to the ring without her feet ever touching the ground.

But now her dainty toes were in the wet grass, and she didn't like it one bit.

The white bitch had been happy enough when the class was standing under the tent. But, apparently, moving was another matter. She could see that involved going out in the downpour, and she didn't want any part of it.

"Good timing for us," Sam muttered under his breath.

I nodded in agreement. *Best timing ever.*

Crawford was the consummate professional. He never lost his cool. Instead, he merely turned the white bitch in a small circle to get her feet moving. Then he reached down and chucked her lightly under the chin to bring up her tail and focus her attention on him.

That did the trick. She was a Standard Poodle, after all. She might take a minute to make her displeasure clear, but she wouldn't disobey a direct order. Finally, away the handler and Poodle pair went.

The rest of the class followed.

While the white bitch was hopping and skittering around up front, Coral treated the jaunt around the outside of the ring like her own personal picnic. She floated over the wet grass as if it was her preferred surface. And when she and Davey were once again beneath the tent, the Poodle treated the spectators to an exuberant four-footed bounce in the air—just to make sure everyone knew how much fun she was having.

This time I did laugh. Sam and Aunt Peg, both of whom believed in behaving with decorum at ringside, kept their reactions to a restrained smile.

"Did you see that?" Kevin's eyes were wide with delight. "Coral can fly!"

"When she wants to," I said. "That's a happy Poodle thing. Now let's be quiet and watch the rest of the class."

One by one, Mr. Connelly performed the individual examinations. After that, it didn't take him long to place Coral at the head of the line. Having reshuffled the bitches into his preferred order, the judge simply motioned everyone over to the place markers rather than sending them all out in the rain again. To my surprise, Crawford and his pretty bitch were placed fourth of the five.

"I thought he liked Crawford's bitch," I said to Aunt Peg. "I know she didn't show well, but fourth seems like an unexpectedly steep drop."

"A judge can overlook a lackluster performance if a dog is really deserving otherwise," she replied. "But despite Crawford's best efforts, that bitch simply refused to settle and cooperate with him."

The first go-around wasn't the only time the white bitch had balked at the rain. She'd also resisted during her individual examination. By the end of the class, both her head and her tail had begun to droop. Though Crawford had remained expressionless throughout, he'd probably felt the same way.

"You know how important it is that a Poodle have a superb temperament," Aunt Peg continued. "One might even say it's a defining characteristic of the breed."

I nodded. I'd been lectured about this before.

"Mr. Connelly didn't drop the white bitch down in place because she didn't show well," Sam put in. "He did it because he decided that her repeated refusals to work with her handler meant that her temperament was lacking."

"And a lucky thing that was for us," Aunt Peg said in a low voice. "Because I'm not sure we'd have beaten her otherwise."

Davey stuffed the blue ribbon in his pocket and remained in the ring with Coral. As he set her up, the Puppy Bitch winner came back to join him. Mr. Connelly briefly gave both bitches a good look. Then he pointed at Coral for the win.

"Yay, Davey did it!" Kevin tilted his head up toward mine. "Can we go now?"

"Not yet," I told him. "Davey still needs to win again."

If he didn't succeed in beating the Winners Dog for Best of Winners, all the effort we'd gone to today would be for nothing.

Crawford came over to stand next to Aunt Peg. Terry, his hand cupped about the white bitch's muzzle, walked around beside me.

"Since I'm outside the ring rather than in, I might as well come over here and root for the competition," Crawford said wryly. "I expected Connelly to love my bitch. I thought we might have a shot at taking the variety."

"He *did* love your bitch," Sam pointed out. "Until she decided to defeat herself."

"Finicky female," Crawford grumbled.

Terry snickered under his breath. Then he used his free hand to reach over and poke me. "Don't say it."

"Say what?" I flicked him a glance.

"Whatever it is you're thinking."

"I wasn't thinking anything," I said innocently. *Finicky female, indeed.*

Coral and Davey were once again at the back of the line. There were two Standard Poodle champions up front, followed by the Winners Dog. Coral, the Winners Bitch, was behind him.

The judge gave both specials a thorough examination.

Then he turned to his two Winners. He compared the Poodles to each other standing still, then he sent the pair around the ring together.

The white dog puppy was striking, but so was Coral. They both possessed beautiful breed type, but she had him beaten on maturity and movement. To my eye, Coral looked like the easy choice.

Not that anything about winning a major was ever easy.

Aunt Peg was muttering directions at the judge under her breath. "Hurry up and do it," she told him. "It shouldn't be taking you this long to decide."

Finally, Mr. Connelly rearranged his line. He placed one of the champions in front, then beckoned to Davey to bring Coral forward. She was put in the second spot. That meant Best of Winners. And since both specials were males, Coral would also be Best of Opposite Sex.

Outside the ring we all went still, holding our breath as we waited for the judge to point and make it official. When he did, the five of us erupted in happy applause. Kevin tossed in a few cheers for good measure.

After the long journey we'd undertaken as a family, it felt amazing to have reached our goal. There'd been stumbles and setbacks along the way, but Davey had persevered. And in the end, he'd accomplished a major feat by handling Coral to her championship himself.

Even Crawford was pleased by the outcome. "Thank goodness your bitch is finally out of my way," he said to Aunt Peg. "Now maybe *I* can get something finished around here."

We all laughed at that.

Kevin pulled his hand free and ran over to the in-gate. Davey and Coral were standing near the placement marker as the judge handed out the ribbons. Luckily, the quick-thinking steward caught Kevin before he could go flying into the ring.

"Did you win enough?" Kev asked his brother.

"We did." Davey looked somewhat stunned by the outcome. He held up the two rosettes: blue and white for Best of Winners, red and white for Best Opposite Sex. "We actually did."

Nobody minded that it was still raining. After that, everything about the day seemed utterly perfect to us.

Chapter 28

Our show day concluded with a flurry of activity. Finishing Coral's championship was a big achievement. Despite the relentless rain, we were all determined to get a win picture taken to mark the occasion. The weather had wreaked havoc on the Poodle's coat, however, and we only had a few short minutes to make repairs.

As soon as Davey and Coral exited the ring, Sam and Aunt Peg took over. Using combs, brushes, and hair spray, they went to work on Coral's soggy mane coat and drooping topknot. Terry observed their frenetic activity only briefly before he thrust the white bitch's leash into my hands and joined in. Even Crawford decided to get involved.

Meanwhile, Kevin and I just did our best to stay out of the way.

By the time the show photographer arrived, Coral's impromptu glam squad had succeeded in making the Poodle's show side—the only view that would be visible in the picture—look almost as good as she had when she'd first entered the ring. That was a truly masterful performance.

Davey led Coral back into the ring and posed her for the picture. The judge was standing beside them. Davey handed him the two rosettes, then paused and looked around.

"Aunt Peg, you have to be in the picture too," he said.

"No, this is your moment," she told him. "Yours and Coral's."

Davey shook his head. He'd battled with Aunt Peg plenty over the terms of their often uneasy partnership. And he'd lost as many skirmishes as he'd won. This time he was determined to prevail.

"No," he said firmly. "There isn't going to be a picture unless you're in it, too. This is *our* moment."

Sam reached over and gave my hand a squeeze. Maybe because he heard me sniffle and figured that might stop me from crying. It came close. Later, I would blame my teary eyes on the photographer's flash.

I gazed at my older son with love and admiration for what he'd accomplished. I'd never felt so proud.

Early Saturday morning, I was once again awakened by my phone. This time it was ringing. I knew who it had to be. No one was in more of a hurry to get things moving than Aunt Peg with a plan.

I had no idea why I had to hear about it at seven a.m., however.

Faith was on the floor beside the bed. She sat up and watched as I lifted the device to my ear.

"What now?" I said.

"And a cheery hello to you, too," Aunt Peg retorted. "It's a beautiful morning. Yesterday's clouds have given way to beautiful sunshine."

"Thank you for the weather report." I started to disconnect. Her next words stopped me.

"You and I have an appointment at Graceland School at nine."

"We do?"

"Yes. I've spoken with Emily, and she's expecting us. I told her we had information she'd want to hear concerning her Dalmatians. I thought the rest of our news should be delivered in person."

You think?

Despite Aunt Peg's blithe certainty, I wasn't at all sure Emily would be understanding about the fact that the three puppies she'd lived with since spring didn't belong to her. In my mind, there was a small chance she'd be happy to be relieved of their care—and an even larger one that she'd simply refuse to let them go.

And possession was nine tenths of the law. Or so we'd been told when Beau was found.

"Nine o'clock," I said groggily. "See you then."

Sam opened one eye. I knew the phone had awakened him too, but he'd pretended to sleep through my conversation with Aunt Peg. "Are you going somewhere?"

"Not until later," I said. With luck, I might be able to sleep for another half hour.

Kevin stuck his head through the bedroom doorway. "Who was on the phone?" he asked. "Was it Aunt Peg?"

I nodded.

"Is she coming over?"

"No." I lowered my head to the pillow. "Go back to sleep."

"Can't," Kev said.

"Why not?"

"I'm already awake."

Me too, but that wasn't stopping me from trying to reverse the process. I closed my eyes. Maybe that would work.

"Bud needs to go outside," Kevin told me.

"Take him downstairs and put him out," I mumbled. "In fact, take all the dogs with you."

"Bud's hungry too," Kevin added.

"Bud's always hungry." The idea of more sleep was beginning to feel like a distant dream.

"He wants breakfast."

I lifted my head again. "Are you going to keep talking until I get out of bed?"

"Yes." Kevin grinned. It was a good thing he was cute.

"I'll go," Sam said. He pushed back the covers and dragged himself out of bed. "I'm awake anyway."

"I love you," I said to my husband's retreating back.

"You'd better," he muttered.

Once again, I had to leave Faith behind. She and I had a conversation about it before I left.

"This meeting is all about Emily's Dalmatians," I told her. "They're rambunctious, untrained puppies. They'd drive you crazy."

Faith considered that. She wasn't convinced. *But I'll miss you.*

"I know," I said. "I'll miss you too. But I'll be back soon."

"Sheesh," said Davey, passing by with an apple in his hand. "You should know better than to tell her that."

I rose to my feet. "What?"

"That you'll be back soon. These days you're always running off somewhere."

"Aunt Peg and I need to talk to Emily," I said.

"About her dogs, right?"

I nodded.

"You should tell her not to let Mia handle them."

I'd started to go. Now I turned back. "Why?"

"Mia hates it when they run loose all over the place. And she gets mad when they don't listen."

"That's not their fault," I said.

Davey took a bite of his apple. I would have reminded him not to talk with his mouth full, but I wanted to hear what he had to say.

"I'm just saying Mia has a temper," he told me. "And she acts different when adults are around than she does when it's just kids. I don't think she likes dogs much. Or maybe she just doesn't like those dogs."

Fifteen minutes later when I arrived at the school, Aunt Peg's minivan was already parked in the small lot. A couple other cars were there as well, Emily's sturdy SUV and a small blue Subaru. I wondered who else would be at the school on a Saturday morning.

It didn't take long to find out. When I entered the admin building, the sound of conversation and the smell of fresh paint led me to the kitchen at the end of the hallway.

Aunt Peg was seated at the trestle table with an open box of scones in front of her. Emily stood at the foot of a tall A-frame ladder. Mia was at the top of the ladder, holding a paint roller. A paint-filled rolling pan was balanced on a pail shelf beside her.

There was another ladder nearby, and drop cloths covered most of the floor. I stepped carefully as I made my way over to the table. Despite what I'd told Faith, Posey, Pansy, and Poppy were nowhere to be seen. Considering the task at hand, that was probably a good thing.

Emily heard me come in and gave me a small wave.

"I thought you painted that wall ten days ago," I said.

"Second coat," Aunt Peg informed me.

"Actually third," Emily corrected. There was a paint smudge on the front of her T-shirt. "It turns out it's hard to cover smoke damage."

"When I got here, both of them were up on ladders," Aunt Peg told me. "*Some* people like to spend their Saturday mornings productively."

The subtext of that comment was clear. I chose to ignore it. Instead I sat down and helped myself to a scone.

"It's not like I have a choice." Emily opened a cupboard, got out three plates, then came over to join us at the table. "With the camp running five days a week, any extra jobs have to get done on our days off."

I glanced at the woman at the top of the ladder. During the break in activity, she'd pulled out her phone. "Some day off, huh, Mia?"

"I don't mind," Mia replied evenly. She didn't bother to look up.

"Mia never minds," Emily said cheerfully. "I swear she's like the Energizer Bunny. She's always ready to help out whenever something needs to be done."

Emily was busy passing out plates, and Aunt Peg was holding out the bakery box to offer her a scone. Neither of them saw the spiteful look Mia gave her boss as she picked up the paint roller and went back to work.

Having spent time with Emily over the past two weeks, I was aware of how much responsibility she'd been delegating to her assistant. During previous school sessions, Emily was always very much in charge. This summer, however, things were different. With all that had happened recently, it made sense that Emily would rely more on Mia. But maybe she'd been working the young woman too hard?

"How come Miles isn't helping with the painting?" I asked.

"Physical labor isn't my brother's forte," Emily said with a laugh. "If there's work to be done, he can always find an excuse to be somewhere else. This morning he decided to take a trip over to the Greenwich library."

"He'll enjoy that," Aunt Peg commented. Greenwich had a fabulous library.

I looked over at the woman on the ladder. "Hey Mia, do you want to come down and join us?"

Her hand didn't pause until she reached the end of a stroke. "No thanks," she said over her shoulder. "I'm good."

"See what I mean?" Emily was breaking her cranberry scone into small pieces on her plate. "Mia's always good."

Except perhaps when Emily's Dalmatians were around, I thought. I glanced across the table and caught Aunt Peg's eye. It was time to move things along.

Emily must have felt the same way. Her fingers were still crumbling her scone, but she had yet to put a single piece in her mouth. "You told me you had information about the puppies," she said. "Is there something I need to know?"

"I'm afraid there is," I told her. "It turns out that Will didn't own those puppies when he gave them to you."

Emily frowned. It looked as though she was about to protest.

Aunt Peg didn't give her the chance. "Melanie and I have managed to locate the Dalmatians' real owner. We talked to him about them yesterday."

"I don't understand." Emily was still frowning. "Are you saying that you told some random person about my dogs without getting my permission first?"

"Rory Scott isn't just some random person," Aunt Peg replied. "He's the puppies' breeder. The person who brought them into existence, and raised them for the first three months of their lives."

"But . . ." Emily sputtered. She still looked skeptical. "How did you even find that man? I never knew where the puppies came from. So how could you have known?"

"Aunt Peg figured it out," I said. "She could tell by looking at them that they were part of someone's valuable breeding program."

"Valuable?" Emily repeated. Her gaze swung back and forth between us. "You mean those dogs sitting outside my pen are worth a lot of money?"

"No," Aunt Peg interjected quickly. "What Melanie meant is that the puppies' bloodlines have value for their breeder."

She was right to correct me. There was no point in telling Emily the puppies' real worth—or letting her know how much their breeder wanted them back—just before asking her to give them up.

"But," Emily said slowly, "they're my puppies."

"Actually, they're not," I replied. "Will didn't own the puppies. He never should have given them to you in the first place."

"But what was he doing with them?" she asked—then abruptly stopped and threw up a hand. "Never mind. I'm not sure I even want to know."

Aunt Peg could never resist delivering a lecture. She opened her mouth to tell Emily anyway. I glared at her across the table. She glared back briefly, then popped a piece of scone between her lips instead.

After a minute, Emily answered her own question. "The puppies were just collateral damage from one of Will's crazy schemes, weren't they?"

I nodded.

"Dammit," she swore. "They didn't deserve that."

"No, they didn't," I agreed. "But at least by placing them with you, Will put them somewhere they'd be safe and well cared for."

Aunt Peg snorted under her breath. We both knew that her standard for adequate puppy care was a good deal higher than Emily's. But I wasn't about to let her bring that up either.

"Something caught in your throat?" I asked sweetly.

"Oh!" Emily's gaze flew to Aunt Peg in alarm. "Let me get you a glass of water." She hopped up and ran to the sink.

"I'm fine, thank you," Aunt Peg called after her. "There's no need to make a fuss."

Emily returned to the table. She placed a glass of cold water in front of Aunt Peg. "So what happens now?"

"If it's all right with you, we'd like to come back tomorrow with Rory Scott," I said. "As you might imagine, he's very anxious to see the puppies."

Emily shook her head. "I guess I don't really have a choice, do I?"

"Not if you want to do the right thing," Aunt Peg replied briskly. "Rory has been frantic with worry about them."

"Tomorrow just seems so . . . quick," Emily said.

The sooner, the better, Rory had told us. Of course, he was on the other side of the equation.

"It's probably better to do it when the camp isn't in session," I pointed out.

"And then he'll want to take the puppies away with him?" she asked in a small voice.

"I should think so," Aunt Peg said. The woman had about as much sensitivity as a cactus. She pushed back her chair and stood up. "I'll talk to Rory and let you know what time he can come. Does that suit you?"

"I guess so," Emily agreed unhappily.

I stood up too. Aunt Peg didn't wait for me. Her business concluded, she was already striding from the room.

Over on the ladder, Mia's arm continued to move rhythmically as she ran the paint roller up and down the wall. Her back was to us, and she'd made no attempt to join our conversation. But I knew she had to have been listening to every word. Mia didn't miss much.

Emily walked me to the door. I stopped to give her a hug before leaving.

"I'm sorry things turned out this way," I said.

"It's probably for the best." She sighed. "Those puppies were a lot of bother anyway."

"That doesn't mean you didn't fall in love with them."

Emily looked up. "What makes you think I did?"

"Because you haven't even asked about what else I've been doing. Or who I've spoken with about Will's murder."

"Oh, that." She sniffled.

Yes, *that.*

"I'll worry about that later," she said. "Right now, I'm having a hard enough time dealing with this problem."

Chapter 29

The following morning I was once again on my way back to Graceland School. My human family was getting used to my repeated absences. Faith was taking them harder. Once again, I'd promised to make it up to her when I got home. This time, I knew I was going to have to come up with something really special.

I pulled into the school property and parked in the lot beside Miles's silver Lexus. Since he hadn't come up with another excuse to duck out, I was guessing that today's get-together interested him more than painting the kitchen. Or maybe Emily had asked him to be there to act as her champion. Miles was clearly protective of his sister. I hoped he wouldn't turn out to be a problem.

As I started toward the smaller building, I saw Aunt Peg's maroon minivan turn in the driveway. She and I had decided against telling Rory Scott where his puppies could be found. He and Emily had conflicting interests when it came to the future of the three Dalmatians. We definitely didn't want Rory to take matters into his own hands and go racing to the school on his own.

Instead, Aunt Peg and I had every intention of acting as middlemen for Rory's meeting with Emily. Hopefully, we'd be able to direct the proceedings toward an amiable conclusion. Rather than divulging Emily's address, Aunt Peg had given Rory directions to her house. Now the two of them were arriving together.

I stopped and waited for them so we could all go inside at the same time. Before the van was even parked, the passenger side door flew open. Rory Scott hopped out and looked around eagerly, as if he expected to find his missing puppies gamboling around the parking lot.

"He's been like that ever since he arrived at my house," Aunt Peg said as she got out and came over to stand beside me. "The man is a veritable whirlwind."

"He's impatient," I said. "I don't blame him."

Now Rory was staring back and forth between the two school buildings, as if trying to decide which one to charge toward first. He spun around at the sound of my voice. Apparently, he'd been so busy looking for his dogs that he hadn't noticed me standing there.

"Hi!" Rory said. "You're Melanie, right? Where are my Dalmatians?"

"I don't know. I just got here too. Let's go inside and meet Emily, and we'll find out."

"Yeah, sure, the teacher." Rory's gaze returned to the weathered clapboard buildings. "That's really a school?"

"A nursery school," I told him. "Emily runs it."

"Looks like both of Will's exes made out better than he did."

Considering that Will was dead and the police were searching for his killer, Rory wouldn't get any argument from me.

"Let's move along, shall we?" Aunt Peg said. "Emily is expecting us."

As we approached the building, the door opened. Miles stood framed in the doorway. "Emily is out back with the puppies," he told us as he inspected Rory with an unfriendly stare. "The thought of possibly having to say goodbye to them isn't easy for her."

I introduced the two men. They shook hands briefly. Rory was anxious to move on. Miles continued to stand in front of us, blocking our way.

"I hope you've brought proof that those Dalmatians are yours," he said.

Rory didn't appear to be surprised by the request. Nor by Miles's attitude. He stared right back. "Let me get a look at them first. Then we'll worry about establishing ownership."

We walked through the building and exited through the back door. Right away, we saw Emily and the puppies. They were playing in the big field beyond the children's playground. I watched as Emily threw a tennis ball and Posey took off in pursuit.

Poppy and Pansy were the first to notice our approach. When the two Dalmatians came running in our direction, Emily turned and saw us. She and Posey followed more slowly.

Miles was at the front of our little group. Poppy and Pansy raced right past him. They also ignored Aunt Peg and me. Before they'd even reached Rory, the two puppies were already whining under their breath. Without breaking stride, they launched themselves straight at him.

Rory quickly dropped to his knees in the grass. He held out his arms to gather the puppies in for a hug. They both scrambled onto his lap, hopping up and down with joy as they covered his face with kisses. Within seconds, Posey had arrived to join the mêlée. The red-haired man and the three Dalmatians rolled around on the ground together.

I could hear Rory quietly murmuring something to the puppies. His hands were everywhere at once, moving rapidly to make sure each Dalmatian received a proper greeting. Whimpers came from deep within the puppies' throats. It sounded as though they were talking back to him.

I told myself that what I was witnessing wasn't definitive proof of ownership. But it sure looked like it to me.

Emily had hung back when Posey ran on ahead. Now she came forward to stand beside us. Her arms were crossed tightly over her chest. Her expression was carefully neutral, but I knew she had to be hurting inside.

"So," she said with a quiet sigh, "I guess that's that."

Aunt Peg and I both nodded. Miles still looked skeptical. How could anyone not be moved by the emotional reunion taking place in front of us?

Maybe he wasn't a dog person, I thought.

Eventually, Rory wriggled out from beneath the Dalmatians and stood up. He wiped his hand on his pants, then offered it to Emily. "Rory Scott," he said. "Thank you for taking good care of my puppies."

"I was happy to do it." She glanced downward at the lively trio bounding back and forth between them. "I guess this means there's no doubt?"

Before Rory could answer, Miles stepped in. He didn't look happy about the way things were going.

"You can't know with certainty that these dogs are your missing puppies," he said. "All Dalmatians look the same."

Aunt Peg, Rory, and I shared a look. He couldn't have been more wrong.

Definitely not a dog person, I thought.

"Emily told me what transpired yesterday," Miles continued in the same steely tone. "Apparently these puppies possess considerable value. You can't expect my sister to give them up simply because you allege to have a prior claim. Frankly, I don't see any reason why she should believe you."

"Miles, please . . ." Emily placed a hand on her brother's arm.

He shrugged her away. "Let me handle this, Em. I'm looking out for your best interests. This man should have proof that the puppies belong to him. If such a thing actually exists, I'd like to see it."

I'd already seen enough to be convinced. So had Aunt Peg. I expected Rory to bristle at the implied insult, but instead he just shrugged.

"I have their papers in the car. And a boatload of pictures on my phone. Pictures of these puppies with their dam when they were just babies, and then every week after that until they were stolen." Rory smirked in Miles's direction. "Even someone who thinks all Dalmatians look alike should be able to see the markings clearly enough to make a valid comparison."

Aunt Peg went with Rory to retrieve his things. The puppies trailed along after them. I remained behind with

Emily and Miles. As soon as Rory was out of earshot, Emily turned on her brother.

"Stop it," she hissed. "You're making things worse."

"Don't be stupid," he shot back. "From what I can tell, his claim to these puppies isn't any stronger than yours is."

"I don't *have* a claim to them," Emily snapped. "Will showed up out of the blue and dumped them on me. He never said where they came from. And Rory's story sounds perfectly plausible to me."

Miles's face pinched in annoyance. "You know what Will was like. He was Rumpelstiltskin, always trying to spin gold out of straw. And this guy was an accomplice of his. This was probably just another one of their scams. Now that Will's gone, Rory is finishing it on his own. That doesn't mean you have to be taken in by him."

His gaze moved to me. "You're her friend, Melanie. Tell Emily I'm right."

"I can't do that," I said. "I believe Rory's telling the truth. Poppy, Posey, and Pansy are his missing puppies."

"He probably only wants them back because they're worth money. You told Emily they were valuable."

"No," I replied carefully. "I told Emily that the puppies had great value for their breeder. They're the last three bitches out of Rory's best Dalmatian. They're the continuation of his line."

Miles just stared. "That all sounds like gibberish to me. Maybe you're in on this deal too. Is that it? Is Rory paying you to back his claim?"

"Miles, cut it out," Emily snapped. "Right now. I don't want to hear another word from you."

Her brother started to reply. She shook her head firmly.

"Will made his way in the world by taking advantage of people. He was always on the lookout for whatever weakness he could exploit. His Mr. Good Guy persona was just a sham, and by the time I knew him well enough to realize that, I hated him for it. If I can do one small thing to make up for some terrible deed Will committed, I'm going to do it."

Good for you, I cheered silently.

Emily grasped her brother by the shoulders and turned him around. She gave him a nudge toward the buildings. "Go inside now. I'll be along in a few minutes, as soon as things are settled out here."

"You don't get it, Em. I'm trying to help you—"

"I don't need your help, Miles. You have to leave this to me. Please?"

Miles's expression was thunderous, but he did as his sister requested. Shortly thereafter, Aunt Peg and Rory returned with the puppies. Rory showed Emily the dogs' AKC registration papers and win photos of both their parents. Then he brought out his baby pictures.

I was already convinced the Dalmatians belonged to Rory. Emily appeared to be too, but she stepped in for a closer look anyway. Her shoulders slumped as she scrolled through the photos and compared them to the puppies that were eddying around our legs.

After a minute, she cleared her throat softly and looked up. "When do you want to take them?"

"Now," Rory stated boldly. "We brought three crates with us in the minivan." Then he saw Emily's expression and softened his words. "If that's all right with you?"

"I guess so." She nodded unhappily. "All three of them?"

"They're all mine," Rory told her. "It only seems fair."

"I'm sorry, Emily, but Rory's right," Aunt Peg agreed. "It's the only thing to do."

Emily bit her lip. "It's going to seem very quiet around here without them. Maybe I could come and visit them sometime?"

"Sure." Rory was magnanimous in victory. "Why not?"

"Emily named the puppies," I told him.

She nodded, then pointed to each Dalmatian in turn. "That's Posey. This one's Poppy. And she's Pansy." Each puppy looked up and pricked her ears at the sound of her name.

Watching and listening, Rory winced slightly. "I'm not much for flowers myself. Could be those won't last long."

Aunt Peg nailed him with a hard look. "During the transition period, using familiar names will help the puppies adapt to their new surroundings."

"It won't be much of a transition," Rory shot back. "These puppies aren't going to new surroundings. They're going home."

After that, there didn't seem to be much more to say. Poppy, Posey, and Pansy ran on ahead as we all walked toward the parking lot. Aunt Peg and Emily took the lead. When Rory hung back, I slowed my steps too.

"Is everything all right?" I asked him.

He'd gotten everything he wanted. So I hoped he was happy.

Rory glanced at Aunt Peg ahead of us. "She's taking the credit, but I'm guessing you're the one who actually set this up. Am I right?"

"Yes," I replied. I didn't even hesitate. I was happy to be acknowledged for a change. Even if I didn't deserve it.

"That's what I thought. At the dog show, you asked me some questions. Maybe I could have said more than I did. But I wasn't sure I could trust you then."

I waited in silence for him to continue.

"Look at things from my perspective. When you showed up out of nowhere and told me you could get my puppies back, it sounded too good to be true. If there's one thing I've learned in life, it's to be suspicious of good fortune that lands in your lap for no reason. You know what I mean?"

I could see that. Especially since most of Will's and Rory's schemes had probably been based on people's failure to heed that exact warning.

"But now things have changed. You've done me a real solid here today. So maybe I owe you a little something in return. Unlike some people, I'm a guy who pays my debts. Maybe I could elaborate some on what I said before."

"Yes," I said, trying not to sound too eager. "That would be helpful."

"I knew Will was in trouble. He owed money to a guy he'd cut in on a deal that had gone south. Most times, people who've been had like that, they take their lumps and move on. This guy didn't. He told Will to make good on his losses or else. That was why we set up the poker game to begin with. Will needed cash, and he needed it quick."

"But the poker game didn't help," I remembered. "Instead it made things worse. Rather than making money, you lost even more."

Rory grimaced at the truth of that statement. "After that, Will had to be pretty desperate. Because that's when he swiped my puppies. He thought I'd cough up the money—but I couldn't. I didn't have that kind of cash lying around either."

"And then Will disappeared," I said.

He nodded. "What your aunt said the other day, I expect she had things right. Will was hiding from someone who wanted to hurt him."

We'd almost reached the parking lot. Aunt Peg and Emily were loading the puppies into their crates. I was running out of time to get answers.

"On Friday, you told me you had no idea who Will was afraid of. Now that you've got your puppies back, has your memory improved?"

"I still don't have a name for you, if that's what you think."

"It doesn't have to be a name," I said. "Just something to point me in the right direction."

When Rory spoke, he lowered his voice. I leaned closer to make sure I wouldn't miss a thing.

"All I know is that whoever the guy was, the reason Will couldn't dodge him is because it was someone he was close to. Maybe even family. Someone like a brother. You know?"

A frisson of shock rippled through me. "Yes," I replied softly, "I do."

Owen Grace had lied to me once. This time I'd have to work harder to pin him down. I wasn't about to give him the chance to lie to me again.

Chapter 30

When I got home, I was just as ready for a treat as Faith was.

Before anything could come up to stop me, I grabbed the Poodle's leash and hustled her out to the front of the house, where I'd left my car. When I opened the car door, she hopped onto the back seat eagerly. Within seconds, we were on our way.

I glanced back at Faith over my shoulder. "Aren't you even going to ask where we're going?"

Happy! Happy! Her bright expression and wagging tail were enough of an answer for me.

Faith didn't care where we were headed, as long as it was just the two of us. She probably expected me to take her to the park. Or possibly to visit friends. But after all the absences she'd had to deal with lately, this needed to be a special occasion.

So Faith and I were going out for ice cream.

There was an ice cream shop with a drive-up window in a nearby village. I'd decided on a cup of vanilla ice cream for Faith and a mint chocolate chip cone for myself. The Poodle stood up on the back seat and poked her muzzle out the half-open window as I stopped beside the drive-thru. A cheery young woman wearing a retro soda jerk hat leaned out to give Faith's nose a pat.

"Is that a Doodle?" she asked.

"No, she's a Standard Poodle. Her name is Faith."

"That's a big Poodle." The girl smiled. "I hope she's getting some ice cream too."

"Of course."

She took my order and returned in minutes. Thoughtfully she'd tucked a stack of extra napkins onto the cardboard tray. I drove to the other side of the small lot and parked the Volvo in the shade. I slid down all the windows, then I climbed in the back with Faith.

She lay down on the seat and held her cardboard cup between her front paws. I sat beside her with my cone. She lapped up her ice cream quickly. I took my time and savored every bit of mine. Faith finished first. After she'd licked the last of the vanilla ice cream off her nose, I broke my empty cone in half and split it with her.

Faith and I had been sharing ice cream since she was a fluffy puppy with curious dark eyes and feet that were too big for her body. Now the Standard Poodle was nine years old. Her muzzle was gray, and her joints occasionally stiffened. She enjoyed a heartfelt cuddle more than a brisk run.

I knew I wouldn't have Faith with me forever. Most

days, I simply refused to think about that. Instead I cherished moments like this one. The sun was warm, and the ice cream was delicious. Right now, Faith and I had all the time in the world to be together.

"I love you," I told her.

The Poodle's gaze softened. Her tail flapped up and down happily. *I know!*

It didn't get any better than this.

The following morning, I dropped the boys off at camp and headed back to Southbury. The last time I'd gone to visit Owen Grace, I'd expected him to know I was coming. This time, I was hoping to surprise him. Although if Owen wasn't at his office on this fine summer morning, the surprise would be on me.

When I opened the front door to the quaint building that housed Owen's legal practice, I was hit with a blast of cold air. In the ten days since I'd been here, someone had fixed the air conditioning. The fake flowers in the hallway had been dusted too.

But when I walked to the end of the hall and let myself into the office whose brass plaque announced, OWEN GRACE, ATTORNEY AT LAW, nothing had changed. Just as before, Randy was seated behind her desk, gazing down at her phone. Once again, she took her time about looking up.

On the way to Southbury, I'd thought about the fact that I intended to ask Owen some uncomfortable questions. I'd decided it was a good thing that he and I wouldn't be alone in his office in case our conversation took a bad turn. But now, staring down at the receptionist, I realized I'd probably given her too much credit. Randy barely looked capable of taking care of herself, much less coming to my rescue.

I closed the door behind me with a sharp rattle. Then I cleared my throat.

Slowly her eyes rose. Then they narrowed—as if Randy thought I might look familiar, but she had no idea why. I wondered if Owen was actually paying her to take up space in his reception area, or if hers was a volunteer position. Either way, he wasn't getting his money's worth.

"I'm here to see Owen Grace," I said.

Randy glanced in the direction of the appointment book. Since I already knew what came next, I circumvented the move by asking another question.

"Is Owen in?"

"I'll have to check," she replied.

We'd been here before too.

"No need," I said breezily. If she was going to check, Owen must be in his office. "I'll just let myself in."

Before Randy was even out of her seat, I'd already moved past her. Since she applied herself to her job with the speed of a sloth, it wasn't much of a challenge. I didn't knock, I just opened the door.

Inside the room, Owen was standing beside a bookshelf lined with weighty legal tomes. His finger was resting atop the spine of one as if he was about to pull it out. Casually dressed in khaki pants and a navy blue polo shirt, his cheeks ruddy from the sun, Owen looked as though he might have just arrived at the office from an early morning round of golf.

He was already frowning when he turned to see who'd interrupted him. The sight of me standing there didn't appear to improve his mood at all.

"Sorry." Randy popped up behind me. "She didn't give me a chance—"

"Don't worry, it's fine." Owen flashed her a quick smile. "Close the door, and go back to your desk."

He waited until the door had clicked shut before addressing me. He stepped away from the bookshelf, planted himself in the middle of the room, and crossed his arms over his chest. "Well, Melanie Travis, you're back to interrupt me again. To what do I owe the pleasure this time?"

It wasn't the most effusive greeting, but at least he'd remembered my name. "With a receptionist like Randy, your life must be filled with unexpected interruptions," I said.

"Summer help." Owen shrugged. "She's my neighbor's niece. He's been encouraging her to go to law school. He thinks she's going to be the next Robert Kardashian."

I snorted out a laugh. "The next Kim Kardashian seems more likely."

Owen looked briefly amused. I decided to take that as an invitation. I walked across the room and sat down in the same leather chair he'd offered me on my previous visit. For some reason, that amused him again. He strode behind his desk and sat down.

"I didn't think we had much more to say to each other after the last time you were here," he said.

"I didn't either. But things have changed."

"What things? All I know is that my brother is still dead, and the police still haven't arrested Emily."

"I told you before—she didn't do it."

Owen frowned. "Telling me and convincing me are

two very different things. And as I recall, you never got past the first part."

"Last time I was here, you told me you kept your brother's business dealings totally separate from your own."

"So?"

"Now I know that's not true."

"And how would you have come by that knowledge?" Owen inquired skeptically.

"A few months ago, Will tried to make a deal with Peyton Hancock," I said.

"I don't know anything about that." The reply was quick and automatic. Then curiosity got the better of him. "What kind of deal?"

Owen's swift denial had sounded genuine. I noted, however, that he hadn't had to ask who Peyton Hancock was. Or what connection the man might have had with his brother.

"Will told Peyton that he could convince Emily to vacate the Graceland School property quickly and with minimum fuss. That would free up the land so the Hancock family could sell it for considerably more than her lease had been earning them."

As he listened, Owen's fingers had begun to drum quietly on the desktop. I hoped that was a sign of contemplation and not impatience.

"I assume Will wanted to be handsomely compensated for providing such a service," he said.

"Of course." I gazed at him across the desk between us. "You don't sound surprised by that."

"Surprised? No." Owen sighed. "I knew Will longer than anyone. I was well aware of how he operated. There's probably nothing you could tell me about my brother's seemingly endless intrigues that will surprise me."

"How about this?" I challenged. "Will gave Peyton your business card. He told him you were his attorney. And that should Peyton wish to reconsider turning him down, any further business would be conducted through you."

He was already shaking his head before I'd even finished speaking. "That's not right."

"Are you calling Peyton Hancock a liar?"

"Of course not," Owen snapped. "I'm calling my brother a liar. And it wouldn't be the first time. Considering Will's proclivity for disreputable behavior, you can imagine how useful he thought it was for his brother to possess a law degree."

That admission caused him to wince visibly. It looked as though my questions were getting on his nerves. *Good.*

Owen growled under his breath. "Having trouble convincing one of your grifter cronies to make good on a debt? Toss down my card and threaten to sue. See a crack in a sidewalk? Hit the ground and threaten to call your brother—who will sue for pain and suffering. Unless, of course, the store owner would like to pay handsomely to make the complaint disappear."

"I thought accidents and personal injuries were your specialty," I said mildly.

"*Legitimate* accidents," Owen ground out. "I make my living helping people whose cases have true merit. I have no need for clients who are looking to rake in big bucks through dishonest means. I'm nothing like my brother. I told you that the last time you were here."

I wasn't convinced, but I nodded anyway. Anything to keep Owen talking.

"In my business, reputation matters," he said. "How would it look if word got out that I was willing to abet the shady deals that kept paying my brother's way back to the roulette wheel and the craps table?"

"Pretty bad," I agreed.

"You got that right," Owen snapped. "Handing out my business card was a stupid maneuver Will used to make himself appear more important than he was. Giving one to Peyton wasn't the first time he'd done it, and I'm sure it won't be the last."

My breath lodged in my throat. I didn't say a thing.

It took Owen several seconds to realize why. Abruptly the realization that his brother would never attempt to use him again took hold. His face cleared of all emotion. Then his shoulders slumped, and he sat back in his seat.

"I'm sorry," he said. "That was uncalled for."

"Not entirely," I replied. "I asked the questions."

"Losing a sibling is a terrible thing. Especially when you're not even sure how you should feel. Of course I'm grieving Will's loss. But there's also a sense of relief that he won't be around to screw up my life anymore."

"Families are tough," I said. I knew that from firsthand experience.

Owen gave a clipped nod. "Are we done here?"

"There's one more thing," I said.

"I'm sure you'll understand if I ask you to make it quick."

"I was talking to one of Will's associates—"

Owen stood up and walked out from behind the desk. He was ready to see me out. "If Will owed him money, you can tell him there's nothing for anyone to claim."

"No, it's not about that. The man told me that Will had been in desperate financial straits. That he was in debt for a large sum of money to someone he couldn't avoid. Someone who could hurt him if he didn't pay."

Now Owen looked exasperated. "Considering what happened, it doesn't take a genius to figure that out."

"He said Will needed to raise money fast because he was afraid of someone in his family." I rose to my feet. "Maybe his brother."

"Me?" Owen stopped in shock. Then his tone sharpened. "I'm willing to swear that Will wasn't talking about me. I'm sure your mystery informant didn't mention me by name. He didn't, did he?"

"No," I admitted. "He wouldn't give me a name."

"It figures."

As Owen strode across his office and opened the door, I quickly thought back. I was trying to remember what Rory's exact words had been. "He said the person Will was afraid of was someone close to him. Someone like a brother."

Owen gestured toward the open doorway, indicating I should leave. "That makes more sense then."

"What does?"

"Someone *like* a brother is entirely different. The guy was probably talking about Will's best friend, Brad Luft. Those two had everything in common. They were closer than Will and I ever were. Thick as thieves, you might say."

Chapter 31

I guessed that let me know who I needed to talk to next. When I'd spoken to Detective Sturgill, I'd made a point of telling him that Brad was mixed up in what Will was doing. Then, Sturgill hadn't been impressed by the information I'd passed along. Maybe, this time, I could turn up something that would pique his interest.

First, I called Frank at The Bean Counter and told him to reserve me a table. Since the café didn't take reservations, my brother gave me some grief about that. I had to promise him free babysitting before he eventually acquiesced. Brad was easier to convince than my brother.

I called and offered him a free lunch.

"Why?" he asked suspiciously.

"Because we need to talk. I have new information about Will's death that I know you'll want to hear."

After a pause, he said, "Where?"

"Same as last time. The Bean Counter."

"Will your brother be there?"

"Probably," I said. "But don't worry. You're bigger than he is."

Brad grumbled a little more before we settled on a time. But by then I already knew that he'd be coming. Frankly, I was pretty sure I'd had him at "free lunch."

I arrived at The Bean Counter a few minutes early. Frank saw me and motioned toward an empty booth in the café's only dark corner. Considering his reaction when Brad and I had eaten here the previous week, I figured that was my brother's idea of a joke.

"Very funny," I said, stepping up to the counter. "But I need to order first."

"No, you don't." Frank grinned. "You and your guest will be eating the specialty of the house."

Oh joy.

"You mean the current specialty? Or something you're thinking about adding to the menu?"

"The latter. Lucky you, you'll be the first to sample it."

Some of Frank's culinary creations were nothing short of genius. Others belonged in the trash can. Unfortunately, you never knew which option you'd be served.

"Will you at least tell me what's in it?" I said.

"Of course not. I want you to be surprised."

Like that was a good thing.

"Soup, salad, or sandwich? You can tell me that much."

"Sandwich," he replied. "And that's all you're getting."

I poured a drink and sat down. Brad walked in a few minutes later. He started to head to the counter, but I stood up and waved him over. He helped himself to a giant-sized cup of Diet Coke, then joined me in the booth.

"I thought you were buying me lunch," he said.

"I am. My brother decided to make us the specialty of the house."

"What is it?"

"I don't know. He didn't say."

Brad frowned. "Then how does he know we'll like it?"

"That's the whole idea," I admitted. "Frank's trying out a new dish."

"Like he's using us as guinea pigs?"

Or crash dummies, I thought. Take your pick.

"I'm sure it will be something good," I said aloud.

"It better be," Brad muttered. "Otherwise, what was the point of my coming all the way over here?"

The point was for me to find out how much Brad knew about Will Grace's murder. Not that I had any intention of telling him that.

"Enjoy!" Frank said cheerfully. He slid two platter-sized plates onto the table in front of us, then quickly left.

I stared down at my lunch. The sandwich itself was massive. Beside it, Frank had piled a mountain of french fries. Brad and I would be here all afternoon if we had to eat all this.

While I hesitated, Brad looked eager to dig in. He lifted one edge of the big ciabatta roll and peered inside. "Let's see," he murmured. "Looks like pulled pork, plenty of barbecue sauce, provolone cheese, coleslaw." He leaned down to give the sandwich a delicate sniff. "And maybe some sweet pickle relish. I take back what I said before. This thing has potential."

Frank was back behind the counter, making himself look busy. He pretended he wasn't watching us, but I

knew better. Since Brad was already tearing into his
sandwich with gusto, I took that as a good sign and gave
my brother a subtle thumbs-up. Now he could go back to
running his café and leave us alone.

"You told me you had new information about Will,"
Brad said presently. Half his sandwich was already gone.
Now he was stuffing fries into his mouth. "What is it?"

I had cut my large sandwich into quarters. Each piece
still looked like a whole meal to me. I picked one up and
was nibbling around the edges, while trying to keep its
overstuffed ingredients from falling out. It actually tasted
pretty good.

"The new stuff I learned was about you," I said.

Brad abruptly stopped chewing. His mouth was so full
that his cheeks bulged outward. He managed to talk
around that problem. "What's that supposed to mean?"

"I know you didn't tell me everything you knew last
time we were here."

"So what?" He shrugged. "It's not like I owe you any
explanations."

"Sure," I said easily. "But you're going to have to talk
to someone. If not me, then maybe Detective Sturgill of
the Stamford Police."

Brad swallowed heavily. Trying to look nonchalant, he
wiped his greasy fingers on his napkin.

"You do know who Detective Sturgill is. Right?"

"I guess." He grabbed his sandwich, took a bite, then
made a show of chewing it. Like that was the only reason
he wasn't talking.

"If you prefer, I can go and tell him what I've learned.
Detective Sturgill and I have worked together before."

Okay, that was stretching the truth—maybe almost to
the breaking point. But Brad wouldn't know that.

"I'm sure he'll be happy to hear what I have to say."

"Which is?" Brad growled.

"I know you're hiding something important. Two people I've spoken with have pointed to you as the person most likely to have been involved in Will's murder."

Brad's hand slammed down on the tabletop hard enough to make me jump in my seat. Out of my eye, I saw Frank give us a sharp look. I waved him off—and hoped he'd listen to me.

"Who?" Brad demanded. "I want names."

"So what?" I echoed his earlier question. "You want names, and I want information. It looks as though we've reached an impasse."

"Look," he snapped, "I don't know what you think I know. But I don't know anything."

"You and Will were as close as brothers. Everyone says so. If Will was in trouble—and clearly he was—he would have gone to you for help first."

"What kind of trouble are you talking about?"

There was only one possible answer. Because where Will Grace was concerned, it always came down to the same thing.

"Money problems," I said. "Will needed cash. Fast. He had to pay someone back, someone who'd threatened him if he didn't come through."

"Okay, yeah." Brad slumped back in his seat. "Maybe he did come to me looking for money. And maybe he was really on edge about it. I would have helped him if I could. But I was as broke as he was."

"When was that?" I asked.

"I don't know. A few months ago."

"April maybe?"

"Sure, I guess."

Will had proposed his deal to Peyton Hancock around the same time. Then he'd set up the disastrous poker game with Rory Scott. That had led to the theft of Rory's Dalmatians. April had been a busy month for Will Grace. It was beginning to look as though he'd spent most of it running scared.

But who was the person he was so afraid of?

"Who did Will owe money to?" I asked.

Brad didn't say a thing. He just shook his head.

"Maybe there was nobody else," I mused aloud. "Maybe the person Will was in debt to—the one he was so scared of—was you."

Brad's face grew red. The man looked like the poster boy for heart attacks. He grabbed for his soda and gulped some down.

"Don't be stupid," he said after a few seconds. "Of course it wasn't me."

"Sorry." I shrugged. "I've eliminated everyone else. Yours is the only name left."

"You're wrong."

I stopped breathing. I didn't move or make a sound. I didn't want to do anything to spook him. Any minute now, Brad was going to stand up and go storming out of the café. I really wanted him to tell me what he'd been holding back before he did so.

"All I know is there was some kind of family connection," Brad said finally.

"Family?" I frowned.

Just that morning, Owen had sent me to Brad. Was Brad now trying to send me back? Maybe the two of them were playing me for a fool. Or maybe one of them was legit, and the other was guilty as sin.

"It was a relative of his," Brad said. "You know Emily."

Damn, I thought. *Not Emily.*

"Yes."

"It was some guy Will knew through her. An in-law." He paused and smirked. "Will never said the guy's name. He used to call him the Outlaw. That's who was yanking Will's chain."

I had a suspicion I knew who he was talking about. But I wanted to be sure. "What else did he tell you about him?"

"Nothing, really. All I know is that he didn't live around here. That made Will feel like he had some breathing room when the guy first started making threats. Although I guess that didn't last." He paused and thought back. "He came from one of those snowy states up north. I think he worked in a school or something."

And there it was. The final piece of information I'd needed locked into place.

Damn, I thought. How had I missed that earlier? *Not a brother. A brother-in-law.*

"Did you tell that to the police?" I asked him.

"You're kidding me, right?" Brad snorted. "I'm not stupid. The last thing anyone needs is for the police to think you know stuff. Because then they start wondering what else you might know. And where Will was concerned, there were always more secrets tucked away. It was much safer to never even start that conversation."

"Oh, it's going to get started, all right," I said.

Brad quickly slid out of the booth. Then he leaned down and stabbed his index finger toward my face. "You better make damn sure you leave my name out of it. You hear me?"

Frank suddenly materialized behind him. He placed a heavy hand on Brad's shoulder. "Hey, buddy, the whole place hears you. I think it's time for you to go."

"You got that right!" Brad snapped.

Frank and I both watched as he pushed his way through the room. Brad yanked open the café's front door and ran down the outside steps. Frank waited until he was out of sight before turning back to me.

He surveyed the half-full plates on the table with a sigh. "That wasn't about the food, was it?"

I almost laughed. Trust my brother to think about his own interests first. Then I stood up and gave him a hug instead.

"No, Frank, it wasn't about the food. Brad loved your new sandwich. I think you should put it on the menu."

He smiled. "Maybe I will."

"Thank you for coming to my rescue," I said.

I hadn't needed him to. But Frank would be happy to hear that anyway. My brother lapped up praise like a puppy.

"Anytime," he told me.

"I'll keep that in mind," I said.

As soon as I got to my car, I put in a call to Detective Sturgill. He wasn't there, but I was offered the opportunity to leave a message. So I did.

The officer who was manning the phones probably hadn't expected as much detail as I gave her. But she said she was writing everything down. And if you can't trust a policewoman, who can you trust?

I told her I was calling with regard to Will Grace's murder. At that point, I could have skipped ahead and given her Miles Harlan's name. But I knew Detective Sturgill. He never wanted to hear about conclusions that seemed to appear out of thin air. So instead I started by laying a strong foundation of evidence.

I gave the policewoman the timeline of events that began with Will being in dire need of funds in the spring. I mentioned his meeting with Peyton Hancock and his futile attempts to borrow money from both Rory Scott and Bradley Luft. Those disclosures were followed by an account of Will's subsequent disappearance when he'd been unable to come up with the cash he needed.

Then I reminded Sturgill of the things that had taken place at Graceland School in the days leading up to the murder. First, Will's Dalmatians had been put in jeopardy. Then his antique truck had ended up in a pond. After that, his ex-wife's school had been set on fire.

Looking back now, it seemed clear that Emily had never been the real target of those escalating threats. They'd been orchestrated by Will's killer, and their purpose had been to draw Will out of hiding. They'd obviously had the desired effect because two days after the fire, Will Grace appeared in Stamford.

And he was dead.

Shortly thereafter, Emily's brother, Miles, had also showed up at the school. Supposedly he was there to provide his beleaguered sister with support. I suspected, however, that he'd actually come to keep a close watch on how the investigation was proceeding.

Because Miles was the person Will Grace had owed money to, the man he'd been afraid of all along.

After delivering that dramatic pronouncement, I paused to take a breath.

"You finished?" The officer blew out a weary sigh. She sounded like she was really hoping I'd say yes. "Because I've got plenty here to get you a callback from Detective Sturgill. I'm thinking maybe you want to explain the rest of this to him in person."

If only it was that easy.

"Sure," I said. "Thank you."

I started the car, intending to head home. Then I abruptly changed my mind, when something else occurred to me. Maybe Miles had a second reason for showing up at Graceland School. Maybe he'd wanted to keep an eye on his sister too. He might have felt the need to ensure she didn't say anything that could get him into trouble.

Because suddenly I realized that Emily had been right in the middle of this fracas all along. So now I had to ask myself: *How much did she really know?*

Chapter 32

I turned in the opposite direction and headed toward Graceland School. Camp ended in less than an hour, and Sam was expecting me to pick up the boys anyway. So it only made sense to go there. Before the day's session was over, however, I intended to find Emily and make her tell me the truth.

I was happy to see that Miles's Lexus wasn't out front when I arrived. That helped. I had no desire to see him. I texted Emily once I'd parked the Volvo in the lot. She quickly wrote back to tell me she was in her office.

I let myself in the building and strode down the empty hallway. Emily's door was half-open. She was sitting behind her desk, frowning at her computer screen. When I knocked, she glanced up and smiled.

Emily closed the computer, then beckoned me into the

room. "It's nice to see a friendly face. It feels so quiet around here now that the puppies are gone. It's only been one day. I can't believe how much I already miss them."

"I'm sure you do. They were a big part of your life for three months." I pulled over a chair and sat down. "I didn't see your brother's car when I came in. Is Miles around?"

"Not if his car's gone," Emily said with a shrug. "He must have gone out. Miles gets bored hanging around the school all day. I think he'll be heading home soon."

"To New Hampshire?"

She nodded. "Miles expected the police to have things wrapped up by now. But the investigation is still dragging on, and he says there are important things he needs to get back to."

I didn't believe that for a minute. I wondered if Emily did—or if she was covering for her brother. Maybe Miles had felt the authorities' net closing around him. New Hampshire shared a border with Canada. Maybe he was already on his way there.

"You and I need to talk," I told her.

"Oh?" Emily didn't guard her expression closely enough because she suddenly looked wary. "About what?"

"I think you know."

She managed a wobbly smile. "Don't tell me you've managed to scoop the police."

"No, but I have gotten some things figured out. You told me you had no idea what Will was doing in the woods behind the school on the night he was killed. That wasn't true, was it?"

Emily stared at me. She had to be wondering how much I knew. And how much she ought to admit.

"Maybe not entirely," she said after a pause.

"Did you speak with him?"

"Just briefly."

"What did you talk about?"

Her chin lifted. "Money, what else? As usual, Will needed some. He tried to persuade me to give it to him."

"And you didn't," I said.

"Of course not. What would have been the point? Maybe he'd have used it to pay off whoever he owed *this time*. But sooner or later, he'd have been back for more. Will refused to understand that his mistakes weren't my problem anymore."

"Will was in trouble," I said. "Did he tell you someone had threatened to harm him if he didn't pay up?"

"He did, but I didn't believe him," Emily snapped. "Will's whole life was one drama after another. I thought this was just more of the same."

"Did he tell you who he was in debt to?"

The wary look came back. Emily's expression immediately shuttered. "No. He didn't."

I was pretty sure she was lying. But I could circle back around to that later.

Instead I said, "Why didn't you tell anyone that you spoke to Will on the night he was killed?"

"Why do you think?" She snorted. "Doing so would have made me look guilty. Will was my ex-husband. His body was found near my property. I knew the police would be examining our relationship under a microscope. If I'd admitted I was the only person who knew he was here, that detective would have snapped handcuffs on me the very first day."

"So instead you impeded their investigation," I pointed out.

Emily just shrugged, as if the move still made perfect sense to her.

"Did you shoot Will?" I asked.

The question—coming from me—seemed to surprise her. "No, of course not."

"So if you didn't kill him, that must mean you *weren't* the only person who knew he was here. Right?"

Emily bit her lip and took her time about answering. She cast her eyes around the room as if she was looking for a way to escape. "Maybe."

"And maybe you know who pulled the trigger," I said.

This time, she didn't reply at all. So I kept talking.

"You knew all along, didn't you?"

That accusation finally goaded her into responding.

"No!" Emily cried. "In the beginning I had no idea. None at all. Otherwise, I never would have asked for your help."

I nodded. At least that part made sense.

"But then you couldn't help becoming suspicious," I prompted.

Emily wasn't dumb. While I'd been blundering around in the dark, she'd already had the pieces of the puzzle neatly lined up in front of her. All she'd had to do was put them together.

She might have shied away from doing so for as long as possible. But eventually, Emily had to have come to the conclusion that was now glaringly obvious to both of us.

"I talked to Miles right after I found out what had happened," she said. "I was in shock, and he was the first person I called. Later, it occurred to me that he hadn't asked many questions. And that he seemed to already know about things I hadn't told him. But I still didn't realize." Emily stopped and shook her head. "How could I have realized? The whole idea was impossible."

"I understand that."

"But then Miles showed up here—after I'd told him not to come. He was the one who insisted. And once he was here, he kept bugging me to talk to the police. He wanted to know all about their investigation." Her gaze lifted. "He asked about you too. And why you were poking your nose into everything. He told me I was stupid to let you keep coming around."

"You weren't," I said. "Your instincts about that were spot-on. But now you have a decision to make. What are you going to do?"

Once again, I'd asked a question that surprised her.

"There's nothing I can do," Emily replied sharply. "Miles will go back to New Hampshire, and we'll both put this behind us."

She had to know that was a fantasy, I thought. A man had been murdered. Perhaps not a very good man—but even so, she wasn't naïve enough to believe that the police wouldn't follow their investigation to its conclusion. Whether or not Miles left the state.

"I'm sorry, Emily," I said. "But that's not how this is going to end."

"You're right," a deep voice said from behind me. "It's not."

Slowly, I turned in my seat. Miles was standing in the doorway.

So Emily's brother wasn't on his way to Canada. That was too bad. Miles wasn't holding a weapon, but he still exuded a palpable air of menace. I wished the puppies had been here to warn us of his approach.

"I thought you were out," I said.

"I was. But it looks like I returned just in time."

Emily stared at him, wide-eyed. "How much did you hear?"

"More than enough."

She shoved back her chair and stood. "Then you know what you need to do. Go upstairs and pack your bags. You can leave right now."

"And go where?" Miles's lips pursed in annoyance. He knew better than to believe his sister's fanciful solution. "There's no point in my going anywhere until I've fixed things here."

I didn't like the sound of that. I grasped the arms of my chair and stood up too. Now at least we were all on equal footing.

Emily stepped out from behind her desk. She moved to stand between me and her brother. "Don't do something stupid, Miles. There's nothing here that can be fixed. Things have gone too far."

"You need to get a lawyer and talk to the police," I told him. "Explain to them what happened. It will be better if they hear it from you first."

"First—before they come for me, you mean?" Miles growled. "That's not going to happen. Because you're not going to have a chance to tell them what you know."

I'd already told Detective Sturgill everything I knew. At least, I'd tried to. Hopefully, the message I'd left hadn't been too garbled in the retelling.

"Don't talk like an idiot," Emily snapped. "Forget about what Melanie said. Just go. Get away from all this. Go someplace where the authorities will never find you."

Where would that place be? I wondered. *La La Land?*

"I'm not running away," Miles shot back. "I have a life. I have a job. I'm not going to let everything be ruined just because I happened to be there when your irresponsible ex-husband had an accident with a gun."

An accident? That was a new idea. Next, it might occur to Miles to argue self-defense. Whatever kept him talking was fine by me. I'd listen to as many stories as he wanted to spin. I would even pretend to believe them.

"You," he said, pointing in my direction. "You're coming with me."

I braced my feet and crossed my arms over my chest. Whatever Miles had in mind, I didn't want any part of it. "I'm not going anywhere."

He reached around behind him. When his hand came forward again, it was holding a gun. The weapon must have been tucked in the back of his waistband.

Miles pushed Emily to one side. Then he lifted the barrel and pointed it at me. "I said *move*."

My head jerked up as a bell chimed in the other building to signal the end of the camp day. *Dammit.* The timing couldn't have been worse.

Emily caught my eye. I knew she was thinking the same thing.

"Just keep the kids safe," I said to her. "All of them. I'm going with Miles."

"Melanie, don't—"

"I have to. You know that as well as I do."

Emily wanted to continue arguing. She didn't want to accept the truth of what I was saying any more than I did. But neither of us had a choice. After a moment, she nodded and stepped aside to let me pass.

Miles grabbed my upper arm. He poked my ribs with the gun's muzzle. Like he thought I wouldn't be frightened enough with the weapon six inches away. Fat chance of that. At this close range, any shot he took wouldn't miss.

"Go to the children," I said to Emily. "Now."

She turned and ran from the room.

Through the office window, I caught a quick glimpse of campers pouring out of the other building to gather in the school's front yard for pick-up. Then Miles yanked me away. I stumbled after him, out into the hallway. He and I walked toward the rear door.

At least we were heading away from the children. But the end of the camp day also meant that he and I would be alone behind the school. There'd be no one around to notice that something unusual was happening.

"Where are you taking me?" I asked as we exited the building.

"You'll see," Miles replied grimly. "Just keep walking."

Together, we strode toward the woods at the back of the property. Those trees had provided ample cover for Miles's first dirty deed. It must have made sense to him to repeat what had worked before.

Miles was bigger and stronger than I was. And he had a gun. Out here in the open, I'd have no chance of escaping. But maybe once we reached the woods, I could convince him to let go of my arm. It would be darker there, and the uneven footing could work to my advantage. Considering our size difference, dodging between the tightly packed trees would be easier for me too.

We walked past the Dalmatians' empty pen. It was a shame the puppies weren't here to provide a distraction. Then again, who knew what Miles might be capable of? Maybe he would have shot them too. The thought made me cringe.

Miles must have felt my small tremor. He looked down at me and frowned. "Just a little farther now."

As if *that* was what I was worried about.

"You're making the biggest mistake of your life," I said.

"No, not even close," Miles retorted. "The biggest mistake of my life was letting Will Grace funnel my life savings into one of his bogus investments. I should have known better—but Will always did talk a good game. He had a real gift for making larceny sound like it was the best thing that could happen to you."

"So that's why you killed him?"

"It was an accident," Miles said again. "I didn't want Will dead. I wanted my money back. I only intended to threaten him. I needed him to understand that I meant business."

"You were the person behind all those other 'accidents' that happened here too, weren't you?"

Miles cast me a quick glance. "You're smarter than you look. Emily never did figure that part out."

"She'll never let you get away with this," I said.

"I'm not worried about that," he replied. "I'll convince her I was only doing what had to be done to protect both of us—and her school. She'll be upset at first. But in the end, she'll go along."

I knew he was wrong about that. He had to be.

We were at least sixty yards away from the school now. The first line of trees was just ahead of us. The woods beyond them looked dark and ominous. Or maybe that was just my state of mind.

Abruptly I stopped walking. That jerked Miles to a halt too.

He motioned with the gun. "Not out here. Keep go-ing."

As if he thought I would be a willing participant in my own demise. The man was delusional.

"Let go of me," I said. "There's nowhere I can run now. I won't be able to walk between the trees with you hauling me around."

His grip slackened slightly. It wasn't enough. The moment Miles released me, I intended to be gone. I'd dash into the woods before he even had time to think, much less react. I took a step away from him and yanked hard.

Then suddenly Miles did let go, and my whole plan went to hell. Instead of running like a swift and graceful gazelle, I stumbled over my own feet and fell down on the ground. Like an idiot.

The same ankle that I'd broken in February, twisted beneath me. Pain made me suck in a sharp breath. I swore vehemently. I wouldn't be dashing anywhere now.

I was so busy berating myself that it took me a moment to realize that Miles and I were no longer alone. A pair of official looking shoes stepped into view. Relief washed through me as I realized what that meant.

"Miles Harlan, we have you surrounded," Detective Sturgill said. "Put your weapon down on the ground and put your hands up."

Epilogue

Later, I found out that Emily had called the Stamford Police Department the moment she was out of sight. Detective Sturgill had not only received my earlier message, he'd also understood most of it. So he and his partner were already close to the school when Emily's frantic call came through.

Detective Sturgill put in a call for extra backup. Then he came up with the idea to use the Earleys' property as a means of accessing the woods behind the school. That maneuver ensured that he and his partner remained unseen as they circled around to get ahead of us and lie in wait.

Unlike my plan, the detective's had come together beautifully.

Even better, Detective Sturgill had overheard much of

what Miles and I had been talking about as we approached
his hiding place. He'd been listening when Emily's brother
confessed to killing her ex-husband. He'd also heard
enough to realize that Miles intended to shoot me too.

Miles, who'd been full of bluster and bravado when it
was just the two of us, offered no resistance at all when
the police suddenly appeared in front of him. He quickly
laid down his gun and surrendered. I watched with satisfaction as he was handcuffed and taken into custody.

Detective Sturgill was looking very pleased with himself when he extended a hand to help me up. I was pretty
pleased with him too. He would probably never admit it,
but he and I worked well together. Almost in spite of ourselves, we were turning into a decent team.

After Miles was arrested, the police questioned Emily
extensively. In the end, they decided not to charge her as
an accessory to her brother's crime. That she'd acted to
thwart Miles's plan to commit another murder, then read-
ily confessed to everything she knew, were both mitigat-
ing factors in their decision.

Miles hired a lawyer who entered a plea of self-
defense on his behalf. He was granted bail, then made
himself scarce while awaiting trial. Before he left, Miles
revealed to Emily that her assistant, Mia, had been working as his well-paid, on-site accomplice.

Confronted by Emily, Mia admitted to the role she'd
played in engineering the alarming events that had taken
place at the school prior to Will's death. She blamed poor
judgment and massive college debt for her regrettable behavior. Mia claimed to have been entirely unaware of
Miles's endgame and insisted she never would have par-
ticipated in his scheme if she'd known it would culminate
in Will Grace's murder.

Emily was devastated to discover that someone she'd believed in and relied upon had betrayed her trust. She received scant sympathy from me, however. I found I was feeling much the same way.

With Mia suddenly gone from Graceland School, Emily stepped up to take charge of running the camp. To all outward appearances, she managed the remaining two weeks of the session with her usual energy and enthusiasm. It was clear she was working hard to return her life, and her livelihood, back to normal.

Even as I admired Emily's resilience—and accepted her heartfelt apology—I knew it would take our relationship a long time to heal, if indeed it ever did. She and I remained cordial, but the easy camaraderie we'd once shared was a thing of the past.

In early August, Aunt Peg and Emily held the A Day in the Country Breed Showcase and Benefit. Boosted by Aunt Peg's television appearance, the united efforts of dozens of purebred dog breeders, and the country fair atmosphere supported by delicious food and live music, the event was an even bigger success than they'd anticipated.

Enough money was raised for Emily to be able to approach negotiations with Peyton Hancock with a degree of cautious optimism. There she learned that he'd recently been cornered by one of his siblings whose two-year-old twins would soon be in need of a topnotch nursery school. Peyton had been asked to pull strings to ensure the duo's enrollment at Graceland. After that, it didn't take long for the Hancock family to formally renew Emily's lease.

A few weeks after Miles was arrested, Aunt Peg called to tell me she'd be picking me up early the next morning. She and I had already held a lengthy postmortem of the events surrounding Will Grace's murder. So I had no idea what she could be up to now.

"You're not going to tell me where we're going?" I asked.

"Certainly not. It's a surprise."

"A surprise I'll be happy about?" It was a fair question. Giving Aunt Peg control of any outing was a risky venture.

Now she sounded smug, however. "Oh, I think you'll be quite pleased."

Well, that piqued my interest. When her minivan pulled up to the house, I ran out and started to hop in the front seat. Then I realized that spot was already taken. Rory Scott gave me a friendly wave as I slipped in the back instead.

As I fastened my seat belt, I took a look around the interior of the van. There was an enclosed dog crate in the back. It appeared to have an occupant.

"Is there a dog back there?" I asked as Aunt Peg backed out of the driveway and sped away.

"Not a whole dog," Rory told me with a grin. "Just a puppy."

I swiveled around in my seat for a closer look. Through the small, wire mesh panel, I saw a white head dotted with black spots. A pair of dark brown eyes stared back at me.

"Posey, is that you?"

The sound of a tail thumping happily against the side of the crate answered my question. "Good girl," I told her. "You'll be out of there soon."

I turned around to face forward again. "Is Emily expecting us? Or are we surprising her too?"

"She knows we're coming," Aunt Peg replied. "But I

didn't tell her why. I merely said we needed to stop by to tie up some loose ends."

"So what happened?" I asked Rory. "You were desperate to get your three Dalmatian puppies back. And now you're going to give one away?"

"I was desperate," he agreed. "Honestly, I'd given them all up for lost. So regaining even one would have been wonderful. Two seemed like a multitude of riches. But now that I have Poppy and Pansy safe at home in my kennel, their dam's bloodline is secure."

I nodded, noting happily that Rory hadn't changed the puppies' names. Emily would be pleased about that.

"If the puppies had never disappeared in the first place, I wouldn't have kept all three," he continued. "I'd have retained the two best ones for my breeding program—and let the third pick go to someone else. So that's what I'm doing."

"There's no need to tell Emily that Posey was only third choice out of three," Aunt Peg said firmly. "No one wants to hear that about her own puppy."

"Emily won't care," I said. "She'll just be thrilled to have one of her girls back."

Emily was waiting for us in front of the school when we arrived. Sitting in the shade on one of the Adirondack chairs, she rose and came over when Aunt Peg stopped the minivan nearby.

She greeted Aunt Peg with a big smile. The look she gave me was more tenuous. But when Rory came around from the other side of the van, Emily's smile died entirely.

"What's wrong now?" she asked.

"Nothing," I said. "In fact, something is very right. You'll see."

When Aunt Peg opened the minivan's back door, I could hear Posey scrambling in her crate. Her nose was pressed against the crate's front gate. By the time Aunt Peg had unfastened the latch, the puppy's low whines had turned into happy yips.

Emily was walking around the back of the van to see what was going on when Posey came flying out of her crate. The puppy leapt up into Emily's arms. Surprised, Emily staggered back slightly. Rory braced a hand on her shoulder for support. Tears gathered in Emily's eyes. Posey's pink tongue came out to lick them away.

Their giddy reunion went on for several minutes. Finally Emily lowered the wriggling puppy to the ground at her feet and caught her breath. She swiped a hand across her face. She couldn't stop smiling.

"You'd better be planning to leave Posey here." Emily stared at Rory with her hands propped on her hips. "Because I'm not letting you take her away from me a second time."

He nodded. "As I understand it, you didn't end up with my puppies by choice. But you stepped in and took good care of them anyway. If not for that, I might never have seen any of them again. Under the circumstances, this seemed like the least I could do."

He had that right, I thought.

"One puppy is much easier to train than three of them," Aunt Peg said to Emily. The two women had become close as they'd worked together on the school benefit. "But you'll still have to put in the time."

"I know," Emily agreed. "Will you help me?"

"Of course," Aunt Peg replied. "We'll start tomorrow."

Shortly after that, it was my family's turn to welcome new puppies. Aunt Peg had brought Willow over to our house two weeks before she was due to whelp so she could settle in and become accustomed to her new surroundings. Willow was already well acquainted with our Poodles, so it only took a day or two before she was part of the pack.

Aunt Peg departed for her judging assignment, leaving us with strict instructions to call her the minute something happened. Even if it was in the middle of the night. Perhaps mindful of Aunt Peg's orders, Willow chose a reasonable hour to deliver her puppies.

We had set up a whelping box in our bedroom and Willow had been nesting for days, so we knew her time was near. The sun had barely gone down when she began to pant and pace restlessly. I offered her some cool water, but Willow had other things on her mind.

This wasn't her first litter, and she knew what to do. Within half an hour, Willow was lying down in her box. Sam and I were right beside her. Davey and Kevin were watching from the bed nearby. Contractions rippled down the length of Willow's body. She was ready, and so were we.

When the first puppy arrived, Sam broke the sac and made sure he was breathing. Then Sam moved out of the way so Willow could reach around to examine the puppy for herself. He rolled on the floor of the whelping box as she began to lick him vigorously.

Each time I watched a new life enter the world, it felt like a miracle. Fresh beginnings like these filled me with wonder. They renewed my hope for the future. I reached over and gave Sam's hand a squeeze.

"Here we go again," I said.

Dear Readers,

For years Melanie Travis has starred in her own mystery series, with Aunt Peg hovering—not altogether quietly—in the background. Eager to share her opinions and dispense advice, Peg has always grabbed center stage whenever she's had the chance. Now I'm delighted to announce that she'll have the opportunity to be totally in charge when she gets her own mystery to solve.

At long last, Peg will have everything her own way. Or will she?

Rose Donovan is Peg's sister-in-law. She's been a thorn in Peg's side for forty years. But somehow, when Rose decides to join a local bridge club, she can't think of anyone she'd rather have as her partner than Peg. Apart, these two women can be difficult. Together, they're more trouble than a sack of cats. Perhaps it's no surprise that when a member of the bridge club is murdered, Peg and Rose are named as suspects.

I had a great time writing *Peg and Rose Solve a Murder*. Peg has been a voice inside my head for so long that I loved being able to finally let her out to do her own thing. I hope you'll give her book a try. Otherwise Peg will never let you hear the end of it—and trust me, nobody wants that.

Happy reading!

Laurien

Chapter 1

Peg Turnbull was standing in the hot sun on a plot of hard-packed grass, staring at a row of Standard Poodles that was lined up along one side of her show ring. She'd been hired to judge a dozen breeds at the Rowayton Kennel Club Dog Show, and she couldn't imagine a better way to spend a clear summer day. Judging dogs involved three of her favorite things: telling people what to do; airing her own opinions; and of course, interacting with the dogs themselves.

A tall woman in her early seventies, Peg had a discerning eye and a wicked sense of humor. In this job, she needed both. Aware that she'd be on her feet for most of the day, she had dressed that morning with comfort in mind. A cotton shirtwaist dress swirled around her legs. A broad brimmed straw hat shaded her face and neck. Her feet wore rubber-soled sneakers, size ten.

Though her career as a dog show judge had taken her around the world, today's show was local to her home in Greenwich, Connecticut. Peg had arrived at the show-ground early. She'd begun her schedule at nine o'clock with a selection of breeds from the Toy Group. Now, two and half hours later, she finally found herself facing her beloved Standard Poodles.

As she gazed at the beautifully coiffed entrants in front of her, Peg knew exactly what she was looking for—a sound, elegant type dog displaying the exuberant Poodle temperament. Having devoted her life to the betterment of the Poodle breed, and spent the previous decade judging numerous dog shows, Peg was well aware there were days when those coveted canine attributes could be in short supply. Thankfully, this first glimpse of her Open Dog class had already indicated that this wasn't going to be one of them.

Peg flexed her fingers happily. She couldn't wait to get her hands on the Poodles. She was eager to delve through their copious, hair sprayed coats to assess the muscle and structure that lay beneath. It was time to get to work.

A throat cleared behind her. "Peg?"

Marnie Clark was Peg's ring steward for the day. While Peg evaluated her entries and picked the winners and losers, it was Marnie's job to keep things running smoothly. That was no small feat. To the uninitiated, the arrangement of classes, record keeping, and points awarded could appear to rival a Rubik's cube in complexity.

Marnie was an officer of the show-sponsoring kennel club. She was bright, vivacious, and two decades younger than Peg. Peg's Poodles and Marnie's Tibetan Terriers were both Non-Sporting Group breeds. The two women had known and competed against each other for years.

Reluctantly Peg turned away from the four appealing Open dogs to see what Marnie wanted. The woman was holding up an unclaimed armband. The fifth Standard Poodle entered in the class had yet to arrive.

Absent? Peg wondered. Or merely late?

Each exhibitor was responsible for being at the ring on schedule. However, busy professional handlers with numerous breeds to show could sometimes find their presence required in more than one ring at the same time. In those cases, it was up to the judge to decide whether or not a concession would be made.

Peg glanced at the armband and lifted a brow.

Marnie wasn't supposed to tell her the missing exhibitor's name—a nod to impartiality that didn't fool anyone. The dog show world wasn't large. As soon as the handler arrived, Peg would recognize him or her, just as she knew the other exhibitors currently in her ring. As long as a judge remembered to evaluate the dogs on their merits and not their connections, that didn't have to be a problem.

Marnie obviously agreed. "It's Harvey," she said under her breath.

The steward nodded toward a big, black Poodle waiting just outside the gate with the handler's harried looking assistant. Peg hadn't seen the young man before. He must be new. He was casting frantic glances toward the Lhasa Apso ring farther down the row of enclosures.

Peg took a quick look herself. Yes, indeed, there was Harvey—standing in the middle of a class of Lhasas that he very clearly wasn't winning. The handler was glaring at the indecisive judge as if he wanted to throttle her.

Peg felt much the same way. In her opinion, anyone who didn't want to have to make tough choices shouldn't apply for a judging license. Peg presided over her ring with the deft precision of a general inspecting troops. People might not agree with every decision she made, but they all respected her ability to get the job done.

Peg turned back to Marnie. "Give the young man the armband. Tell him to bring the dog in the ring and take him to the end of the line. You can switch Harvey in when he gets here."

"I already tried that," Marnie told her with a sidelong smirk. "The poor guy looked like he might faint. I wouldn't be surprised if this was his first dog show."

"And possibly his last." Peg felt an unwanted a twinge of sympathy. It was no wonder that Harvey's assistants always looked stressed. The handler had entirely too many clients to do each one justice.

On the other hand, she was well aware that Harvey's Open dog was a handsome Standard Poodle who compared favorably with the others now in the ring. Unless she was mistaken, the dog only needed to win today's major to finish his championship. Harvey would be devastated if he missed this chance.

Peg sighed. Time was a valuable commodity for a dog show judge. And now hers was passing. She was done dithering.

"I'll start the class but take things slow," she said to Marnie. "Harvey has my permission to enter the ring when he gets here. But for pity's sake, do try to hurry him along."

Ten minutes later, Harvey made it to the ring in time, but only just. Peg leveled a beady-eyed glare in the handler's direction as he took possession of the big Poodle at the end of the line. Her meaning was clear to everyone in the vicinity. She'd granted Harvey leniency this time, but he shouldn't make a habit of needing it.

After weighing the merits and flaws of her male Standard Poodle entry, Peg was further annoyed when her earlier speculation proved to be true. She ended up awarding Harvey's dog the title of Winners Dog and the coveted three point major that went with it. With an outcome like that, Harvey would never learn better manners. But darn it, the dog had deserved the win. So what else was she supposed to do?

Peg hated it when her principles found themselves at odds with each other.

It didn't help that Marnie was laughing behind her hand as she called the Standard Puppy Bitch class into the ring.

"Wait until you get approved to judge," Peg said as they crossed paths at the judge's table. "Then I'll come and make fun of you."

"As if you'd stoop to stewarding," Marnie sniffed. Then winked. Stewarding was a difficult and often thankless job and they both knew it.

The Standard Poodle bitch classes passed without incident. Peg took the time to reassure a nervous novice handler whose lively puppy couldn't keep all four feet on the ground. The woman left the ring delighted with her red second place ribbon in a class of just two.

In the Open class, Peg purposely paid scant attention

to a local handler who'd brought her a black Standard bitch that wasn't at all her type. The man had shown under Peg on many previous occasions. He would have known that she preferred a more refined Poodle, not to mention one with a correct bite. He would also have been aware, however, that Peg and the Poodle's owner were friends.

No doubt he was hoping to capitalize on that relationship.

The implication made Peg steam. If the handler had the nerve to think that would sway her decision, he deserved the rebuke she was about to deliver. With a dismissive flick of her hand, Peg sent the pair to cool their heels at the back of the line. Then she awarded the class, and subsequently the purple Winners Bitch ribbon, to a charming apricot bitch she hadn't previously had the pleasure of judging.

After that, Best of Variety was an easy decision. It went to a gorgeous Standard who was currently the top winning Poodle on the east coast. The apricot bitch was Best of Winners, which meant she shared the three point major from the dog classes. Her elated owner-handler pumped Peg's hand energetically when she handed him his ribbon.

"You certainly made someone happy," Marnie commented as she turned the pages of her catalog to the next breed on the schedule.

"Yes, and my fingers may never recover." Peg smiled. "He was so excited by the win, I was afraid for a moment that he might burst into tears. Were we ever that young and enthusiastic?"

"Of course we were. It's just that it was so long ago now, we're too old to remember what it was like."

Peg turned away and surveyed her table. If Marnie was old, what did that make her? Perhaps it was better not to think about that.

She grabbed a sip of water from her bottle, then flipped her judge's book to a new page. Miniature Poodles were up next, and they'd drawn a big entry. Dogs and handlers were already beginning to gather outside the ring.

More fun coming right up.

"I wonder what that lady's story is," Marnie said. "Even in beautiful weather like this, dog shows hardly ever draw spectators anymore."

Not like in the good old days, Peg thought. She was arranging her ribbons and had yet to look up. "What lady?"

"Over there." Marnie gestured discreetly. "She's sat through four different breeds. There's a catalog in her lap but she looks like she hasn't the slightest idea how to read it."

"Maybe she just loves dogs," Peg said happily. *Welcome to the club.* She straightened to have a look, then abruptly went still. "Oh dear."

Marnie was heading to the in-gate. It was time to start handing out numbered armbands. She glanced back at Peg over her shoulder. "What?"

"That's my sister-in-law, Rose."

"Okay. Then that makes sense."

"Not to me," Peg muttered.

Marnie returned to her side. "She's really a relative of yours?"

Peg nodded.

"And you hadn't noticed she's been sitting there for an hour?"

"Apparently not." Why would she waste time perusing

the ringside when she had all those lovely dogs in her ring?

"Right." Marnie didn't sound convinced.

Now that Marnie and Peg were both looking in her direction, Rose lifted a slender hand in a tentative wave. Her pleasant features were framed by a firm jaw and a cap of short gray hair was brushed back off her forehead. She was perched on the seat of a folding chair with her head up and her back straight. Rose had always had excellent posture.

Marnie smiled and waved back. Peg remained still.

Marnie gave Peg a little push. "Go say hello to her."

"I think not."

"Don't be silly, you have plenty of time."

Peg drew herself up to her full height. Even in sneakers, she neared six feet. "Not now. I have Minis to judge—"

"You're running early. I won't call the puppy dogs into the ring for at least two minutes."

"Rose can wait. I have a lunch break after Minis. She and I will talk then. Or maybe we won't." Peg pulled her gaze away. "Her choice."

"I see." Marnie bit her lip. It suddenly sounded as though this had ceased to be any of her business. "Then let me just finish handing out these armbands and we can get started."

Peg refused to let herself be distracted by her sister-in-law's presence as the first class of Miniature Poodle dogs filed into the ring. She had a job to do. Numerous exhibitors had honored her with an entry, and each of them deserved her complete attention.

Still, it was hard not to sneak a peek in Rose's direction every so often. What on earth was she doing here? As far as Peg knew, Rose didn't like dogs. Nor did she like Peg.

That feeling was mutual.

Animosity had sizzled between the two women since Peg became engaged to her beloved, and now dearly departed, husband Max more than four decades earlier. In all the intervening years, neither Rose nor Peg had managed to put the things that were said during that rocky time entirely behind them. Max was Rose's older brother—and a man for whom Peg would have done anything. Yet even he had never succeeded in forging a friendship between the two most important women in his life.

Peg plucked a stunning white youngster from the Puppy class and awarded him the points over the older dogs. She suspected once she'd seen the rest of her Mini entry, he would win Best of Variety too. That would be a bold move on her part. People would take notice. There was bound to be talk.

As she waited for the first bitches to enter the ring, Peg allowed herself a small smile of satisfaction. The white puppy was a star in the making. He would finish his championship handily, and she would be known as the judge who'd discovered him.

Buoyed by the prospect of that success, she allowed her gaze to flicker briefly in Rose's direction. It aggravated Peg that she felt compelled to gauge her sister-in-law's reaction. It aggravated her even more than to see that there was none.

Rose had set aside her catalog. Now her hands were

folded demurely in her lap. Her expression was bland, her features arranged in a mask of resigned complacency that Peg knew infuriatingly well.

Of course Rose hadn't noticed anything unusual. She probably couldn't tell the difference between a Miniature Poodle and a hamster.

That brought Peg back to her earlier thought.

It was never good news when Rose appeared. Peg wondered what the woman wanted now.

Chapter 2

Peg finished her Mini Poodle judging by making the handsome white puppy her Best of Variety winner. Since she put the dog up over two finished champions, her selection caused some minor grumbling among the other exhibitors. Not that anyone would dare say anything to her face, of course.

"Don't worry," Marnie told her. The show photographer had been called to the ring so they could take pictures of the morning's winners before the lunch break. They were waiting for the man to appear. "I've got your back."

"Thank you," Peg replied. "I wasn't worried, however. Should I be?"

"You didn't hear what Dan Fogel said as he left the ring."

Fogel was a busy and successful professional handler with a very high opinion of himself and his dogs. He clearly hadn't been pleased when Peg moved the white puppy up from the middle of the line and placed it in front of his specials dog.

"And I don't want to either," Peg said firmly. "Considering all the breeds he handles, Dan shows under me frequently. If a momentary lapse in judgement caused him to say something unfortunate, I'm better off not knowing about it. I'd hate for it to taint my opinion of him in the future."

"Your loss. He used some rather colorful language." Marnie grinned. "For what it's worth, I'd have done the same thing you did. There wasn't a better moving dog in the variety ring than that puppy."

Once the photographer arrived, a dozen pictures were taken in quick succession. Everybody knew the drill. Pose the dog, hold up the ribbon, smile, flash! Done, and on to the next.

"Lunch time," Marnie said happily when they were finished. "I can't wait to get off my feet for a few minutes."

"You go ahead." Peg glanced toward the side of the ring. "I'll catch up."

Apparently the extra time Peg had spent taking photographs had been the last straw for Rose. Now she was squirming in her seat. Peg didn't blame her. Those folding chairs weren't meant for long term use.

"Sounds good." Marnie followed the direction of Peg's gaze. "I'll save you a place."

The two women exited the show ring together. Marnie headed toward the hospitality tent. Peg went the other way, striding around the low, slatted barrier that formed the sides of the enclosure. She stopped in front of Rose, who looked up and smiled.

"Good morning, Peg."

"Afternoon, now," Peg replied smartly. There was another chair nearby. She dragged it over and sat down. "Imagine my surprise to find you sitting outside my ring. What are you doing here?"

"I was curious. I came to see what you do for a living."

Peg wasn't buying that for a moment. But she was willing to play along. "And?"

"It's rather boring, isn't it?"

"Not to me." Peg's smile had a wolf-like quality, more a matter of bared teeth than shared humor.

"Perhaps not. I'm sure you know more about these things than I do."

Having been immersed in the sport of purebred dogs for the majority of her adult life, Peg knew more about *these things* than ninety-nine percent of the world's population. She might have been tempted to point that out except it sounded as though Rose was trying to be agreeable. And that immediately made Peg suspicious.

"If you found the judging boring, why did you stay?" she asked pleasantly.

Rose shifted sideways in her seat. Now she and Peg were face to face.

"I think it's time you and I got to know each other better."

Peg's mouth opened. Then closed. She could have sworn she already knew more about Rose than any sane person would ever want to know.

"Why would we want to do that?"

"Because despite our differences, we're family."

Family. Hunh. As if that was a good excuse.

Peg's eyes narrowed. "What are you up to?"

"What do you mean?" Rose's reply was all innocence.

Abruptly Peg was reminded that her sister-in-law had found a vocation early in life. She'd entered the convent straight out of high school and spent most of the intervening years as Sister Anne Marie of the Order of Divine Mercy. Rose had perfected that serenely guileless look during her time in the convent. She still used to it great effect on occasion.

Peg wasn't fooled. Having been called both a heathen and a sinner by Rose in the past, she disdainfully thought of the expression as Rose's *nun face*.

"As entertaining as it is to spar with you," she said. "I'm sure you can see that I'm quite busy today. If you have something to say to me, please do so. If not, it's time for my lunch."

The other woman sighed heavily. That was Peg's cue to stand up. Somewhere on the showgrounds there was a rubbery pre-wrapped sandwich calling her name. And a trip to the port-o-potty wouldn't go amiss either.

"Wait," Rose said. "Give me a minute."

"I've already given you three."

"Sit back down. Please?"

It was the novelty of hearing the word *please* that did it. Peg thought that might be the first time she'd ever heard Rose voice such an appeal. She swished the skirt of her shirtwaist dress to one side and sat.

"Go on," she said.

"I want to join a bridge club. And I want you to join with me as my partner."

"You're joking."

"No." Rose frowned. "Why would I joke about something like that?"

"Because it's funny?"

It was funny, wasn't it? Any moment now, the two of them would dissolve in laughter. Not that they'd ever done so before. Belatedly it occurred to Peg that it didn't appear to be happening this time either.

Instead Rose was simply sitting there, staring at her. Her calm manner was almost unnerving.

"A bridge club," Peg repeated. Apparently it wasn't a joke. "I would think you'd be too busy for a frivolous pastime like that."

"Of course I'm busy. But I can't spend all my time doing good works." Rose managed to deliver that statement with a straight face. "Besides, bridge isn't a frivolous game. You should know that. You used to play."

Yes, she had. But how did Rose know that?

"You mentioned it once." Rose answered the unspoken question. "You were talking about living in a dorm when you were in college. You said every night after dinner, you and your friends would go down to the living room for demitasse and bridge."

Peg was slightly stunned. "That was fifty years ago."

"Even so. You talked about it."

Peg shook her head. She barely remembered playing bridge, much less having a conversation about it later. And with Rose of all people. How had that come about? She had no idea.

"I never went to college," Rose said in a small voice.

"No. You left home to become a nun instead."

"I had a vocation."

Even Peg wasn't mean enough to point out that Rose's vocation had apparently vanished like a puff of smoke when—after more than three decades in the convent—she had met a priest and fallen in love. Peter and Rose had recently celebrated their tenth wedding anniversary, however. So there was that.

"I realize now that there are many things I missed out on in my youth," Rose said.

"That was your choice," Peg pointed out.

"I didn't know that then. I was young enough and naive enough to think that God had made the choice for me. Now that I'm older, I realize that there are many paths to eternal salvation."

"And one of them includes playing bridge?" Peg regretted the words as soon as they'd left her mouth. In all the years she and Rose had known each other, they'd never had a conversation quite like this. All at once, Peg didn't want to be the one responsible for shutting it down. "I'm sorry. That was uncalled for."

"No, I get it. You're skeptical. I probably deserve that."

"Yes, you do."

"That goes both ways."

Peg snorted. "Don't tell me you're waiting for an apology."

"Of course not." A small smile played around the corners of Rose's mouth. "I know better than that. But I didn't come here today to fight with you."

After a pause, Peg shrugged. "It wasn't on my calendar either."

The two women shared a look of mild accord. It wasn't quite rapprochement, but perhaps a small step in that direction.

"I gather you're missing lunch on my account," Rose said. "I passed a food concession on my way in. Maybe I could buy you a salad?"

Peg nearly laughed. "Thank you, but no. Obviously you've never had dog show food."

"That bad?"

"Probably even worse than you're imagining."

"All right, then." Rose reached down into a canvas tote beside her chair and pulled out a shiny red orb. "Apple?"

Peg accepted the piece of fruit. She studied the apple from all angles, then took her first bite. "Maybe you should tell me something about your bridge club. I haven't played the game in years. I may not be up to their standards." She cocked a brow in Rose's direction. "Or yours."

"You don't have to worry about that. My friend, Carrie, belongs to the group. From what she's told me the members enjoy getting together to play bridge, but they aren't seriously dedicated to the game. They don't play duplicate or anything like that. Just plain old rubber bridge, and it's mostly for fun and socializing."

"What about Peter?" Peg asked. "I would think you'd want to play with him."

"His game is chess, not bridge," Rose told her. "Besides, just because he and I are married doesn't mean we have to do everything together."

Peg helped herself to another bite of the apple and stared off into the distance. She and Max had done everything together. Their relationship had been one of moving in tandem toward shared goals and accomplishments. They'd created a family of renowned Standard Poodles, while building a life that suited each of them perfectly. Max had been the other half of Peg's whole. Even a decade after his death, she still felt incomplete without him. Peg would have given anything to have those days to live over again.

"Plus, I like to win," Rose was saying. "So I'd prefer to have a partner who's competitive. Someone cut-throat like you."

Peg blinked, yanking her thoughts back to the present. "Cut-throat?"

"You know what I mean. You make Genghis Khan look like a sissy."

Peg suspected she was meant to be offended. In truth, she didn't mind the comparison. Strength was a virtue in her eyes. Speaking of which, Rose wasn't giving in and going away like she usually did whenever the two of them crossed paths. Maybe she possessed more backbone than Peg knew about.

"Apparently you're not as mild mannered as you'd like people to believe," she said.

"Then perhaps we'd make a good team."

"We'd probably end up fighting with one another."

Rose shrugged. "We fight now, so what's the difference? Who knows, maybe after all these years, we could become friends."

Peg nearly choked on her last bite of the apple. "I highly doubt that."

"Now you sound like a quitter."

"I do *not*."

"A coward, then?"

"I see what you're doing," Peg said mildly. "You think if you back me into a corner, I will give you what you want."

"Not at all," Rose replied. "It seems to me this should be something we both want."

"How do you figure that?"

"Neither of us is getting any younger."

"So?"

"At our ages, life is all about personal connections. It's inevitable that we'll start losing people from our lives. Doesn't that make it even more important to appreciate the friends and family we have with us?"

Family. This was the second time Rose had referenced that relationship. As if things were really that simple. Unfortunately, where the Turnbull family was concerned, complications had always been a way of life.

Peg's heart squeezed painfully in her chest. Rose did have a point about losing loved ones, however. Peg hadn't needed to reach the age of seventy-two before realizing that.

Still, she hated having to admit that Rose might be right about something. So instead she said, "I'll think about your offer and get back to you."

"Don't wait too long." Rose picked up her tote and stood. "This isn't an open-ended invitation. If you dawdle, I might find someone better."

Someone better. Peg blew out a breath. *Right.* Like that was going to happen.

Visit us online at
KensingtonBooks.com
to read more from your favorite authors,
see books by series, view reading
group guides, and more!

BOOK **CLUB**

BETWEEN THE CHAPTERS

Visit us online for sneak peeks, exclusive
giveaways, special discounts, author content,
and engaging discussions with your fellow readers.

Betweenthechapters.net

Sign up for our newsletters and be the first
to get exciting news and announcements about
your favorite authors!
Kensingtonbooks.com/newsletter